In loving memory

Shirley Roselee
and
Patsy Mae

This book is a Self-Published Second Edition from Paisley and Tumbleweed Publishing

# Deadly Intent

The author can be contacted at: www.robinwtitchen.com

ISBN-13: 978-1492820932
ISBN-10: 1492820938

# DEADLY INTENT

## I

Before I learned she was an unscrupulous sociopath in the making, with a cruel and deadly streak in her personality, I believed she was an innocent little girl in need of help.

Being an ex-cop turned forensic psychologist, I'm pretty good at interviewing and reading between the lines, sniffing out facts, and knowing when someone is lying to me. I'm also, usually, very intuitive; although in this particular situation it failed me.

At least I thought I was good at reading between the lines until I met "Little Darling." Just keep that in mind when I relate to you the story of the nine-year-old, 'multiple personality/clairvoyant' patient whose parents brought her into my office for therapy.

\*\*\*\*\*\*\*\*\*\*

It was a perfect start to a beautiful day. As usual, I woke that morning and let Paisley, my rough-coat Jack Russell Terrier, out into the fenced backyard to do her business. I put a mug of water in the microwave and a cup of kibbles in Paisley's food bowl. I refreshed her water and added Folgers instant coffee to my own hot water.

Paisley came in and followed me to my bedroom where I threw on a pair of jogging pants and an old Dallas Cowboys T-shirt from my college days. I put her harness and leash on and gulped the rest of my coffee before we left for our morning run. It was an ideal spring morning just after a rain; the sun was peaking over the Sandia Mountains of Albuquerque, New Mexico, and the birds were singing in the trees.

There are four different routes I choose from when Paisley and I go for our runs, and I switch it up each day so I don't become too predictable and complacent. That's something I was taught early in my childhood by my dad, who was a firefighter, and his two younger brothers, Dan and Richard, who were both career cops.

Uncle Dan, the youngest, retired from the FBI two years ago. Uncle Richard retired from the Dallas Police Department two years prior to that.

My dad's oldest brother, John, was my martial arts instructor my whole life. After serving in the Vietnam War, he went to Okinawa and lived there for twenty years training under a good friend and master in Tai Chi Chuan. While there he also trained in Karate, Taekwondo, Kung Fu, Aikido, and Jujitsu, all of which he became a master or Sensei in.

I am now classified as a master (or sensei) in all of these forms as well. In my spare time I teach classes at the YMCA to keep in practice.

My home rests in the lower foothills of Albuquerque. On this particular morning, Paisley and I left the house and jogged down the block to Golf Course Road.

Golf Course Road runs uphill from downtown to one of the many golf courses in the greater Albuquerque area. It is a wider two lane thoroughfare than standard residential streets with semi-heavy traffic. South of the golf course is a large fenced dog park which was where Paisley and I were headed.

When I turned to make sure it was safe to cross the wide street to the dog park, I noticed a dark grey sedan pulled over to the curb about a block behind us facing uphill—its engine running. I didn't think anything about it at the time. It isn't common, but neither is it unheard of for people to park along the street in this area. The traffic was clear and we jogged across to the park.

Inside the fence, I let Paisley off the leash so she could run at her own pace while I started jogging the quarter-mile track.

Paisley likes to chase birds or sniff and pee on the good smells. She does this while she waits for me to get far enough ahead so she can chase me down. She'll jump against my legs when she catches me before running off to explore more scents, only to repeat 'the chase' again and again. Sometimes I'll break into a sprint to make the chase more challenging when I see her coming. It's a good workout for me and she loves it.

When we left the park that day and crossed the street for the jog home, I saw the same sedan pulled to the other side of the road above the dog park and facing downhill in my direction. The engine was still running.

This caused me some wariness. On the jog home I ran ahead of Paisley at the start of each block—just enough so I could look back at her and see if the sedan was following. It was.

The first time I looked back, the sedan had moved up two blocks keeping pace with me. This held true until right before I turned back onto my street. That's when the sedan sped up and passed me, continuing toward downtown.

I rounded the corner to my subdivision and jogged the rest of the way home. I puzzled over the sedan and ran different scenarios around in my head while I got ready for work.

My typical day's attire consisted of pressed jeans and shirt with a blazer and my cowboy boots. Sometimes I'd opt for dress slacks but the important garment was the blazer or jacket. It makes it much easier to conceal carry one of my guns.

Why do I conceal carry you might wonder? I'll tell you.

As I stated earlier, my former occupation was that of a law enforcement officer—first uniformed patrol, and then plain clothes detective. On occasion I find myself in a situation where one of the unfortunates I assisted in finding new residency in a government-operated institution looks me up. Their intent is not to thank me, but to extract retribution for arresting them.

Some of the people I helped put away were gang and mob members. That's not to say we didn't have our share of perpetrators of other heinous crimes. We did.

One or two of the characters I had a part in putting away came after me for revenge once they were paroled (or escaped, which doesn't happen often, thankfully). Sometimes it's one of their family members or cohorts who will come after me for revenge.

Because of those occasional threats, I keep my grandfather's old duty weapon, a four-inch Colt Python revolver, loaded and in my desk at the office on the off chance I have an unwanted visitor from my past. My conceal carry weapons are my old duty weapon, a Glock G21 .45 auto, or my smaller off-duty weapon, a Glock G26 (subcompact) nine millimeter.

Most days, I take Paisley with me to the office. She's a good little girl and sleeps in her bed beside my desk unless she's following me around the office or goes outside with me to do her business. Although Jack Russell Terriers are very high-energy dogs, they're also very smart, and Paisley knows when I'm working, she has to be calm and quiet. I make sure she gets plenty of exercise outside of work.

One benefit of having Paisley in the office is that she's a good ice-breaker for those clients who have been through a traumatic experience, and most of my clients enjoy seeing her. Once I'm finished with work, she's all about playing, running, and jumping. On this particular morning, I decided to leave her at home since I had a date for lunch.

Jerry and I dated for a while, and although he's funny and interesting to talk to, the romantic relationship never progressed. Instead, it settled into a very comfortable and trusting friendship. We helped each other out when needed, and we frequently went out for dinner or lunch, movies, and social events where a plus one is expected.

Since I was widowed three years prior to this, I haven't felt much chemistry with anyone. I lost my soul mate in a terrible accident and doubt I will ever know love like that again. For some stupid reason that eludes me, however; I keep trying.

Norah, my secretary slash assistant, was already at the office when I arrived that morning; she usually is. She had the good coffee brewed and the mail sorted and stacked on my desk. I noted as I walked in, she was busy transcribing the notes I spent Saturday morning dictating. When you work for yourself, you work when there's work to be done—there's no nine-to-five schedule for the small business owner.

I asked Norah how her weekend was when I entered the office. She followed me into the little kitchenette and told me about her daughter's soccer game and how she scored the winning goal. I enjoy hearing about her domestic life. It gives me a sense of family participation.

I poured myself a cup of coffee and grabbed an individual container of yogurt from the small fridge. I poured some granola over the yogurt and mixed it all together before I headed to my office, coffee in one hand and yogurt in the other.

The phone rang and Norah took the call. I could hear her scheduling another forensic evaluation. One of the defense attorneys wanted his client evaluated to determine if he was mentally fit to stand trial.

In my office, I went through my mail putting the bills in one pile and the checks in another; Norah would handle them for me. That task completed, I started proofing the dictation Norah typed up the previous week. At ten o'clock, my newest client arrived for her appointment.

**********

# II

The parents of the little girl I referred to earlier were convinced their little darling was off her rocker. Who would have thought any differently when one minute you're talking to Little Darling and the next you're talking to Joe Blow? I first counseled with Little Darling's mom and dad to get some background information. Dad was pretty quiet, and didn't seem to know a lot, except that his "little miss" seemed to be two different people.

He related that one day when she was seven years old; he walked in the front door of their home after work. Instead of running to him yelling, "Daddy, Daddy, I missed you!" dressed as usual, she strolled into the foyer with a swagger. She was dressed in oversized rolled-up jeans, a muscle T-shirt under a flannel button-down shirt, and tennis shoes, all of which she took from her brother's closet.

She spoke in a deep, raspy voice. "'Bout time you got here, bub. You're late and holding up dinner." Needless to say, ole Pops was a bit put out by this display, so he asked Mommy Dearest what was going on.

I switched my gaze, with raised eyebrows to the mother who shrugged and nodded—her mouth in a pout.

Now Pops was a neat little dandy who was decked out in a tailored three-piece, pin-stripe suite and wore Italian leather loafers. He had a neat haircut and a perfectly trimmed van dyke—the perfect attire and appearance of a bank president which he stated he was. He was six foot tall and muscular, but he had the beginnings of a rounded midsection from overstuffing his face and lack of exercise. He wasn't a bad looking man in spite of his lack of a neck, his long beak-like nose, and his squinty eyes.

He also came with a nice health insurance policy befitting one with such a position and social status. That made me happy. I tire of trying to run down (figuratively speaking) deadbeat clients. Fortunately, I don't have a lot of those. The state or individual law enforcement agencies pay the bill for the bulk of my business—the forensic studies I do for them. A number of my clients are people with private insurance, as in Little Darling's case. I have several who are cash paying customers, and a few indigent cases which I handle pro bono.

Little Darling's mom was one of those high-society dames. She was perfectly attired and coiffed, with impeccably applied make-up, and beautifully painted gel nails.

She carried a Coach handbag and displayed a lot of flashy diamond jewelry. She was a platinum blonde with a Jessica Rabbit figure. The only downside was her high-pitched, whiney voice that just about drove me crazy.

*I'm sure glad she's not going to be my client. I don't want to spend any more time listening to her talk than necessary,* I thought as she narrated her side of the story.

"So what transpired that day and when did you notice your daughter had changed her behavior and dress?" I asked Mommy Dearest.

"Well," she squealed, "I was at a meeting for the Ladies Community Benefit, where we were making plans for the neighborhood-wide garage sale and fundraiser. Little Darling was at home with the babysitter. Everything was fine," she dragged out the word fine in an exaggerated sing-song, "when I left the house." She stuck out her hand, flopping at the wrist and continued.

"She was dressed in her favorite pinafore dress and matching accessories. She loooves dressing nice and making sure her appearance is appropriate for social interaction."

Mommy dearest patted her chest above her ample and exposed cleavage. She gazed skyward before she turned her eyes on me and pouted her lips again.

"When I got home, Little Darling didn't come to greet me as she usually does, so I called her. She appeared all dressed up in her brother's play clothes and *talking* funny. I was taken aback, so I asked her what was going on.

"She answered me with this weird, adult-like voice, and I looked around to make sure there wasn't someone else in the foyer playing a trick on me.

"She said, 'First of all, lady, I ain't this little darlin' you keep hollerin' for.'

"*Ain't!* Can you believe it? She actually said '*ain't*' like it's a proper word. She has never said '*ain't*'. Can you imagine?" She paused, waiting for me to respond.

I nodded. "Go on."

"Then she said, 'I dunno who that brat is.' *Brat? Really?* She's calling herself a brat now.

"My children have never, *EVER* heard me *or* their father refer to them as brats. I just don't know where she got this language."

Mommy dearest reached a hand over and patted Pops on the knee before continuing. "We don't have a television in the house because we believe it's a bad influence. Nothing but junk, you know?

"Anyway, the next thing she said was, 'My name is...' Oh dear!" Mrs. Pops fanned her face with her hand. "'My name is Rocky Polanski. Nice to meet you.' And then she stuck her hand out like I was supposed to shake it or something.

"That's when I called Isabella. Isabella's the babysitter. Anyway, I called Isabella into the foyer, and I asked her what kind of game she had been playing with the children.

"She said, 'Geez, Mrs. Pops, they were in their rooms doing homework all afternoon. We weren't playing any games at all.' 'Is that right?' I asked her giving her a stern look.

"She nodded and said she was in the dining room doing her own homework, and the children were upstairs in their rooms doing their homework. 'I checked on them several times to make sure they weren't fooling around.' she said to me.

"Well, let me tell you, I knew something was going on because Little Darling has *never* behaved in such a hooligan manner before. I was just appalled; let me tell you, I was.

"That's when Isabella looked at Little Darling, and her eyes grew as big and wide as saucers. If it hadn't been such a serious situation, I would have laughed." Mrs. Pops closed her eyes and shook her head. "But, of course, I didn't."

I touched the side of my head to make sure blood wasn't seeping from my ears; her voice was painful to listen to. It took every ounce of decorum within me to maintain my professional demeanor. I was unusually jumpy this morning to begin with, which didn't help matters.

"Go on." I remained calm and professional on the outside.

"Well, then Isabella asked Little Darling, 'What are you doing? Why did you change your clothes?' And Little Darling looked at her and asked her in that *weird* voice, 'You got a smoke I can bum, sweetheart? It's been a while, and I'm about to have a nicotine fit.'

Mommy dearest grimaced before continuing. "Isabella bent over, slapped her knee, and laughed until she was in tears. I couldn't believe she was laughing. There was nothing funny about it.

"Well, that was the last straw. I glared at Isabella and told her to stop laughing this instant. Then I grabbed Little Darling by the shoulders, turned her around, and I ... and I..."

Mrs. Pops closed her eyes again and patted herself on her ample chest. "I swatted her on the behind before sending her to her room. I instructed her to change into her own clothes." Her voice dropped in a conspiratorial tone and she leaned toward me.

"We don't normally spank our children, but I lost control. I was so frustrated and ... well, I was *scared!*"

"What did she do then?" I asked.

"Well ... she went to her room to get changed I thought. But when Pops got home, she greeted him in the manner he already told you."

"I see." It sounded a lot to me like a child acting out or playing pretend and being stubborn about it, but I didn't tell them that.

"How long did this behavior last?" I glanced at the father hoping he would answer. No such luck. Mrs. Pops chimed in with her squeal.

"After she greeted Pops and he called me to the foyer to see what was going on, I swatted her behind again. I repeated that she must go change into more appropriate clothes for a little girl. She went up the stairs without another word, and when she came to the dinner table she was fine. During dinner I asked her why she was pretending to be a little boy hooligan, and she looked at me in confusion.

"She asked, 'What do you mean, Mother? I was in my room doing my homework, and I fell asleep.'"

I couldn't help but wonder if this nine-year-old actually spoke that formally or if it was wishful thinking on Mrs. Pops' part.

"I told her what she had done earlier. She laughed ... in a nervous way and said, 'Oh mother, you're so funny. I wouldn't put Bubbas clothes on for *anything*. They smell funny and besides, they would be too big.'

"I said, 'But you did, dear.' Then Pops told her she was never to do that again because she had upset me so.

"Pops doesn't like for anything to upset me, not even the children. He's such a good husband." At that she turned a beaming smile on Pops and batted her false eyelashes a couple times.

*Yeah, he just doesn't want to listen to your grating whine,* I thought.

"And then what happened?" I resigned myself to the fact that Pops wasn't going to help me out, but I wished he would respond instead of his wife.

"Then we dropped it. We figured she was playing around and it wouldn't happen again since Pops told her to stop."

"And she always obeys when Pops tells her something?"

"Oh yes. Always, because she knows if she doesn't, she will be punished."

"And how is she usually punished?"

"Well," said Pops before clearing his throat. "It depends on the infraction, of course. Usually she's grounded from her phone, computer ... all her electronics, including games, and she's sequestered to her room for a specified period of time. If it's a serious infraction, which has never happened, we would consider a spanking. Thankfully we never had to resort to that. Well..." He coughed and cleared his throat. "...with the exception of Mother's swats that day."

"When you say 'sequestered to her room,'

what exactly does that consist of and for how long?"

"Again, that would depend on the infraction," chimed Pops again. "On one particular occasion, we sequestered her to her room for one week. She had wandered off to the neighbor's backyard to play with their dog and no one knew where she had gone. We called and called and she never answered, so we called the police. They found her back there after a lengthy search. The neighbors weren't even home at the time and she had no permission to trespass. That was serious, so the punishment was more severe."

"And what exactly does that entail? Does she stay in her room after she returns home from school? Does she take meals with the family? Is she allowed friends, or no friends? You stated you remove all electronics. What else? What *exactly* is included in that sequestering?"

Pops sighed and explained. "We remove all electronics, books, toys—everything except the furniture and pajamas for the allotted time. We deliver her school books and homework assignments daily if it occurs during the school week. We lock her dressing room door so she only has the bed, and her desk and chair for studying. She is not to leave her room or attached bathroom until the designated amount of time is up.

"She is to meditate on her behavior and why it was egregious. We take her food to her room and collect the dishes exactly forty-five minutes later.

"Once every evening, either Mother or I go to her room and talk to her about the situation and what she meditated on that day."

"And on this particular occasion, this went on for a week? She wasn't allowed to leave her room for a week?"

"Why, yes. That is correct."

"I see." *Wow, no wonder this child is acting out.*

I glanced from Mom to Dad as they sat in their chairs with deadpan expressions. They gave me the creeps. It seemed they were waiting for me to tell them the whole scenario is perfectly normal.

"After the incident of the personality change, did she behave and act herself again?"

"Yes, for a while," answered Pops.

I addressed my next question to him, hoping he would continue to take the lead in this conversation.

"How long did her normal behavior last?"

"Oh, goodness," squealed Mrs. Pops.

*Oh great!* I thought.

"We didn't have any more problems like that until about six months ago. That's when that hooligan kept showing up."

"That's correct," interrupted Pops. "It started again about six months ago. It was right after we returned from vacation in Paris, France. We were there for a month so we could immerse the children in the culture. They take private French lessons, you know, and Mother felt it was important to let them experience the language in day-to-day life.

"They were not allowed to speak English the whole time we were there. Bubba stayed on with my second cousin to continue his education.

"When we got home, Little Darling went up to her room to unpack and put her things away before dinner, but when she came down, she was in Bubba's clothes again. We tried to get her to go back upstairs and change, but she kept insisting her name was Rocky. When we finally convinced her to go upstairs and change, I told Mother the next time we should play along and maybe that would get all this craziness out of the child's head.

When she came down the stairs, she was still dressed in Bubba's clothes.

"She said, 'Look here, folks. My name is Rocky Polanski. I'm forty-three years old, and I'm *not* going to put some tacky dress on for *nobody*, ya hear? I'm through playing these games with you people. Now give me some grub, I'm starving!'

"Well, as you can imagine, Mother just about fainted dead away. I had to calm her down and get her up to bed with some tranquilizers and a cold rag on her head. When I came back downstairs, Little Darling had finished eating and was picking her teeth with a wooden toothpick. I decided to play along and see where this would lead.

"I always wondered what it would be like to be a detective and find the truth about something." He puffed his chest out and cocked an eyebrow. "So, as I was eating my dinner, I commenced to have a conversation with her just as I would with an adult gentleman.

"'So Rocky, what do you do for a living?'

"She replied in her very male, raspy voice, 'I'm a runner.'

"'A runner? What do you mean a runner?'

"'Come on, man. You know ... a runner. I run numbers for the racket and get kickbacks.' That's what she said ... just like that. 'Oh, so you have a pretty good income then, right?' I asked her ... him ... her." He waved his hand as if waving away a gnat. "You know what I mean."

"Right. Go ahead." I nodded.

"She said, 'Sure, man. It's okay.'

"'What do you do with your income?'

"'Awe, I play the stock market mostly. I do pretty good for an old bloke, too. I have a nice little nest egg socked away someplace safe.'

"'You do?' I said. 'Where do you keep your nest egg?'

"'What kind of fool do you take me for, man? I'm not telling you. You might take it from me ... what with you wanting me to wear dresses and all. You're not all that trustworthy right now as far as I can see.'

"'Oh, I see,' I told her. 'You're smart to be so cautious. When it comes to money, you never know who you can trust. I know because I'm the president of a bank and we have to be very careful about things like that.'

"Then, out of the blue, she went rigid in her chair, closed her eyes, and said in a soft, far-away voice, different from Rocky's but not Little Darling's either, 'Invest five thousand dollars in Pickering Caniby Kravutz & Co.'

"I asked, 'What?', but she didn't say anymore. After a few minutes, she started acting like Rocky again and continued as though nothing happened. I didn't know what to think."

"I can imagine. What happened next?"

"Well, we talked a little while longer, and 'Rocky' said he was tired and going to bed. After he left the dining room, I cleaned up the kitchen for Mother and went into my study.

"I know it sounds crazy, but I wanted to research the company she ... uh he mentioned. Sure enough, they were about to make a large acquisition so I set up some reminders to watch the growth. I wasn't about to invest on my little girl's or ... Rocky's recommendation, but I was curious. I'm sure you understand."

"I do," I told him. "Did you track the investment information?"

"I did, and I was surprised. It was a real winner ... like she had inside information. If I had invested five thousand dollars when

Rocky gave the recommendation; I would have made at least eighty thousand on the investment. It was odd the way he hit it on the nose like that."

"Do you have any other information about Little Darlings behavior for me?"

"Well, that's about it," Mrs. Pops squealed. "I can't think of any other pertinent information. I just want my little girl back. I can't *stand* that ruffian she pretends to be."

"Thank you for this information. I would like to talk to Little Darling now." I stood from behind my desk to escort them back to the reception room.

**********

In the reception room, Little Darling sat in one of the chairs, her feet dangling, crossed at the ankles. She had a Kindle in her hands and had apparently been reading before we came into the room. The incongruence of her pretty 'little girl' dress, ankle-length lace socks, and shiny, black patent Mary Janes, and the contrasting adult makeup, shoulder-length brunette 'big hair' adult hair-style, and oversized 'diamond' jewelry surprised me. I couldn't believe what I was seeing. The hair and make-up appeared as though professionally applied.

I walked over and squatted down in front of the child, and she looked into my eyes. This little darling had the prettiest baby blues I had ever seen and her smile, although quite pretty, was forlorn. My heart went out to her, and I wanted to help more than with any client I ever had.

If I had only known the truth behind her eyes, things would have been very different. I must have been hormonal or something that day. There's no other explanation as to why I was so taken in by these people—hormonal blindness.

"Hello, Little Darling, I'm Doctor Jeffries. I would like to talk to you about your parents' concerns. Will you follow me to my office?" She didn't say a thing but instead tipped her head in a nod and slid off the seat. She took my hand in hers, and I led her down the hallway to my office. Before closing the door, I asked if she would like a bottle of water or a soda. She responded with a shake of her head and a, "No, thank you."

I turned to close the door while she took a seat in the chair her father had vacated. Instead of taking my usual seat across the desk from her, I sat next to her where her mother was seated earlier and turned to face her.

"How are you doing?" I asked.

She shrugged. "Okay, I guess."

"Why do you guess? Don't you know how you're feeling?"

She shrugged again and shook her head.

"Are you afraid?"

"No. Not really." She smiled. This time, her smile was like warm sunshine and sandy beaches ... happy. I liked her smile.

"That's good because there isn't anything to be afraid of. Why don't you tell me a little about yourself?"

"You already know about me. My parents told you everything I'm sure. They said they would."

"Yes, that's true. They told me a lot. But I would like to hear from you." I leaned back in my chair and crossed my legs.

"You see ... the way one person sees a situation may not be the same way another person sees it. That causes a difference in the way people respond to situations and what they think about them. Do you understand?"

Little Darling nodded indicating she was following me. I folded my hands in my lap and smiled at her.

"That's why I need to hear from you—what you know about the situation, what you think about it, and what, if anything, you want me to help you with." I leaned forward to stress my next statement. "I assure you that anything you tell me is kept confidential. Do you know what confidential means?"

She nodded. "It means you won't tell anyone else, right?"

"That's right. I won't tell your parents or anyone else, except if something bad is going on and the courts or police need to be called in to stop it. Are you being mistreated?"

She stared at me without moving so much as a muscle. I waited. Silence filled the room until she took a deep breath and whispered, "I'm scared. My parents keep telling me I'm doing strange things, acting funny, and dressing in my brother's clothes, but I don't remember doing anything like that."

"Okay. Would you like to dress in your brother's play clothes instead of dressing up all the time?"

A frown creased her brow. "No, not really, but I wish I could have my own play clothes and do things outside like the other kids. I never have time. Bubba was allowed to be on lacrosse and baseball teams, but I have to take piano lessons and voice lessons and sewing lessons and cooking lessons—stuff like that, and it's all so *boring*." Her bottom lip stuck out in a pout. "Playing sports looks like a lot more fun. I'm not allowed ... that's all."

"Have you told your parents that you would like to join a sport team or do something outside?"

"I wouldn't be any good at sports." She shook her head looking dejected.

"Why do you say that?"

"My parents remind me how clumsy I am all the time." She sputtered a derisive laugh. "I would either get hurt or hurt someone else. I don't want to do that."

"It takes time and practice to be good at something. You could learn something fun if you were given a chance. Maybe we can talk to your parents about that. What would you be interested in?"

"I don't know—probably nothing. I just want to go outside and play with the other kids."

"Have you ever met anyone named Rocky?"

"No."

"Your brother never had a friend named Rocky or maybe someone at school you might have seen in passing, or heard about?"

"No. The first time I heard the name Rocky was when my parents told me I called myself that, but I don't remember ever doing it."

Her bottom lip started to quiver and tears pooled in her baby blues.

"Do you ever lose time, Little Darling?"

"What do you mean?" She swiped at her eyes.

I grabbed a tissue from the box on my desk and handed it to her. She patted her eyes in order to avoid smudging her makeup.

"It's like one minute you're doing something and the next thing you remember, you're somewhere else or doing something else and you have no memory of what happened in between."

"Oh! Yes, but I just thought I was sleeping or daydreaming and didn't remember it."

"Have you ever come back to your senses in a different location minutes, hours, or even days later?"

"No, I've pretty much always been in my room when it happens, except one time. I was..." She blushed and looked at the floor.

"You were where? What were you doing?"

"I was naked in my brother's room when I—what you said—came to."

"Was anyone in the room with you?"

"No."

"What happened next?"

"My clothes were thrown up against the wall under the window. I grabbed my clothes and got dressed as fast as I could before my brother got home."

"And...?"

"I went to my room. That really scared me until I remembered a girl from school who told us about her father. She said he sleep-walked, and I decided that must have been what I was doing."

"But you never lost time anywhere else in the house except that one time in your brother's room and in your bedroom?"

"No."

"Did you ever wake up somewhere outside the house? Maybe the neighbor's backyard or something like that?"

"No! Never. Just in my bedroom and that one time in Bubba's room."

"Tell me, Little Darling, how are you at math?"

"Pretty good, I guess. I get straight A's in everything. If I don't, I get punished."

"That's a lot of pressure put on you, isn't it?"

"Yeah, but it's for my own good. That's what my parents tell me. It's hard, though, and sometimes I, uh, umm..."

She looked at the floor again for a long moment while I waited patiently.

"Sometimes..." She paused. "You won't tell anyone, right?" She turned her gaze up to me.

"That's right. I won't tell anyone. You can tell me anything."

"Well, sometimes I cheat because I don't always have all the answers." Her eyes started to well up with tears again and she brushed them away.

"I really don't like it, but I don't want to be in trouble. If I didn't cheat, I would be locked in my room all the time, and I hate that. I feel like a prisoner ... like Rapunzel or something."

Little Darling began to cry. I grabbed another tissue and slipped it into her hand. When she began to calm down, I reached over and patted her knee. "I'm sorry, Little Darling. It's okay to cry and be angry about it." She wiped her eyes and blew her nose.

"Please, please don't tell anyone."

"I won't. It's just between us." I waited a few minutes to let her compose herself before I asked, "Can you tell me about your punishments? What happens when you're sent to your room, and how long does it last?"

"I'm locked in my room, usually only over the weekend, but a couple times it was for a long time. They would call my school and tell them I was sick, and they would pick up my homework and bring it to my bedroom. One time, the first time, it was like..." Her eyes grew large. "I don't know ... a month, it felt like."

"That's a really long time."

She raised her hand out to the side of her body, palm up. "I know." She nodded. "It was *forever!*"

"What do you do when you're locked in your room?"

"Nothing to do." She sighed, looked to the floor, and shook her head. She sighed again and raised her eyes to mine.

"I open my bedroom window and sit and listen to the kids playing in the park across the street. I watch them doing all the things I want to do but am never allowed to do."

"Like what?"

"Riding bicycles, playing hopscotch, running around and chasing each other, shouting and laughing, or sitting in the grass and talking—a lot of different things."

"Okay, what else do you do?"

"Sometimes I'll run a hot bath—as hot as I can stand it—and lie in it until the water is cold and my skin is all wrinkly. I think a lot, trying to figure out what is wrong with me, and I sleep a lot."

"What do ...?"

"Sometimes I'll exercise—jumping jacks, running in place, dancing to music in my head, that kind of stuff." She frowned again. "It gets pretty boring."

"What do you mean, 'what's wrong with you', do you mean what's wrong because you're in trouble and locked in your room, or what's wrong because you lose time?"

"No, just..." Another heavy sigh. "...why can't I go out to play with the other kids, and why am I locked up ... stuff like that. Bubba has *never* been locked up that I know of, and he gets to go out and play *all* the time."

"I see. Well ... I don't know why your parents won't let you go out and play. Have you ever asked them?"

"Yes, but they say it's not *lady-like* and not to question them. They say they know what's best for me. I guess they do, but sometimes I wonder."

"What else happens when you're locked in your room? Do you get to go have meals with your family?"

"No, they bring me a tray three times a day, and I have to eat right away because they take it away pretty quick."

"What else happens? Does anyone come and spend time with you, maybe your parents or your brother? Anyone?"

"My mom or dad would come in to tuck me in at night and talk to me."

"What was that like? What would they talk to you about?"

"Mother would sit on my bed and talk ... always about what I did, if I thought about my behavior, and why I deserve to be punished. She never asks me how I'm doing or why I did whatever I did. She *never* hugs me or anything. She just tells me how it is.

"If it's Father, he would sit on my bed and talk the same way, but he would rub my arm or hold my hand in his. Sometimes he would hug me and rub my back, but he never asks me how or why or anything like that either."

"How did your father's touch make you feel—comforted or weird?"

She shrugged and grimaced. "It was okay, it was nice to be hugged. They don't usually touch me at all, ever."

Little Darling stiffened her back, and her eyes went vacant. She stood from her chair and walked over to the wall beside my desk. She raised her arm as though she had something in her hand and turned her hand like she was trying to unlock something.

"Must ... get ... jewels." Her voice became higher pitched and had a bit of a British accent.

"Where are you now?"

"Bus ... station."

"Are you trying to unlock something?"

"Locker ... one ... nine ... seven."

"What's in the locker?"

"My ... jewels."

"Why are they in a locker at the bus station?"

"He ... stole ... them."

"Who stole them?"

"He ... did."

"Who am I talking to now?"

She dropped her hand to her side and stared at the wall, "Barbara ... I'm ... Barbara. I ... want ... my ... jewels ... back."

She turned and looked at my desk. "This ... not ... bus ... station. Must ... get ... there."

"Okay, why don't you have a seat now, and I'll see what I can do about getting you to the bus station."

She walked mechanically to her chair and sat back down, stiff backed.

"I'll be right back. Will you be alright for a moment?"

She was still in the altered state and gave a single nod of her head. I left the office door open and walked down the hall to talk to her parents.

"Has she ever referred to herself as Barbara before?"

They looked at each other a moment before turning to me. Both Mom and Pops appeared startled at the inquiry.

Pops shook his head. "No. Never."

"She just changed her demeanor and told me her name is Barbara and that she must go to the bus station to get some jewels out of a locker. Do you have any idea what this might be about?"

"No. Mother, do you?"

"No!" Mrs. Pops squealed.

"Has she ever been to the bus station or seen either of you put something in a locker at the bus station?"

"Absolutely not. She has never been to the bus station for any reason." Pops was adamant.

"Thanks. I'll be right back." I turned and went back to my office. Little Darling was still sitting in her chair, stiff backed and with a vacant stare. "Are you doing alright, Barbara?"

She nodded in the affirmative, and I went back to the reception room.

"She hasn't changed her demeanor from Barbara. I would like to take her to the bus station and see what happens. If she comes out of it before we get there, I'll explain what happened and tell her where we're going. She probably won't have a clue as to what to do from there, but I would like to see what she does."

"That sounds good to me. We can take my car, and I'll drive. That way you can sit in the back seat with Little Darling and watch her." Pops pulled his keys from his pocket. Mrs. Pops nodded with enthusiasm.

I was going to take her myself but with Pop's offer, I thought it might be a good idea to observe her the whole time. I'd never witnessed anything like this before.

I told Norah where we were going, and then I went back to my office and asked Little Darling, A.K.A. Barbara, to come with me to the bus station. She stood from her chair and woodenly followed me out to Pops' car without saying a word.

When we got to the intersection where I would have gone straight, Pops turned left to get on the interstate.

"Where are you going? The bus station is on Lincoln Avenue."

"I have to make a stop first. It won't take long."

"I wish you wouldn't. I'd like to get there before she comes out of this trance, not to mention you're still on the clock. I charge by the hour."

"It'll just take a minute. Besides, no cost is too great to help Little Darling."

I didn't like this turn of events and the hair on the back of my neck started standing on end. I was beginning to feel duped and trapped. I looked over at Little Darling, and her demeanor hadn't changed since leaving the office.

Pops and Mrs. Pops seemed different. They were happy and excited which made no sense to me. The thought of the sedan on my morning run popped back to mind.

*This is the same car. I'm sure of it!*

All of a sudden, Little Darling turned her face toward me, smiled, and said in her normal voice, "This is fun, isn't it?"

I turned to see what she was talking about and was clubbed in the side of my head with something hard.

My hand darted to my head and I turned to see Mrs. Pops holding a short-wooden club. She sported a sinister grin, and in my daze I saw the club coming at me again. The pain of another strike drew brilliant stars in my vision before everything went black.

**********

# III

When I woke, my head was pounding and my eyes had trouble focusing. I closed my eyes, hoping the pounding in my head would go away. Buzzing filled my ears and I wasn't sure if it was from a nearby bee hive or the blow to my head.

The air was pungent ... musty but mingled with the smell of oil, rust, and dirt. I wrinkled my nose a little and opened my eyes a slit to test my vision. After a brief blurring they focused on pitchforks, shovels, and sickles hanging on pegs along the wall behind the skeleton of an old tractor across from me.

I was hog-tied and gagged, lying on my side in the middle of a barn. I listened for any sound of life around me before moving. It was dead quiet. I didn't want to alert whoever tied me up that I was awake. I needed a little time to assess my situation and get my head cleared.

I tried lifting my head a couple of inches and the dizziness swam from the top of my head to the pit of my stomach. Fear washed over me as I realized I might throw up and drown in my own vomit. I laid my head back down and closed my eyes concentrating on breathing—a few deep breaths in through my nose and slow exhalations through my mouth around the gag to settle my stomach helped.

The queasiness passed, and instead of moving my head, I tried to reach my boot where I kept my Cobratec knife. I pulled my bound ankles toward my reaching hands tied behind my back. I arched my back to assist the reach. I was finally able to grab the hem of my jeans and pull my legs closer. I felt for the clip to my knife at the top of my boot.

*It's gone!*

Above the buzzing in my head, I heard footsteps approaching from outside scuffing gravel. A door behind me squealed as it slid open. I didn't hear it close and noticed a little stream of light from the open door reaching into the barn and slicing across my body. I wondered if there was another person following, but I didn't hear additional footsteps.

"Hi, Doc," I heard Little Darling say. She skipped over to me and kicked me hard in the back. "Wake up, wake up!" She was in a cheerful mood.

I groaned and rolled over onto my back, the pain from the kick spreading.

"Oh, did I hurt you?" Her sass and sneer provoked my ire and there was nothing I could do about it.

I looked up from the floor to the smirk on her face.

"I forgot to tell you something. I have also been taking acting classes since I was five years old. I'm pretty good, huh? I've even been in a few commercials. We were hoping you wouldn't recognize me, but we had an explanation if you did."

"Tabatha!" a gruff voice barked.

She jumped and turned to the door. It wasn't Pops, and I didn't hear this person approaching.

"I told you not to come in here. Go on back to the house. *Now!*"

"You can't tell me what to do." She stamped her foot and turned back to me. She kicked me in the ribs, turned back to the door, and skipped away.

I groaned and watched her turn at the door.

"Okay, George. I just wanted to wake her up for you." She raised her right hand wiggling her fingers at me.

"Bye, Doc. It's been a lot of fun, but I won't be seeing you again. No one will." Cackling, she skipped out of sight.

"Kids!" George muttered. "Can't stand them."

He came around and squatted down beside me. He poked his fat, dirty finger in the goose egg on my forehead.

"Ouch, that's gotta hurt. Mary's a real mean one. She likes bouncing her wooden club off of folks' heads. Betchya never even saw it coming."

I stared up at him wishing he would take his whiskey breath away from me and let me hurt in peace. Instead, he grabbed my shoulders and pulled me up into a sitting position.

Again, the dizziness assaulted me, and I hung my head taking a couple deep breaths to try and keep the bile down. I could see a small pool of dried blood where my head had been.

George untied the gag. I coughed and then croaked out, "What's going on, George?"

"Now, don't you worry about that. You just drink a little water here and think about your life. The Mongoose will be here tomorrow to talk to you."

*The Mongoose!* I recognized that moniker, but I couldn't quite place it. My head was swimming, and I couldn't think clearly.

"Who ... who's The Mongoose?"

"You think on it, Jeffries. You just think on it while you wait." He put a tin cup to my lips. The cup wasn't particularly clean and the water wasn't cold, but it didn't smell bad and it felt good on the back of my throat. After a couple sips the cup was removed. I cleared my throat.

"More." I croaked and took a couple more sips before George took the cup away and set it down. He checked the ropes to make sure I wasn't able to get loose.

"I'll be back in a little while to check on you. Don't go anywhere." He laughed a rough laugh, almost a growl, as he left the barn and closed the door behind him.

Alone at last, I reached my arms around to my left side and felt in my front jean pocket for my keys with a pen knife on the ring. As I expected, my pockets were empty, too. *If I can get on my feet and over to one of the sickles on the wall, I'll be able to cut the ropes on my wrists*, I thought.

I tried scooting across the floor but made little progress so I stretched out and rolled to

the ancient looking car I hadn't seen earlier—
the dizziness came in waves, but subsided
the more I moved.

The old car was in front of the tractor but
pushed further back in the barn. With my
back braced against the old rusted quarter
panel, I pushed with my feet until I was in a
standing position. Once I had my balance, I
hopped to the wall where the tools were.

I was in luck! One of the sickles was hanging
low enough to slip the ropes at my wrists over
the blade. I nicked the side of my wrist and
winced but kept working at cutting my
bindings. The blade was rusted and dull.
Warm blood ran down my hands, and I could
hear it plopping on the cement floor at my
feet.

My bindings were at last severed, and I
dropped to untie my ankles. I checked the
cut on my wrist and ripped off a strip of cloth
from the bottom of my button-down shirt. I
wrapped it around my wrist and tied it tight
to staunch the blood flow. It was deep, but
thankfully it didn't hit an artery.

I stood and looked around trying to think
clearly. A trickle of hazy light bled into the
gloom through the cracks in the plank wood
walls of the barn. I couldn't see any of my
belongings ... like my gun or knives ... so I
took down the sickle before I went to the door

and listened. I didn't hear anything but the buzzing in my head. I eased the door open just enough to slip out, worried about the grating squeal I heard when Tabatha came in.

Standing flat against the outer wall, I looked around. It was dusk, and night was falling fast. There were no street lights in sight. The sky was almost dark and it was overcast. I gave thanks for the heavy clouds blocking out any light from the emerging moon and stars.

The house was around the corner of the barn to my right, and the lights were on in the kitchen. Peeking around the corner, I could see three people sitting at a table through the open window. They were talking and laughing but I couldn't make out any of the words. Mrs. Pops' voice—Mary I presumed—was as grating as before. I could hear that.

Pops' car was in the drive at the far, dark side of the house. Next to it was an old Chevy pickup truck.

I crouched down low and ran across the yard to the car staying out of the illumination of the porch light. I didn't see any light coming from this side of the house, so I eased the car door open and slipped into the driver's seat reaching for the ignition. No keys. I checked the floorboard, the visor, and the console but found nothing.

*Why don't the bad guys leave their keys in the car like they do on television shows and in the movies? Sure would help.*

I pulled the wires to hotwire the car but nothing happened. I figured they must have removed the battery or distributor cap—something to keep the car from running. Even though I know little about cars, I know there's a way to do that.

I eased out of the car closing the door with a soft 'click' and went to the pickup. I went through the same process—nothing. As I exited the truck and closed the door I heard a screen door slam.

"Where you going, baby?" Mary squealed.

"Just going to check on our little rat in the trap. Be right back," George hollered back.

I ran, crouched, to the dark side of the house and cut across the side yard to the field beyond with a tree line about seventy feet away. I stumbled into a ditch ten feet before reaching the trees and landed with a jolt on my hands and knees. I came close to cutting my face with the sickle when I fell.

I knew I didn't have much time, so I stayed low and belly crawled as fast as I could toward the trees. I entered the tree line and glanced back to see if I was being pursued.

So far I wasn't. I was creeping through the trees toward the road when I heard George yelling.

"Eric, get the guns. She's *gone.*"

I heard George's feet hit the front porch at the same time the screen door to the house slammed open and banged closed. I could see by the porch lights that another man met George on the front steps and tossed him a long gun—probably a shotgun, but I couldn't tell from where I crouched.

"Hurry up. The Mongoose is going to kill us if she gets away." Eric sounded a lot like Pops.

I didn't think they could see me in the cover of the trees, especially with it being such a dark night, but I stayed low and ran for the road.

I heard the hood of the car slam and then the car door thump closed. "She tried hot-wiring the car, George. She can't be far. Look for her footprints and follow them. I'll take the car and search toward the road."

George didn't say anything, so I figured he was already looking for my tracks. Hopefully he wouldn't find them, but I wasn't counting on that.

Looking over my shoulder, I saw the car backing up to turn around and come down the rutted drive. I didn't want the lights to hit me, so I stayed low and ran, changing my course. I ran to my right, away from the drive and parallel from what I guessed would be the road.

I still hadn't heard anything from George but from his silent entrance into the barn earlier, I knew he was pretty light on his feet. He had a rifle or shotgun too, so I was a bit worried.

I was trying to be as quiet as possible while running through the woods, but to me it sounded like a herd of elephants running through the trees. Limbs were slapping and scratching me, one hitting me right across the bridge of my nose and under my right eye. I could feel the blood trickling down my face from a cut from a thorn or sharp twig.

I stay in good shape so the exertion wasn't a problem—the terrain was. I couldn't see very well in the darkness of the night and the cover of the trees. After running up a slight rise, still inside the small woods, I stepped into open air. I landed awkward on my left toes and fell to my knees, went head over heels rolling down a steep embankment and ended in a deep creek. I was soaked, water sluicing across my face. Somewhere during the fall I lost my sickle. The splash from falling in the water sounded like a tidal wave in the still, dark night, and I decided I didn't have time to look for it.

I jumped up and starting running down-stream on the narrow muddy bank. I ran out of bank and was running in the water, splashing as I went. The stream turned to my right toward the farm and snaked around a big boulder to my left changing directions again. The water was getting deeper, making it more difficult for me to run, so I got on my belly and pulled myself along with the current.

I heard a splash behind me and George cussing up a storm. The water was up to my waist by then. I waded to the edge of the stream and ran up the bank making sure I left footprints. I circled around and eased back over the bank and into the stream behind George.

I could see George's flashlight beam ahead of me go up the bank where I left the stream, and then it was bouncing along at the top of the bank in my direction. His head was bent following my footprints as I floated by.

I watched him pass me and then turned my head back downstream paddling. I remained as quiet as possible.

The light beam bobbing on the bank above me moved out of sight as the creek made another slight curve to the left, pulling me along with it. Beyond that the current became so strong I couldn't resist it. It pulled me along another curve before spilling into a river, the banks spreading and flattening a little but the depth deepening.

I looked back over my shoulder for the light beam but only darkness pursued me in the river. Turning back downstream, my left leg slammed into a large submerged rock, and then my right shoulder hit a boulder that rose above the water. The current was very rapid now, and I was fighting to keep my head above water—getting pulled under and turned around several times.

I was beginning to panic when there was a break in the clouds while my head was above water. I could see I was in white-water rapids. Boulders spread out on both sides of me in the river. The banks were narrowing and growing steeper.

Watching the boulders, I tried to keep my feet in front of me and worked at directing my body away from the rocks as much as possible. Deflecting my body from the boulders with my feet and hands jarred me all the way up to my throbbing head. My joints ached, but I knew if I hit my head and passed out, I would be fish food. I also knew I could get sucked under and trapped beneath debris, never to emerge again if I wasn't careful. I kept glancing off the boulders and scraping over submerged rocks and debris.

As the moon slid back behind the clouds, I went feet first over a ledge. I scraped my back on the rocks at the edge and hit the back of my head before plunging into a pool eight feet below.

I kicked for the surface, and as the water calmed into a gentle flowing river, I rolled onto my back and floated, catching my breath and trying to assess the damages.

I didn't find any apparent broken bones but the all over pain was real. I sure didn't need another knock on the head; I already had a screaming headache. I rolled back over and swam to the bank to my left and crawled out onto a small sandy beach area.

I had gone through so many curves and turns I was disoriented and didn't know in which direction the farmhouse lay. For all I knew, I was in their backyard, but I doubted it.

I didn't want to go back in the direction I came and there was a jetty of rock narrowing the river, preventing me from going further on the beach. I had to either get back in the river or climb the steep bank—almost a cliff. I was too tired to climb but afraid of more rapids.

I searched the beach area and found a small pack trail behind dense grass that rose up the side. I started up the gentle rise.

I moved as quickly and quietly as I could in spite of the pain I was in. When I made it to the top, I stopped and listened for any sound of pursuit; I heard only the sounds of nature.

I eased my head up over the edge and looked around. In the distance, I saw what appeared to be streetlights twinkling. I didn't have a clue where I was, but at least I was near enough to a town I might have a chance to get some help.

I could see traffic along a highway far to my right, so I started off straight ahead on the rough terrain—toward the town and parallel to the highway. I figured I would skirt around to the opposite side of the town from the highway once I got closer.

The moon started drifting in and out of the clouds after I had stumbled about halfway to the edge of town. That gave me enough light to travel a little faster. When there was enough light, I checked behind to see if anyone was following and saw only darkness.

Approaching the edge of town, I squatted down at the edge of illumination from the nearest lights and watched for any sign of life. I didn't want to run into a trap, and I knew Eric could already be in town looking for me.

Before me was a large parking lot with a number of trailers and a few big rigs in front of a squat, wide warehouse. Not seeing anyone, I prepared to run to the nearest building to melt into the shadows. As luck would have it, the moon slipped behind the clouds again.

I still had the streetlights and security light to contend with, but they also allowed more shadows for me to slip through while I moved. I didn't want to stay on the outskirts of town. That was where Eric would start his search for me.

**********

After slinking and dodging from building to building, shadow to shadow, and down dark but thankfully vacant alleys, I made it to a wide thoroughfare with a number of fast food restaurants and closed office buildings. Across the street and two blocks down from my location stood a Shell gas station and convenience store. I backtracked through the alley I was in to the dark, quiet street at the other end. I cautiously made it to the cross street the gas station was on.

I hid behind a dumpster next to the building and watched the parking lot and entrance across the street for anything that might be of concern. Even though my clothes and hair had dried for the most part during my trek across land, I knew I was a bloody mess and because of that, I would stand out like a sore thumb. I didn't want the clerk or some concerned citizen to call the cops on me.

I needed to clean up so I could move around without being so conspicuous, and I needed to get to a phone.

While I was watching the gas station from the shadows before crossing the street, I noticed a couple of times that the customers were going around to the side of the building. I guessed that the doors to the bathrooms were on the outside of the building instead of in the store. At least that's what I hoped it was and not some kind of drug-dealing location.

After assessing the situation, I slipped through the shadows to the busy thoroughfare and waited next to the building for a lag in the traffic. When it occurred, I ran across the street.

Once I got to the other side, I continued to run until I reached the back of the building. The door to the men's bathroom was on the back side of the building, and around the corner to the other side was the door to the women's bathroom.

I tried the knob and it was locked, but a female voice rang out in a sing-song from inside, "Just a minute ..."

After a few minutes, I heard the toilet flush, sink water run, and some paper rustling. The door opened, and I stepped up to catch it before it closed in the event it locked automatically. The woman coming out looked startled at first, but she gave me a nervous smile and handed me the key.

"Here you go, honey!" she said before rushing around the corner.

I stepped inside closing and locking the door behind me. Looking in the mirror I saw that I was even more of a wreck than I imagined. No wonder the woman rushed away.

There were bruises, scratches, and cuts all over my face and neck, and I was caked with mud and dried blood. My clothes were ripped and caked also. I turned the water on, cupped my hands, and drank until I was sated. I stripped down to my bra and panties lowered my head as close to the faucet as possible and started splashing water on my hair. I used soap from the dispenser and washed my hair as best I could. When finished I washed my face and neck.

The soap stung the scrapes and cuts something fierce, and the water ran blood red before changing to clear as I rinsed. I was relieved to see I wasn't still bleeding. I used paper towels and wrapped them around my hair to soak up the excess water.

I scrunched up two paper towels to use as a wash cloth. With the dispensed soap, I worked up a lather and washed my torso, arms, and legs before inspecting my wounds. The only deep cut was the one on my wrist and possibly a gash on the back of my head where I was first clubbed; the others were simply painful and ugly.

Rinsing was a little more difficult, but I got the bulk of the soap off. I figured a little soap residue wasn't the worst thing that had happened to me. I finger-combed my hair toward my face to hide as much of the damage as possible and looked in the mirror. My appearance was much more presentable.

I washed the makeshift bandage and wrung the excess water out before I reapplied it to my wrist. I pulled it as tight as I could without cutting off circulation. The wrist was still oozing blood. No surprise there.

I picked up my jeans from the floor and could see they weren't going to ever look any better. They were ripped and caked with mud and blood. I rinsed as much of the muck off as possible and put them back on. The wet fabric was cold and clingy against my skin. I shivered.

Next, I picked up my blouse. Again, I had to rinse it out but other than the blood stains and the torn-off strip at the bottom for my wrist, it fared a little better than the jeans.

The blazer was another matter altogether. I tried fixing it up as much as I could, but it was hopeless. I checked the pockets and was happy to find a twenty dollar bill that had accidentally been tucked in the lining of the inside breast pocket. The seam had popped open and I hadn't gotten it mended. That twenty was going to come in handy. I wadded up the battered blazer and shoved it into the trash. I pushed my feet into the mud caked and misshaped boots and prepared to step back outside.

I turned the light off and waited for my eyes to adjust to the dark before I opened the bathroom door and looked in both directions. When I saw that no one was around, I stepped out of the doorway and let the door close silently behind me, keeping it unlocked.

I gave silent thanks for my dark blouse and jeans which aided me in slipping through the shadows. I didn't know how long it would take for help to arrive and I might still need to hide in the shadowy recesses.

I stayed close to the wall, easing up to the front corner of the building. Peeking around the corner I saw Eric's car at the pumps, and the two goons, George and Eric, walking out of the store. As they walked to the rear of the car, I could hear George.

"... then I found where she went back into the river. I followed the edge, looking for footprints where she might have gotten out again, but I think the water swept her away this time. She's probably drowned and pinned under a log in the rapids. We'll never see her again."

"What are we going to tell The Mongoose?" asked Eric. "I'm not taking responsibility for this. You were supposed to make sure she couldn't get away."

"I checked her ropes!" George barked back. He glanced around and lowered his voice. "I don't know how she got loose. She's dead now and that's nothing short of what The Mongoose wanted anyway."

"He's going to kill us, you know!"

"Let's wait until daylight and go back to search the river bank," suggested George. "We can do a better search then.

"If she did get out, she has nowhere to go. It's a long walk across some rough terrain to get to town. We cleaned out her pockets, so even if she made it to town, we should be able to find her. Where's she going to hide? She doesn't even have a dime to her name to call for help, and if she goes to the cops, we'll hear about it."

"Sounds as good as any plan I could come up with right now. Get in the car and we'll head back to the farm; daybreaks not too far away." Eric got into the driver's seat while George got in on the other side. They eased out into traffic and were gone.

**********

$I$ waited a few minutes after seeing the taillights disappear down the street before I stepped out from the corner of the building. There was a pay phone in front of the store, close to me.

I went inside to drop off the key to the bathroom and break the twenty for some quarters. The clerk looked me over, and asked if I was alright.

"Yeah, my car broke down and I need to call Triple A."

Back at the pay phone I called my old partner and good friend, Morgan Sellers, at his home phone number.

Morgan had been a Marine in El Salvador, came home, and went to school on the G.I. Bill. He got his degree in child psychology.

He was good with the kids, but seeing the abuse and neglect that a lot of these kids dealt with took a toll on him. A fire burned deep inside him for justice and retribution for these kids. He couldn't take it anymore and decided he would be better off putting away the culprits who were hurting children than he was at counseling the kids. His heart couldn't take the pain of witnessing their suffering anymore.

He applied as a patrol officer and got on the force a month after I was hired. After six months, we found ourselves as partners.

Morgan is a big guy who has always maintained his Marine Corps physique. He's built to meet out abuse when necessary, but underneath he's a gentle hearted guy. I don't know of a single fight he ever lost and there were a lot of them. About as many cons would like to kill him as there are who want to get even with me, more even, since he's still at the department.

Morgan picked up on the second ring.

"This better be an emergency," he growled still groggy with sleep.

"And a good morning to you, too," I snapped back.

"Jeffries, is that you? Where are you?" He was wide-awake after hearing my voice.

"I don't know. I was abducted by some thugs for someone named The Mongoose. Does that ring a bell?"

"The Mongoose ... yeah, but I can't place it right now. Look, the cops are looking for you. Your secretary called and told them you left the office with a family and never came back. When she got to work the next day, your office had been burglarized and ransacked. We've all been worried sick about you."

"The next day? How long have I been missing?"

"Three days. Four, if you count today."

*They must have had me drugged.*

"Four days? Oh my God! *Paisley* ... I left her home. She'll be starved or—"

"Hold on there girl. As soon as you went missing, Molly and I went to your place and collected all your half-dead houseplants and Paisley. She's been taking up space in *my* bed, I'll have you know."

He chuckled. "Don't worry. She's fine but wonders where you are."

"Oh thanks, Morgan. I don't know what I would do if something happened to her. What was missing from my office? Do you know?

"No, but the forensic team collected evidence, including finger prints. ARE YOU OKAY?"

"Yes and no. I'm beat up real bad, but no broken bones that I can account for. I escaped and I need help."

"Sure, you got it. You don't know what they might have been looking for in your office, do you?"

"No, I would have to look the place over to see if anything is missing. I'm guessing a file on one of my clients, and Norah should be able to help with that.

"Morgan, the family that came in were fake, even the kid. Her name is Tabatha—that's what they were calling her at the farm where they took me. The dad's name is really Eric, and the mother's name is Mary. I don't think they were a real family, either. There was another guy at the farm where they were holding me named George. I got away and ... long story short, I made it to town. I need you to come pick me up."

"Sure, where are you?"

"Umm, I'm at a Shell station at the corner of ... the only sign I can see says 12th. I don't even know what town I'm in. Hold on a minute."

I fed more coins into the phone and turned to holler at a guy walking out of the store.

"What town is this?"

"Rexburg," he yelled back.

"*Rexburg?* Where's that?"

He started toward me. "Lady, you don't know what state you're in?"

"No, sorry." I shook my head. Thinking on my feet I added, "I was asleep in the back seat of my friend's car, and he woke me when we stopped here. While I was in the bathroom, he took off, leaving me stranded. I'm guessing we're ... somewhere in ...?"

"He wasn't much of a friend from the looks of you. You're in Rexburg, Idaho. Do you need some help or something? I can call the police for you—"

"Oh, no. No! We were on our way to New Mexico, and I guess we didn't get very far. Thanks, though. I'm on the phone with my brother who's not far away. He'll come get me."

"Okay. Good luck, lady." He turned and walked to his car.

"Morgan—"

"I heard. What in blazes are you doing in Idaho? No—don't try to answer that. Hold on. Let me get my cell phone and google Rexburg."

"Okay, thanks. But hurry, will ya?"

I fed more coins into the pay phone and watched the traffic while Morgan looked the place up.

*I hope that guy doesn't call the cops. Apparently someone is on the take in their department.*

"Wow, you're up there by the Snake River, just north of Idaho Falls," Morgan muttered.

"How am I going to get home? I don't want to use public trans. They might be watching for me. Someone on the police department here is on the take. I heard Eric and George say that if I went to the police, they would know about it. Any ideas?"

"When was that?"

"Just before I called you. They showed up here at the Shell station, looking for me, and I overheard them talking before they got in the car and left."

"Yeah, hold on." After a few minutes, he said, "Okay, what's the address there?"

"Hold on." I laid the phone down, walked to the open door of the store, and asked the clerk who was at the counter, "What's this address?"

"15 North 12<sup>th</sup> West."

"Thanks." I went back to the phone and gave Morgan the address.

"Okay, I'm flying up. Can you hide out for a bit? I have a good buddy that served with me in the Marine Corps who's FBI now. He's in Idaho Falls, and he can be trusted. I'll meet up with you guys when I get there."

"I'll manage. Have Molly go to my house and get me some clean clothes and toiletries for you to bring. I'm beat up and my clothes are filthy and in bad shape. Shoes too. My running shoes would be great; my boots are ruined."

"Will do. You need anything else?"

"Food," I said and laughed.

"I'll get there as soon as I can. Hang by the phone while I call Riley, and I'll call you back in a few. What's the number?"

"It doesn't say. I'll call you back in five. Will that work?"

"Yeah, hold tight." He hung up.

I ducked back into the shadows beside the building and watched the comings and goings while I silently ticked off the seconds in my head. After what I thought was about five minutes, I called Morgan back.

"Hi! Riley's on his way. He's more than happy to help and it's a feebee case now since you were taken over state lines. He's driving a blue Ford 500. He's six-two and built a lot like me, and he said he'll be wearing jeans and a button-down blue chambray shirt. He'll go to the pay phone and pretend he's dialing a number. He'll say, 'Is my pal Peabody there?' That's the password. Oh, and he's bald as a cue ball."

"Is my pal Peabody there, got it. Thanks, buddy, I owe you one."

"Be careful, and I'll see you soon. Molly sends her love."

"Love back to her. See you soon," I disconnected before he did this time.

I forgot to ask how long it would take Riley to show up, and I sure didn't want to miss him, so I slipped back into the shadows. The sun was starting to peek over the horizon, and I knew my sanctuary of shadows would be diminishing.

I was starving, but I didn't want to go into the store and take the chance of getting trapped, so I went back to the bathroom and drank more water to take the edge off. When I came out, a lady was approaching to go in. We passed without speaking. After she closed the door, I ducked into the shadow of some bushes. They were against a chain-link fence on the other side of the walkway. This gave me a view of the road, the front of the store, and the phone. I was out of sight from anyone else going to the bathrooms and still close enough to hear what someone was saying on the phone if they spoke clearly.

About thirty-five minutes later, a dark blue Ford pulled up in front of the building by the pay phone. A man fitting Riley's description got out and walked to the phone. He picked up the receiver and dialed without putting any coins in and said, "Is my pal Peabody there?"

"I stepped out of the shadows and said, "Hi, I'm Peabody."

**********

# IV

He stuck his hand out and grinned. "Riley."

Taking his hand, I smiled back. "Mariah Jeffries but my friends call me Jeffries. I'm sure glad you're here."

"We're glad you called Morgan. Sorry, but you look like hell. Come on, let's get out of here and get some breakfast. I'd ask if you're hungry, but I know you have to be."

"I am," I said and laughed. A huge weight had been lifted off my shoulders. I took a deep breath and followed Riley to the car.

I got into the passenger side of the car when he opened the door for me. Before closing my door, he leaned in. "Do you have any injuries requiring medical attention? I have a private doctor that can meet us at the house."

"Other than this cut on my wrist and a split skull, I don't think so. The wrist might need some stitches, and I should probably have a tetanus shot. I'm not sure how bad my head is. I have some other cuts and scrapes, but I'm pretty sure I don't have anything major, no broken bones."

"Good thing." He grinned again and closed my door, walked around to the other side, and slid in behind the steering wheel. He made a call on his cell phone to make arrangements for the doctor to meet us at his house.

In the car, I gave him a rundown of what I could remember. He told me the only thing he knew was what he heard on the news about an ex-cop turned high-profile forensic psychologist from New Mexico who was abducted. As far as he knew, the search had been centered in New Mexico and west Texas until Morgan called him.

He'd called his director when he got off the phone with Morgan and filled him in on the situation. "You'll have to meet with the director to give a formal statement later today," he added. I wasn't surprised.

As we turned into a driveway, he hit a button in the roof of his car and the garage door opened. He pulled in and closed the door behind us before we exited the car and went into the house. The aroma of bacon and eggs tantalized me, and my mouth started to water.

A tall, slender brunette turned from the stove and smiled at me as I walked into the kitchen from the garage.

"Perfect timing." She smiled. "You can wash up in the bathroom." With a spatula in one hand and a frying pan in the other, she nodded her head toward a hallway. "First door on your right."

"Thank you." I turned toward the hall.

I washed up and walked back to the kitchen where Riley was sitting at the breakfast table, and the brunette was walking toward the stove.

"Hi, I'm Jeri, Riley's wife. Go ahead and have a seat," she said over her shoulder. "You look half-starved."

"I am. Thank you for taking me in."

"We're happy to help out a friend of Morgan's. When we're finished eating, you can take a nice hot bath or shower if you like. I have a clean robe you can put on until Morgan gets here with your clothes. In fact..." She turned from the stove and checked me out, "you could probably wear some of my clothes."

"Thanks. That sounds wonderful. The bath—but I'll wait for my clothes ... unless we have to go somewhere before Morgan gets here."

We chatted about trivia, steering clear of the case while we ate. Jeri was a naturally warm and friendly person, and I took an immediate liking to her.

Dr. Bell showed up as we finished breakfast. In the guest bedroom, he took a blood sample to see if they could determine what I was drugged with during my capture. He checked me for signs of concussion and had me strip down to my bra and panties. He took pictures of every wound and advised me the investigation will require new pictures in three days to record any new bruising that hasn't shown up yet. He checked the cut on my wrist, deadened it, stitched it up, and covered it with a bandage. He covered the lesser wounds with a salve and a bandage where needed.

My scalp, he informed me, was split and swollen where I was hit, but not bad enough to require stitches. "The wound is scabbing and looks good." He clucked in satisfaction. My skull seemed to be intact. If I had a concussion from being whacked in the head, he thought it subsided while I was unconscious from the drugs.

He gave me a tetanus shot and checked me over to make sure there weren't any other injuries requiring care. He gave me a bottle of antibiotics to take as a prophylactic—since my open wounds had been exposed to so much filth—and some Tylenol 3 for the pain in case I felt the need of it. Everything else, he told me, looked good.

After the doctor left, I offered to help clean up the breakfast dishes, but Jeri insisted I go soak in a warm tub which sounded great.

In the bathroom, I ran hot steaming water until the tub was just over half-full. I added some fragrant oil that was placed on the counter along with clean towels, a wash cloth, a packaged toothbrush, and a wide-toothed comb for my hair. There was a plush blue, full length bathrobe that zipped up the front hanging on the back of the door. The tub was an old-fashioned claw-foot type that was big and beautiful.

I moaned as I lowered myself into the hot water and leaned back to rest my head against the raised back of the tub, my injured arm, wrapped in plastic wrap, resting over the edge to keep it dry.

The warmth of the water and the fragrance from the oils were so relaxing I couldn't keep my eyes open, and I drifted off into dreamless sleep. When I awoke, the water was cold and I was chilled. My injured arm was numb from hanging over the edge, and I had to lift it with my other hand. I opened the drain to let the water out which had turned a dingy grey.

Rubbing my arm to get the blood flowing again, I stood up and turned on the tap adjusting the temperature. With the water temperature to my liking, I started the shower. I shampooed first and then soaped down and rinsed off.

I was still sore, but my scrapes and cuts didn't look like they would leave any terrible scars with the exception of my wrist. That will definitely leave a scar but not a particularly ugly one. The doctor did a good job sewing it up.

I put on the robe, zipped it closed, turned to the sink and combed my hair and brushed my teeth. When finished, I gathered up my rags and boots and stepped out of the bathroom. I walked down the hall toward the kitchen and saw Riley and Jeri in the living room to my left, so I tapped on the threshold to get their attention.

They both looked up at me and before they could say anything I asked, "Where's the trash? These things are ruined."

Riley stood from the recliner.

"I'll take them. Go ahead and have a seat, and I'll be right back." As he took my things, I clung to my boots for a moment, hesitant to relinquish them.

"I sure hate that these are ruined. They were my favorite pair, but the river pretty much destroyed them."

"We can take them to a boot shop if you want to try and salvage them, but they'll probably never fit right again."

"No, I don't think they'll be worth the cost. I'll buy new ones when I get home."

I continued to hang onto them looking them over.

Riley waited with the rags in his hands while I mulled over trying to save the boots or not. After careful consideration, I put them in Riley's hands and sighed. He gave me a half smile and walked through the kitchen to the garage. I entered the living room and sat on the opposite end of the couch from Jeri. We chatted about her home and hobbies until Riley returned. Jeri said she would leave us to discuss the case.

"You look better. How do you feel?" Riley sat in his recliner catty-corner from the couch.

"Much better ... thank you."

I rested my head on the back of the couch.

"When will we meet with your director?" I closed my eyes.

"Not until Morgan gets here. He called while you were in the bathroom and his flight is due in at two this afternoon. The Albuquerque Police Department is turning the case files over to the FBI field office there, and the field office will transmit them electronically to my office. Once Morgan gets here, we can go to my office and go over everything with the director."

I nodded. "Sounds like a plan."

"He's putting together a detail to raid the farm once we pinpoint its location from the recounting of your story."

"Hmmm, that's good," I was slurring my words, the weight of exhaustion pulling me into another world. The relaxing bath and lack of adrenaline caught up to me, and I could no longer stay awake.

Riley continued talking, but his voice faded away as I drifted off into la-la land.

"Mariah?" Someone pushed my shoulder, and I lurched, startled, opening my eyes. I realized then that I had fallen asleep.

Jeri was standing before me, asking me something.

"Wha—" I cleared my throat. "Is Morgan here?"

"No. I'm sorry to wake you, but I thought you might be more comfortable in our guest room. Morgan isn't due here for a few more hours."

"That would be great, thank you." I pushed myself up from the couch and followed Jeri to the bedroom. She didn't have to tell me to lie down; I stretched out on the bed. Jeri pulled a light blanket from the closet and threw it over me closing the door on her way out. I was asleep before the door closed all the way.

The last thing I heard was Jeri saying, "Sweet dreams."

**********

The sound of men laughing brought me awake. I was confused for a moment. I sat up on the bed and didn't recognize my surroundings until I heard Morgan's voice. Everything rushed back to me. I opened the door and walked out to the living room where Riley and Morgan were talking.

Their conversation stopped as I entered the room. Morgan got up, came over to me, and wrapped his arms around me in a big bear hug.

"Ow, ow ... ouch.    Not so tight; you're bruising my bruises."

"Sorry."  He leaned back to examine me, still holding me at the shoulders.  "I'm so glad you're alright.  How are you feeling?"

"Better.  It's amazing what a little food, a hot bath, and a little sleep can do for a girl."

"Jeri put your things in the bathroom."  Riley nodded toward the hall.

"Thanks."

Morgan let go of me and I walked to the couch.  "Are we in a hurry?"

"No, you have about ten minutes to relax."

I must have grimaced and Riley laughed.

"I'm kidding. Do you need anything? Jeri's making up some sandwiches for a late lunch ... early dinner, and after we eat, we'll go to the office."

"Hmmm, I can't believe how hungry I am again. I guess they didn't feed me those three days they had me drugged."

I sat on the couch with Morgan, and the three of us talked about the investigation in New Mexico after my disappearance.

"Hey, Riley, can you believe she used to be a beauty queen? That ugly mug? Haha," Morgan bellowed.

I could tell by his joking he had been worried about me and was breaking the ice on his uneasiness with his lame joke.

"Really, Mariah?" Jeri asked as she poked her head around the corner.

"Yeah, it's true." I sighed.

"You'll have to tell us about that," Riley said.

"Lunch is ready. Come eat everyone," Jeri cut in.

We went to the dining room where Jeri had soup and sandwiches set out for our meal.

"What do you want to drink? There's fresh coffee, sodas…" Jeri waited for me and Morgan to reply.

We opted for coffee, and she brought a tray with a selection of Keurig coffee pods to choose from. We made our selections, took our seats, and I started to regale them with my past adventures as a beauty queen.

"The summer after graduating from high school, I was approached by the town mayor who was a good friend of my dad's. He asked me to represent our small Texas town in a county-wide beauty pageant that would, through a series of pageants, eventually determine the contestant who would represent the state in the National Miss Universe Pageant.

"My mom and I watched the Miss America Pageant and Miss Universe Pageant on TV for as long as I could remember, and I was really excited. Instead of going off to a University, I decided to stay home and go to the local community college for a while so I could participate in this process.

It was a lot of fun, and I eventually made it to the statewide pageant which was a big to-do. We contestants met in Dallas, Texas, where we were put up in this fancy schmancy hotel with chaperones. We were wined and dined, interviewed on television and radio, and interviewed in person by celebrity judges— well, not all of them were big-name celebrities, but Dan Stovie, the Houston Oilers quarterback, and Judy Minker, the former Miss Texas, were judges. I even have their autographs somewhere.

"Anyway, that's the highlight of my pageant career. I didn't win the Miss Texas Universe Pageant, but it was fun.

"After that I followed my boyfriend to the University of New Mexico in Albuquerque where I majored in psychology. A month after classes started he dumped me for a cheerleader and broke my heart. I graduated four years later with my bachelor's and that summer my dad was killed in the line of duty."

"Oh, I didn't know you came from a cop family," Riley said.

"Well, I do and I don't. My dad was a firefighter, and while he was in a building rescuing a woman, the building collapsed on him. The woman and my father both died. It was later determined the fire was set deliberately, and the arsonist was never caught.

"Two of my dad's brothers, his father, and his grandfather were all career cops though, and somewhere back in ancient history, someone on my mother's side had been a sheriff in Oklahoma. My dad was the black sheep, I guess, but he was good at what he did and loved his job."

"Morgan said you were his partner on the department for a while. What made you become a cop instead of going into psychology?" asked Jeri.

"My dad and I were really close. When he died and they couldn't find the arsonist, I couldn't get past it. I knew I wouldn't be able to find my dad's killer, but I had to do something to get the bad guys off the street, so I applied to the police department in Albuquerque where I was living at the time. I was hired and went through three weeks of classroom training and three months of on-the-job training with a training officer. Then they sent me to the police academy for certification. I graduated third in my class of thirty-eight officers.

"Morgan was hired a month after I was, and we went through the academy together. We worked patrol together as partners for a while after that.

"Tell them where I graduated in our class."

I opened my mouth to blurt a sassy remark, but nothing came to mind.

"Go ahead. Tell them." Morgan was grinning from ear to ear.

I glanced from Morgan to Riley to Jeri.

"Oh, okay. Morgan graduated first in the class ... but I swear he must have cheated."

"Sore loser."

"Braggart."

Everyone laughed.

"Morgan's achievement aside," I stuck my tongue out at him, "when a couple of the old timers retired from the detective division, Morgan and I applied. We were both promoted to detective and worked a number of cases together, including some undercover work.

"I actually applied for the FBI before I left the department and was accepted, but before I got the notice, I decided to go back to school and get my masters in psychology. I was already enrolled by the time the acceptance letter reached me.

"I graduated and worked for a while with a group of psychologists while I got my Ph.D. I really haven't had any regrets until now."

Riley looked at his watch and stood up. "Well, we better get going."

"I'll go get changed. Thanks, Jeri, for breakfast *and* lunch. It was all wonderful."

I brushed my teeth, and dug out clean clothes from a carry-on bag Morgan brought. I dressed and sat on the commode lid to put on my tennis shoes.

When I got in the car with Riley and Morgan, I found a paper grocery sack with my ruined clothes and boots inside.

"I thought you were going to throw these rags away for me."

"Nope. We're keeping them for evidence."

"Oh! Yeah. I should have known that. I guess I'm still a little fuzzy headed."

At Riley's office, we met with his regional director in the big conference room. When Riley introduced me to Director Jim Benton, I extended my arm to shake hands with him. Jim took my proffered hand.

"Nice to meet you, Mariah. We have a file on you at the bureau, and I saw that you once applied with the FBI. You looked like a great candidate on paper and your test scores were right at the top, but then you declined the offer. Mind if I ask why?"

I told him about my dad and the reason I went into law enforcement in the first place.

"By the time I was accepted to the FBI, I decided to go back to school and finish my degree in Psychology."

He nodded. "Well, we've always got a place for a good forensic psychologist as well as good agents."

He had a video recorder set up to record the entire interview. Jim conducted the interview, Riley represented his office, Morgan was there representing the New Mexico investigation, and of course I was present.

Morgan went first with all the information the department had accumulated during their investigation into my disappearance and the break-in of my office. I gave a complete rundown of everything I could remember, and Riley gave an account beginning with the call from Morgan to when we started the interviews.

Once the interviews were finished, we took a fifteen minute break and then came together again in the conference room.

Normally, as the victim, I wouldn't be allowed to participate in the rest of the meeting. Since Jim was privy to my background, and it was believed this case was related to my prior occupation as a law enforcement officer, an exception was made.

"So, I've spent most of the day going over everything we received from New Mexico, ranging from the Albuquerque Police Department, the New Mexico State Police Department, the New Mexico State Forensics Lab, and the Northern New Mexico Division of the FBI. Here's what I've got."

He pulled out a yellow legal pad from a box of paperwork beside his chair.

"The fingerprints found in your office belong to a couple of small-time hoods. A check of your past cases showed that you and Morgan both busted them on different charges.

"The first guy's name is Benny Parra. You busted him on petty theft and misdemeanor assault charges when you were in uniform, Mariah. He was busted for drunk and disorderly as well as possession of marijuana by Morgan when he was in uniform. Parra spent some time in the slammer for assault by motor vehicle on a peace officer after he tried to run down a uniformed officer in his escape from a jewelry heist. Apparently he was the getaway driver. The whole gang was caught.

"You and Morgan were detectives then and headed the sting that took them down. You were both the lead witnesses for the state, and all three of the gang were convicted and spent three years in the state pen except, Larry Smith. He is still serving time; he'll never get out.

"What's the deal on him?" I asked.

"He killed an inmate and crippled one of the guards during a riot, and he's been caught trying to escape three times.

"The prints on the other guy came back as Ricky Saldivar."

"Big Ears Saldivar?" I asked in surprise.

"Yep, the very same."

"I remember him. I thought he was dead."

"Me too." Morgan nodded in agreement. "Yeah, he worked for Compton, that big drug dealer who ran all his money through his trucking company."

"Right." I pointed my finger at Morgan and nodded. "Big Ears was a safe cracker. At first we thought Compton was the head of that organization, but we found out he was working for James Franklin." I drew in a deep breath. "A.K.A. *The Mongoose ... that's* where I know that name from. He was out of Denver, Colorado." I turned to Riley.

"We had to turn our evidence over to the feds since it turned into a multi-state case. You guys ran a great case and busted Franklin and Compton on that murder down in El Paso. Remember, Morgan, we had to testify since we found the key evidence when we ran the search warrant at that trucking company. Turns out it was one of Franklin's businesses. The evidence we gathered tied them to the murder in Texas."

"That's right," Riley said. "They were both sent up for life. Compton was fried down in Texas six years later. We found a long string of dead bodies that we could tie to him spanning Texas, New Mexico, Colorado, Nevada, and Idaho."

"We know he was taking orders from James Franklin but could never prove it," Jim said.

"James Franklin was released a few years back; his sentence was overturned on a technicality. We believe someone higher up in the judicial system is on the take, but we can't prove that either. We've been trying to get something solid on Franklin for years."

"So now we have a good idea why I was targeted. But why wasn't Morgan?" I turned to Morgan. "Sorry buddy. I don't *want* you taken or harmed but you were in on that case too."

"I *was* targeted." Morgan's countenance turned dead serious. "Jim called me. When he heard you made contact and said The Mongoose was involved, the Colorado office was contacted. They shook down one of their snitches who finally gave up the information. Franklin's goons were supposed to take you first and lure me in while I searched for you. They didn't expect you to get away and call me..."

His eyes were on the conference table and his fingers tapped out a little rhythm. "...they missed their opportunity before I flew out here.

"Anyway, as soon as the FBI found this out, Jim called the Albuquerque FBI office and put Molly and the kids in protective custody until we tie this up."

"Good. I'm glad they're safe."

"Me too. So, what do we do now, Jim?"

"Here's the plan."

We all gathered around Jim.

**********

"You and Morgan stay close to Riley. He's in charge of you two." Jim eyed us as he handed out bullet proof vests with "FBI" stenciled on the front and back. Riley's buddy, Sheriff Hargrove, deputized Morgan and me so we could assist on this raid. Morgan and I nodded. We were in the back of a SWAT van, the plans for the raid on the farmhouse where I'd been held captive clear in everyone's mind.

It was another cloudy night, but the moon was fuller and the clouds not as thick as the previous night when I escaped. It was hard to believe I escaped only twenty-four hours ago.

We were parked about a half mile from the farmhouse on a dirt road that turned off the main highway. Two more vans with FBI agents had pulled in before us and were parked in a small clearing out of view from the highway.

Morgan reached under his jacket and pulled out an FN Five-seveN from his shoulder holster, removed the magazine, locked the slide back, and handed the gun to me grip first.

"Oh baby, come to mama." I have true appreciation for this magnificent handgun.

The Five-seveN pistol and its 5.7x28mm ammunition were developed by FN Herstal. Originally, the military and law enforcement were the only entities who could acquire the Five-seveN pistol per certain restrictions, but it has since been made available to the general public in limited lots. They're hard to come by.

Morgan handed me the magazine and I seated it, letting the slide chamber a round.

"I've wanted one of these ever since I shot yours, Morgan. I couldn't justify the purchase before, but I'm going to buy one when this is over!"

Riley smiled. "It's a fine weapon. Morgan says you've spent a lot of time in target practice with that gun. Do you feel proficient enough to carry it tonight?"

"Absolutely. I'm an excellent shot with this weapon; just ask Morgan. What are you carrying, Morgan?"

"Riley loaned me his shotgun and his Colt .45 auto. When this is all over, I'll make you a great deal on the Five-seveN. I ordered a new one, and I should be getting it in a week or two."

Morgan removed his shoulder holster. He handed it to me before he put his vest on. I adjusted the shoulder holster to fit me while Jim gave final instructions.

"Okay, folks, let's lock and load." Jim opened the back door of the van and climbed out.

I holstered the Five-seveN, put on the vest, and then the holster. I followed Jim out the back of the van, Riley was behind me, and Morgan exited last. The driver, Randolph, got out of the driver's seat, and we all approached the group from the other two vans, who were gathered in the clearing.

"Okay," Jim said. "David, you and your team take the north side and approach toward the garage."

"I think it's a barn, Boss."

Jim nodded. "I want two of your men to go behind the *barn* to make sure no one comes out that way and to watch the back of the house. Make sure no one leaves in that direction. You and the rest of your team will clear the barn before heading to the house.

"Jackson, you and your team will approach from the south side. I want two of your men to remain on the south side of the house and watch for anyone trying to exit through any doors or windows that might be there.

"Keep your men away from the back of the house and the barn. We don't want any crossfire accidents.

"The rest of your team will swarm to the front as the rest of us approach head on from the tree line. Stay off the radios until we have the place secured unless all hell breaks loose before then. Let's go!"

We headed down the dirt road and stopped inside the trees before crossing the highway and heading into the trees on the other side of the road. We went straight through the grove and stopped inside the trees before stepping into the open.

We waited there until David's team got in position on the north side of the barn. Once Jackson's team was in place on the south side of the house, the rest of us started across the field toward the front of the house.

The house was dark and looked deserted. I really didn't expect anyone to still be there, but I was disappointed to realize we were not going to clear this up tonight.

All three teams converged on the house and the barn. As suspected, the house was deserted. When we were exiting the house, Jim's radio crackled. "We've got bodies in the barn."

While the rest of the team started gathering evidence at the house, Jim, Riley, Morgan, and I ran to the barn. Laid out side by side on the floor with their hands tied behind their backs were George and Eric shot in the head execution style.

"Where are Mary and Tabatha? Make sure they're not hiding somewhere," I called to Jim.

Jim radioed to the rest of the team to search the house and grounds for the two females. Mary and Tabatha were never found.

In the meantime, the coroner and forensic team showed up. It didn't take them long to get there from where they were waiting a mile north of the entrance to the farmhouse drive. It took us the rest of the night to process the crime scene.

At six o'clock, just as the sun was rising, we made it back to the office. We had a debriefing and planned to take a break. We would reconvene at two o'clock in the afternoon. Riley told Morgan and me that we could stay at his place, so the three of us went back to his house together.

**********

I was beat from the night's activities, and I still had a lot of pain from my ordeal the night before. I took some of the Tylenol 3 that Dr. Bell gave me and went to the guest room to rest.

My sleep was restless with dreams of my capture and escape. When Jeri came to wake me, I felt as though I'd been running for my life for the last three hours. I still felt sleep deprived.

After going to the bathroom and cleaning up, I met Riley and Morgan in the dining room and sat at the table with them. The table was already set. There was a large salad in the center.

"Sleep well?" asked Riley.

"No." I scrubbed my face with both hands trying to get rid of the exhaustion. "I relived my escape in my dreams."

Morgan cocked his head, his brow furrowed. "Did you remember anything new? Sometimes that happens."

Thinking for a moment, I shook my head. "No, I don't think so."

"You want a cup of coffee?" Morgan rose with his empty coffee cup. "I'll fix it for you."

"Sounds great, but I can get it." I rose from my seat at the table and crossed to the kitchen behind Morgan.

I picked out a dark roast coffee and put it in the Keurig. *When I get home, I've got to get myself one of these. Sure is a lot better than instant Folgers, and just as fast.* Jeri had just pulled two homemade pizzas from the oven, and I offered to help cut them while my coffee brewed.

I took my coffee and one of the pans of pizza to the table, and I sat across from Morgan. Jeri followed with the second pan and sat in the chair beside me. After eating, we headed back to the office, leaving Jeri to clean up our dishes again.

Jim wasn't at the office when we got there. I poured myself a cup of last night's left-over coffee and put it in the microwave to heat up. Thick, black, and strong—it was just what I needed. Riley got a Diet Coke and a bottle of water out of the small refrigerator that sat in the corner. He tossed the water to Morgan before popping the top of his Coke. We brainstormed about the case trying to figure out what to do next. Thirty minutes later, Jim came in. He didn't look any more rested than I felt.

"Glad you guys are here." He sat at the head of the table and thumped a travel mug down on top. "Our Colorado division has been keeping an eye on James Franklin. As I told you yesterday, we've been trying to get something to stick on him for a long time. I'm hoping this case will be the one that brings him down for good.

"We have an undercover agent who's been working on getting inside his organization, and she's made a lot of progress. She's been informed of the developments on this case, and she is going to see what she can find out without blowing her cover.

"Colorado was able to confirm that Franklin has not been at his offices or his home since Wednesday after you were abducted, Mariah. They're checking transportation records to see if they can find where he went. He has a private jet and there's no record that it left the hanger in the last two weeks, so..." Jim took a deep breath. "It's possible he took a road trip, and our agent should be able to give us more information shortly to verify that.

"We believe he's in Idaho, either Rexburg or Idaho Falls looking for you, Jeffries. We have eyes and ears in both of these communities looking for him. If he's here we'll find him, but in the meantime, I want you guys to lay low for a while."

"What are the odds he's tracked me to the FBI, and even more important, to Riley's house?" I was concerned for Jeri's safety, and from the corner of my eye I could see Riley was thinking of the same possibility. "Is there some place safe that Jeri can go until this is resolved? I really don't want her caught in the middle of this mess."

Riley scowled and looked at Jim, but Jim raised his hands, palms out, and shook his head.

"Just wait a minute. He doesn't even know you're still alive. For all he knows, you drowned in the Snake River. That being said, yes ... we can put Jeri in protective custody. I'll get a place set up and you can take her there, Riley."

"I prefer to send her to visit her sister in Oregon. Her brother-in-law is a state trooper there, and she'll be a lot safer with them in another state for a little while." Jim gave a brief nod.

Riley stood with a frown on his face. He walked out of the conference room, leaving the door open, pulled his cell phone from his pocket, and turned his back to the door. After a moment we heard him in casual conversation.

"Hi, honey. Why don't you start packing and get ready to take that vacation to Portland to visit Janice and Clive?" There was a pause, and Riley rubbed the top of his bald head.

"No, don't get worried. I just think it's a good time for you to go visit. ... Yes. I'm sure. ... I'll call Clive and fill him in first. After that I'll be home as soon as I can to help you finish packing and take you to the airport. If you talk to Janice, don't say anything about what's going on—Clive will know." Riley cleared his throat. "No, I just don't want you and Janice discussing it over the phone. ... Okay, love you too ... Oh, babe? ... Keep your eyes open for anything unusual. Call me immediately if you need to. ... Yep, see you soon. ... Bye!"

Riley turned back to the room and gave Morgan and me a 'once over' before letting his eyes rove over the rest of the room.

Jim cocked an eyebrow and gave Riley a knowing glance. "I'll requisition the jet to take her there. No sense in alerting anyone of where she's going by using public transportation." He rose from his chair and left the room.

Riley nodded and pushed a couple buttons before putting the phone back to his ear.

"Clive, hi. It's Riley." He leaned on the door jam. "Good, good, but we have a little situation here, and I'd like to send Jeri your way for a visit. ... I can't go into details but there's a slight possibility that some hoods could snoop around the house. ... Yeah. I need to know Jeri is out of harm's way. ... Will it be a problem for her to come and visit right now? ... It shouldn't be for more than a week, maybe not even that long if we wrap things up here sooner."

My stomach clenched at the thought of this investigation dragging on for a week.

Riley laughed. "I know. Once they get together, the visit always seems to be extended. ... Great, thanks! I'll be in touch with the details of her arrival."

He came back into the conference room and sat down.

Jim returned and took his seat. "All set. I told them to have the jet ready and waiting within the next two hours.

Riley nodded. "I'll need to go home and take care of this."

"I understand. Jeffries, we're going to put you and Morgan in a safe house." Jim let his eyes rove around the room and settle on Riley. He cleared his throat.

"Riley, once you get Jeri out of town you can choose to stay at the safe house or your own home. I prefer you stay at the safe house for added protection, but it's up to you." He reached down into the box of files by his chair and pulled up a yellow legal pad. "Now, get out of here and take care of Jeri. Let me know where you'll be once she's taken care of."

Riley stood and before leaving, he gave Morgan and me a sly grin. "I'll be in touch with you two soon. Try to stay out of trouble, will you?"

"You got it. See ya soon," Morgan replied to Riley's retreating back.

Jim gathered up some folders that were spread out on the table, put them in a pile on top of the legal pad, and placed everything in the box next to his chair. He was frowning and deep in thought, so Morgan and I gave him time to think without interruption.

I folded my arms on the conference table and laid my head on them. I either needed to get some shut-eye or have an adrenaline rush to wake me up.

"Why don't you two relax here for a while? I'll go make arrangements for that safe house and be back in a few."

I raised my head at Jim's words. He slapped his palms down on top of the table and pushed himself to a standing position. He stared down at the box of files beside him and nodded his head as if he was having a private conversation, then took a deep breath, sighed, and walked to the door closing it on his way out.

I grunted and laid my head back down. I heard Morgan get up from his chair. I was so tired I drifted off to sleep before I could tell what he was doing.

I was awakened with a jolt by shouting outside the door. I jerked my head up and saw first Riley and then Jim following him into the room.

"HE'S ... GOT ... JERI!" Riley growled as he turned around and squared off with Jim so suddenly Jim almost plowed into him.

At those words, I was wide-awake. Morgan was by Riley's side in two large strides.

"We'll get her back, Riley. I'm sorry." Jim gripped Riley by each arm. "We had no indication he knew Jeffries was alive, much less staying at your place. We'll get her back. I promise."

Riley sat in the nearest chair, put his elbows on his knees, and cradled his head in both hands, sighing. "He better not hurt her ... not one hair on her head. I swear he'll regret it, Jim." His fingers turned white from the grip on his head. I was afraid he would crush his own skull.

Morgan and I glanced at each other before Morgan turned to Jim and asked, "What do we know?"

Riley raised his head from his hands and said in a broken voice, "When I got home, the back door was kicked in and Jeri was gone. This was on the kitchen counter." He handed the crumpled piece of paper he'd been holding to Morgan. I moved next to Morgan so I could read the paper.

In stenciled letters it read, **"NOTHING WILL HAPPEN TO YOUR WIFE IF I GET JEFFRIES AND MORGAN. I'LL BE IN TOUCH."** There was no signature or name.

Morgan handed the paper to Jim, who read it, looked at Riley, and then looked down at the paper again with a scowl. He stood there staring at it.

"This makes no sense. It's not like The Mongoose to be so brazen." Still staring at the paper Jim yelled, "Hector, get me an evidence bag!"

Hector, five-ten, was dressed in a grey suit with a white shirt and a pink and blue diagonally striped tie—his ID badge clipped to his lapel. He brought in the clear evidence bag, and Jim slid the note inside, took the bag, peeled off the strip protecting the gum, and sealed it. He initialed it across the edge of the flap.

"Here, make a copy of this for my file, then take it to forensics and tell them to put a rush on it." He handed the envelope back to Hector. "Close the door on your way out."

Morgan pulled a chair up in front of Riley. Riley looked up with anguish in his eyes.

"We're going to do whatever we have to, Riley. Right now, what you need to do is think like an agent, not a husband. It's important to get your head in the right place. Let's get a plan in place and take this monster down." Morgan's directness inspired Riley.

I learned later that Riley and Jeri were high school sweethearts. Riley's family was killed in a train derailment when he was six. He grew up being shuffled from foster home to foster home until he was placed with a couple when he was sixteen years old. They were an elderly couple who never had children of their own.

Mrs. Smith passed away from cancer while Riley was in El Salvador. Mr. Smith passed away shortly after Riley got home a year later, so Jeri and her family are all the family Riley has—*ever* had, really. Although he kept in touch with the Smiths, and they were good to him, he never really thought of them as family.

Riley nodded and took a deep breath letting it out slow and steady.

"You're right." He stood and flexed his powerful shoulders to release the tension that had built up in his neck. Then he swung his arms back and then forward and shook the tension out of them. "Jim, have we heard from them yet?"

"No."

"I'm going back to the house. I have my sniper rifle locked up in my gun safe. When we hear from him, he'll tell us where to make the swap. I'm hoping he will give us enough time so I can set up out of si—"

There was a knock at the door and Hector poked his head in. "Boss, the agent we have inside Franklin's organization just made contact. She gave me a phone number he called her from. I gave it to the techs to see if they can trace it."

---

"Good job." Jim smiled. "Go on, Riley."

"If he gives us enough time, I'll go ahead to the swap site and get set up out of sight. I'll be able to cover Morgan and Jeffries. I would also like to have a couple other agents take up inconspicuous positions for back-up to take him down. That's all going to depend on how much notice he gives us."

"How do you want to play this, Morgan?" Jim moved to his chair at the head of the table. He sat scooting the box of files at the side of his chair farther back.

"Basically, you two are civilians even though you've been commissioned by the sheriff. We don't deal with kidnappers, and we don't trade for hostages, but if you two want to turn yourselves over to this guy, and I suspect that you do, I will do everything in my power to help get you back safe.

"Riley, we *all* have to be aware that even though they said they'll release Jeri when they get Morgan and Jeffries, there's a big probability they won't."

"I'm in one hundred percent!" Morgan nodded to Riley. "If they take me and keep Jeri, maybe I'll be able to protect her. Jeffries?" He turned to me and waited.

"I've never considered myself a civilian, not even when I was a kid. I've been training with my dad and uncles my whole life for situations like this. Besides, I have a score to settle."

"Good, but let's keep revenge out of it and be professional." Jim cleared his throat. "If we let our emotions get involved, we'll be more vulnerable."

At that, Jim rose from his chair and headed for the door. "Come on, Riley. I'll go to the house with you as back-up while you get your tools."

The recent developments had me wide-awake. While Jim and Riley were gone, Morgan and I studied maps of the area with Hector, familiarizing ourselves with the whole region of Rexburg/Idaho Falls. With luck, we'd have a good game plan no matter where The Mongoose chose to meet. When Jim and Riley got back, we batted around different potential scenarios and strategies.

We had just taken a break, and started out of the conference room, when a young woman— looked to be in her mid twenties, wearing a yellow cotton dress belted at the waist and falling to just above her knees—opened the door and walked into the front office.

She was wearing a pair of yellow heels and carried a white straw clutch under her left arm and a manila envelope in her right hand.

"May I see Agent Jim Benton? Some man stopped me outside the building and asked me to deliver this. He said it was an emergency and that he had to run to the hospital. He sounded frantic and made it seem very important, or I wouldn't have agreed.

Allison, the office secretary who was sitting at the front desk reached for the phone to buzz the conference room.

Jim, having heard the young woman, walked over to her and introduced himself.

"I understand you have something for me?"

"Uh, yes ... yes, sir. Jim reached his hand out, and the lady handed him the envelope. He took it by the corner between his thumb and index finger, turned and handed it to Riley, who also grasped it by the corner in like manner. Hector met Riley, Morgan, and me at the door to the conference room with a couple evidence bags. I pulled the door closed behind us.

While Hector prepared an evidence bag to receive the contents, Riley opened the piece of mail by slitting the top. He carefully extracted a single page with a pair of tweezers that Hector supplied and dropped it in the evidence bag. Hector laid that bag on the table and opened the next bag so the envelope could be placed in it. Once both pieces were under protective wrap, we all crowded around the table to check them out. The only thing on the envelope was 'Jim Benton, FBI." The letter was typewritten:

**Morgan is to go behind the warehouse at the Rexburg Trucking Company at nine p.m. tonight. He is to come alone in the tan GMC pickup that is parked across the street from your office. Hotwire it and come unarmed.**

**Jeffries is to meet at Tautphas Park by the zoo, at nine p.m. tonight. She is to come alone in the white Ford pickup parked across the street from your office. Hotwire it, no weapons.**

**Riley is to meet on Swan Valley Highway three miles east of N 130th East at nine p.m. tonight. He is to come alone in the grey Chevy pickup parked across the street from your office. Hotwire it, no weapons.**

**If any one of them fails to show up at the appointed time, no matter what the reason, or is not alone when they arrive,**

**Jeri dies. If one of them is armed, Jeri dies. If they are tailed, Jeri dies. If anything goes wrong, Jeri dies.**

Hector and I walked to the window and gazed down at the street. Hector let out a low whistle. Parked on the street across from the office were the three pickup trucks. Looking down on them from the third floor, we could see the beds were completely empty.

"Damn!" said Riley and Morgan at the same time, just as Jim walked into the office.

"The lady didn't have any other information. I've got her with a sketch artist to identify the guy that gave her the envelope, but I'm not expecting it to help us much. What do we have?"

Riley handed the letter to Jim, who scanned it. His brow furrowed as he went over it again before saying, "I knew he wouldn't make it easy for us, but I wasn't expecting him to demand a meet with Riley too."

He looked up at the four of us standing before him and handed the letter to Hector.

"I want a copy of each before you get them to forensics—in case whoever did this got sloppy. I'm still not convinced The Mongoose is doing this. It's not his M.O." He walked over to the window and looked down on the street.  Talking to himself I heard, "I wonder why he's providing the vehicles but no keys ... probably pickups because they're easier to search—no tagalongs or secret stash of weapons in the trunk.  Makes sense, but why no keys?"

After a moment he turned.  "Hector, get Martin to pull the images from the security cameras out front.  Maybe we can identify whoever dropped off the trucks; also, see if there's been any reported pickups stolen in the area.

"I think someone else is behind this, but The Mongoose is pulling the strings.  That's more his style.  He's been known to use blackmail and coercion to get people to do his dirty work which makes it difficult for us to get someone to point fingers at him, or to turn them to testify against him.

"We want to capture whoever is doing this for The Mongoose and get Jeri back.  If at all possible, we need to get the goods on The Mongoose too and put him away.

"Morgan, the doctor is in my office to get you ready.  Then you better head out to make your deadline.  You have the furthest to drive.  Is everything else ready?"

"Yes, sir."  Morgan patted his lower back.

"I'll notify the local law enforcement that you are on a time-sensitive case and not to stop you or follow you for any reason. They'll stay out of your way."

"Thanks. I'm gone!"

"Wait for me to come down and get the tags for the locals. I'll be right there.

"Jeffries, you'll be next. Don't be late getting to your *appointment*." He sneered as he said appointment. I grinned and nodded.

"Riley, you'll be last. It's possible only Morgan and Jeffries will meet with someone and you're being kept out of the way. Don't take any chances though. Let's go get Jeri."

Jim left the room to get the identifying information on the three trucks. He'll relay that information to the locals before Morgan pulls away.

I looked at Riley who was standing at the window looking down on the trucks. He had a very dark and menacing look on his face. I sure didn't want to be the one meeting him.

**********

After my turn to meet with Dr. Bell, I went downstairs and hotwired my appointed vehicle. I stepped on the gas and roared away, careful not to exceed the speed limit.

I checked my watch as I turned into the parking lot of the park—it was three minutes before nine. The sun set twenty minutes earlier.

I pulled into the middle of the vacant parking lot and put the truck in park, leaving the engine idling and the lights on. I rolled down my window and waited.

Nine-ten came and went, and I wondered if I wouldn't be meeting anyone after all. Another five minutes went by before a black van pulled into the parking lot behind me with its headlights on high beam. They stopped right behind me but with the bright lights, I couldn't see much in my rearview or side view mirrors. A deep voice boomed, "Hands where I can see them, get out, and walk backwards to me."

I complied. As I reached the tailgate of the pickup, someone—crouched low with a pistol at the ready—ran forward on the opposite side of the truck to search the interior. I continued to step backward until I passed the hood of the van and a cloth bag of some sort was thrown over my head. I didn't resist. My arms were pulled behind my back by large rough hands. I could feel the dry, calloused palms wrapped around my wrists.

A whack on my left wrist, cold metal, and the sound of ratcheting told me they were using handcuffs. Before they got the next cuff on my right wrist, I heard a *thunk*, my hands were released, and a body fell at my feet.

*What the...* I thought. *Run, Mariah, run!*

I pulled the hood off my head with my right hand and grabbed the loose handcuff in my left. I took off at a dead run toward the corner of a building on the other side of the parking lot. Before I rounded the corner, I glanced back and saw a figure dressed in all black leaning over the prostrate body.

I rounded the corner as the bullets started to fly, and I squatted down against the building. I didn't hear any following footsteps so I peeked back toward the truck.

"Tommy! You alright, Tommy?" called the guy who had been checking out the pickup. He pulled off a few more rounds in my general direction.

The figure in black ran to the back of the van, and about fifteen seconds later I saw him pop up and thunk the second guy on the head, dropping him to the pavement. The figure in black followed him down.    I waited and watched.

After only a moment, the figure in black stood and jogged past the rear of the van and around the corner out of the parking lot. I heard what sounded like the rumble of a motorcycle, and through the bushes I saw a single taillight merge into traffic and disappear.

I stood and reached behind my back to the waistband of my jeans and extracted a handcuff key that had been hidden there. I jogged back to the truck and van while I unlocked the cuff from my left wrist.

I checked to make sure Tommy was alive before I stripped the man down to his boxers. I threw his clothes, tied in a knot around his shoes, into the bushes beyond the parking lot. I dragged his heavy, stinking butt to the driver's door of the pickup, hoisted him up face-first into the driver's seat, and cuffed him to the steering wheel. I pushed his feet in, pulled the latch for the hood, and closed the door.

I ran around the hood to the other side of the truck and checked the second man. He was still breathing and unconscious also.

I couldn't find another pair of cuffs, so I untied his shoe-laces and pulled them out. I stripped this man down to his tighty-whities, doing the same with his clothes as I did with Tommy's. I took a few seconds to make sure their bundles where at opposite ends of the bushes.

That done, I dragged him to the front bumper of the pickup and tied his hands to it with good, solid knots. It would take him a while to work the knots loose, but that would give me time to get away. The guns from both men were missing.

I raised the hood of the truck and unhooked the battery, pulling it out and dumping it in the bushes across the parking lot from the clothes. Once they woke and got loose, it would take them a while to find their clothes and the battery ... I hoped.

I checked the ignition of the van and found the keys there, started it up, and drove out of the parking lot. As I was leaving, I saw another van pull into the parking lot.

*Dang, I'm not going to get as much of a head start as I hoped.*

I headed straight toward the office and parked the van in a Walmart shopping center a half mile away. I walked the rest of the way watching for a tail.

Jim greeted me with, "What happened?" when he met me on the front steps. I gave him a complete rundown of the events while we walked up to the office.

"Any idea who that was? Surely it wasn't a random strong-armed robbery," he said.

"I have no idea." I poured myself a cup of coffee. "I just hope it doesn't jeopardize Jeri's or the guys' lives. What's the news on Morgan and Riley?"

"Morgan's been taken. We lost Riley."

"*LOST RILEY?*" I shouted as the full cup of coffee slipped from my grip and shattered on the floor. Coffee and shards of pottery splattered all over our shoes and pant legs. "How did that happen?"

"We don't know yet. His tracking signal went dead shortly after nine. I sent Rodney and Kelly to check it out. They found the pickup in a ditch and two goons dead in the bed. The van was gone. The tracking device was smashed on the pavement at the back of the pickup."

"Hmmm." I grabbed a roll of paper towels off the countertop and bent to clean up the coffee mess. "But Morgan's tracking device is still working, right?"

"Right!"

"Will you pour me another cup of coffee? I'm desperate."

"Sure." Jim pulled another cup off the counter and poured while I finished cleaning up.

"You're thinking, for whatever reason might have provoked him, he killed the two guys sent to collect him and escaped?" I stood and put the wad of coffee soaked paper towels in the trash. I took another couple paper towels to clean up the rest of the broken mug.

"Hmm ..."

"Man, he had a really dark look on his face before I left. He's out for blood. You know that, don't you?" I stood and took my fresh cup of coffee from Jim.

"Yes, I know. We still have Morgan's bleep. As for Riley..." Jim made a face and shrugged rocking his head from side to side, "more or less.

"I wouldn't say 'escaped,' exactly ... something more like going after whoever has his wife. Riley's a good cop. No doubt about *that*!"

Jim shook his head. "But ... he's ferocious and unforgiving when it comes to the people he loves. Mark my word ... there is no one he loves more than he loves Jeri."

"Okay. I understand, I think." I took a sip of the thick, dark coffee. "So where's Morgan?"

Jim gave me the address where Morgan was being held.

"Do you have any agents on site yet?"

"No, they're working Riley's site."

"I'm going to get Morgan and Jeri back. Any plan?"

"Just go case the joint out and see what it looks like. Then let me know."

I nodded. "No problem."

"I'll get some agents headed that way as soon as I can free them up. Morgan and the kidnappers just arrived at that address when we saw your bleep coming this way. Don't do anything. Just watch and report back to me."

"Right. Don't do anything," I repeated sarcastically and gave Jim a look of irritation.

*Let them kill my partner or Jeri while I sit on my hands? No way!* I thought to myself.

"Here's a radio. Be careful!"

We discussed strategy before I collected my gear—the radio, Morgan's Five-seveN and shoulder holster, and Riley's Colt .45 that Morgan had been using. Donning the shoulder holster, I put the colt in my back waistband and scooped up Riley's keys to the Ford 500.

"I'll be in touch," I told Jim as he slipped another piece of paper into my hand. I memorized the note, handed it back and nodded before leaving. I walked out the door and down the front steps to Riley's car which was parked in the lot beside the building.

**********

With my lights turned off, I pulled up on a side street two blocks from the address where Morgan was. They were holding Morgan, and hopefully Jeri, in a single-family residence on a cul-de-sac in a quiet neighborhood.

Staying low and in the shadows, I ran to the side of the garage of the house. A dog barked in the distance. Two big goons were standing on the front porch smoking and shooting the breeze. I could smell the cigarette smoke as the breeze wafted it past the garage.

I slipped around to the back gate. It was not locked and swung open on quiet hinges. The lights were on in the back of the house, illuminating the back patio and leaving the rest of the yard in broken shadows. Conversations were muffled and undistinguishable.

The back door to the garage was unlocked when I tested it, but I didn't enter it yet. I skirted the backyard, staying out of the light, and peeked in the windows on the other side of the house. The furthest window was completely dark, and I suspected the room beyond was a bedroom.

The light was on and the curtains drawn to the other room. There was a slit where the curtains met in the middle that I could peek through. I saw the foot of a bed in the middle of the room. On the other side of the bed was a buxom brunette pressed up against the wall by a big guy. His jeans were bunched down around his knees and it was clear they were enjoying each other's company.

A light came on at the bottom of the house on the garage side. Voyeurism wasn't my thing, so I was happy to leave and check out the other light.

Skirting the yard again, I leaned down to the basement window. The cardboard inside the window had slipped leaving a corner of the window uncovered. Peering in I saw Morgan, stripped to the waist with his arms suspended over his head by a chain hooked into the ceiling. His toes touched the floor.

He appeared to have been used as a punching bag. His head was hanging down toward his right shoulder. I couldn't tell if he was still alive and my rage flared within me.

I tried looking farther into the room, but the cardboard was blocking my view. I thought to try the window to see if it would open, when I heard a familiar voice in the room.

"You ready to talk now, big man?"

*I know that voice ... Who is it?* I couldn't place it. *Why can't I put a name or face to that voice?* It frustrated me! Water was splashed over Morgan and a fist came out and punched him in the torso.

"What's the matter, tough guy? Can't speaka de English?" Morgan mumbled something that I couldn't make out.

*Yay! He's alive.*

"Your friends, Jeffries and Riley, bailed on you, man. They're cowards and left you to suffer the consequences.

"I sent very explicit instructions, and guess what? My papa, The Mongoose, didn't say how you and Jeri were going to die. I have decided I'm going to beat you to death with my own two hands. If you meet sweet Jeri in hell where you're going, you can ask her what flavor of death she was given."

Morgan took another brutal punch to the face before I saw the back of the brute as he moved to a bench to the right of Morgan. I still could not recognize him.

I went to the backdoor of the garage and slipped inside. The only other door, beside the big electric one in front, led into the house. The knob turned, and I slid the door open on quiet hinges.

The hall was empty, but I could hear laughter coming from another room down the hall, probably the one leading out to the back patio. I heard Mary's squealing voice say something about having to leave for an important engagement.

*So she's alive ...*

There was an interior door to my right and another to my left. The door to my right opened to a broom closet, I discovered. The door to my left opened on metal stairs leading to the basement. I closed the door with a soft 'click' and descended the stairs.

At the bottom of the stairs another door stood ajar. I heard Morgan mumble, "You're gonna pay for this. I'll see to it." The guy laughed and there was the sound of more punches.

Peeking in the doorway, I saw the man's back was to the door, so I eased it open with my gun in hand. As soon as Morgan saw me, he raised his legs and wrapped them around his attacker's neck. I grabbed a big wrench off the bench and hit the guy over the head. His body slumped. I turned and locked the door.

"The keys ... over on the bench," Morgan said, grunting as he continued to choke his attacker, who was at best unconscious. I heard a muffled snap and Morgan let the body fall to the floor.

I grabbed the keys, pulled a step stool up next to Morgan, climbed up, and unlocked the cuffs from his wrists. He fell to the floor with a grunt and was slow to push himself up.

"You okay?"

"I'll live"

I started to step down from the stool, but Morgan told me to stay put. He picked up Canfield by the shoulders.

"Here, take his hands and lock his wrists in the cuffs."

It wasn't easy with the dead weight, but we got it done. I pocketed the keys and climbed down. I handed Morgan his gun after he pulled his shirt on, then I headed for the door.

Morgan grabbed me by the wrist before I reached it. "Let's not risk it. We can climb out the window." He grabbed a dirty rag off the bench and stuffed it into Canfield's mouth. "Turn the light off."

I hit the light switch, and Morgan removed the cardboard from the window and pushed it open. It was small, but not too small for us to climb through which we did.

"Where are they holding Jeri? Do you know?" I asked Morgan once we made it out.

"I heard Canfield out in the hall spitting bullets of profanity at some poor schmuck. He was asking where she was and why she wasn't here at the house. The guy said she was in the storage unit on the east side of town. That's all I got."

We made it to the car, and I picked up the radio from the seat and keyed the mic. "This is Jeffries. I have my friend."

"Where's Riley?" asked Morgan just as the radio squawked back, "Roger that. We're converging on the house now."

"M.I.A."

He looked sharply at me before saying, "Explain."

I keyed the mic, "We need a list of all the warehouses and storage units in Rexburg on the east side of town. Apparently that's where they have Jeri."

"Stand by," Jim responded.

"All Jim told me was that Riley's tracking signal went dead shortly after his meet time. When the backup got there, they found the pickup in a ditch and two guys dead in the bed. The van was gone and the tracking device was smashed on the pavement at the back of the pickup."

"Okay, he's fine. He'll turn up sooner or later." He rubbed his wrists and winced. "Remember Kenny Rhode from patrol?"

"Why is no one worried about Riley?" I was getting frustrated with their nonchalance toward Riley's situation.

"Look, he can take care of himself. The fact that the transmitter was smashed on the road tells me he doesn't want to be tracked. He left it there to be found by backup so they would know he was alright."

I sighed. "Okay ... Rhode ... nice guy but kind of a loner. I heard he got into some kind of trouble and had to quit the department to avoid an arrest ... never heard what it was about. Why?"

"He's in with this group. Canfield stood and watched while Rhode used me for a punching bag, but I got the feeling he was reluctant. It seemed to me like he was a new recruit earning his stripes."

"Hmmm ... interesting."

"I'm wondering if he might be undercover or something."

"I guess it's possible, but not likely if he's been in trouble with the law."

Morgan let out a soft groan.

I knew he was hurting, but I doubted he wanted me to mention it. "And that guy we hung; he seemed familiar to me ..."

"Canfield—he's an assistant district attorney who's been running for the Senate. The mayor of Boise, Bentley Dempsey, has been campaigning for him, and there's been a big splash in the news about him."

"Bentley Dempsey, yeah..."

"Apparently Canfield is the son of Franklin, The Mongoose. He's worked his way up Papa's ranks while working his way up the political ladder. Fortunately he won't be winning any more elections; I'm pretty sure he's dead."

"Got your list," Hector said over the radio. "What are we looking for?"

Morgan picked up the radio, "While I was hanging from the rafters, I overheard someone say Jeri was being held in a storage unit in Rexburg, on the east side. We need to find something that is tied to Canfield."

"Canfield! You mean the Senate candidate?"

"Yes. He's been pulling strings for his papa, The Mongoose. Apparently he's the heir apparent. We think Bentley Dempsey is also working for The Mongoose, but we're not sure. He's sure been pushing for Canfield's election to the Senate."

"Okay. There's one place with four storage units registered to Canfield, two to Dempsey, and one more registered to James Franklin. They're all at the same facility on 4th South."

"That's the place. Give us the unit numbers and then fill Jim in and let him know Jeffries and I are headed over there. We'll find her and bring her back or radio him if she's been moved."

"I copy," Jim announced over the radio before Hector relayed the address and unit numbers.

**********

We parked a couple blocks from the storage facility which sat in the middle of a mile-long tract of land. To the right of the facility was a trucking company with two large bay garages for working on the big rigs, a smaller building for the office, and a fenced compound to lock the rigs and trailers in when not on the road.

On the left of the storage compound was a vacant field, approximately the length of a city block. It appeared the weeds were mowed routinely and due for another mowing. A sidewalk ran the length of the tract of land, around the corner, and down the other side of the vacant lot. The facility itself looked clean and well kept. There was a decorative security fence across the front of the storage facility with a gate to the right of the office. The rest of the compound was enclosed in ten-foot-high chain link fencing. Out in front of the security fence, spanning both sides of the locked gate, were big corkscrew willow trees and evergreen shrubbery.

We walked beside the fence, stopped behind one of the big trees, and climbed over into the compound.

We decided to split up and check the individual unit numbers that Hector gave us. They were spread out.

I took the two registered to Dempsey and the one for Franklin. Those started farthest to the left of the rows of units, the last one in the middle section. Morgan took the other four. Those started in the row just past the middle section and spanned to the last row on the right.

Mine seemed clear; they were locked and there was no one about, no sounds from within, and no lights coming from under the doors. I ran to intercept Morgan and assist on his units.

At the end of the last row, a man was standing guard, his back to us. Morgan motioned me down the back side of the row and around the corner so we could approach from opposite ends.

I headed that way, but at the other end I encountered another guard who rounded the corner at the same time I did. We were both caught off guard. I had the quicker reflexes and was able to disarm the guy with a Haito Uchi strike. It rendered him unconscious.

The guy on Morgan's end of the row heard the scuffle, but when he turned to come down the line, Morgan hit him over the head with the butt of his gun, knocking the guy out.

I looked around the corner at my end of the row and saw Morgan wave the all clear. We started down the row to the open unit in the middle and stopped outside the doorway on either side. A man's voice snarled within.

"For the love of whiskey stop your sniveling, woman." He sounded irritated.

I signaled to Morgan that I was going to distract the guy and draw him away from the unit. Morgan nodded. I stepped into view in the open doorway.

"Leave her alone, prick."

The guy, tall—about six-four with a mop of filthy blond hair—jumped at me. I ran from the unit making sure he followed me.

"There's no place for you to run, Jeffries. I'll get you and a feather in my cap for catching you." He cackled at his lame joke while he chased me.

"DAVE! JIMMIE! WHERE ARE YOU?"

He slowed his pursuit, concerned when his friends weren't there to help him.

I ran to the back of the lot where there were a bunch of RVs and heavy equipment.

Rounding a corner out of his sight, I dropped and rolled under one of the larger RV's. I came up on the other side and ran back to the front—smack dab into the arms of the guy I dropped earlier.

I pushed out of his arms, and when he grabbed for me again, I kicked him in the groin. When he bent over in pain, I kneed him hard in the face. His head shot up, and I caught it and rammed it into the side of the RV, knocking him out cold again.

To my misfortune, Blondie heard the scuffle and came tearing around the back of the RV toward me. I took off in a dead run down the back side of a row of units trying to get to the gate. Ahead of me, I saw Morgan and Jeri running for the gate in the shadows. To give them time to climb the fence and escape the compound, I made a sudden turn down the next row of units back toward the RV parking.

I ran to the very back and ducked down behind the blade of a bulldozer and drew my gun. I didn't have to wait long for Blondie to round the corner after me, and to my dismay, the guy I knocked out twice was following behind him in a stagger.

*Good grief. What's it gonna take to keep that Neanderthal down without killing him?*

I slipped around the other side of the dozer, dropped and rolled under a bus next to it, and continued rolling to the opposite side. I popped up and ran to the front of the bus, where I turned and ran down the line, away from Blondie and his henchman. I came up against a fence with a row of dumpsters.

The two men had stopped running, and I could hear them searching for me. I slid down behind one of the dumpsters and moved down the row. The stench was horrific; rotting food and sewage smells were the most prevalent.

I reached my hand up to the side of the dumpster to brace myself, and a monster cockroach skittered across the back of my hand toward my wrist. I shook it off and reached behind me to grab the fence.

*Roaches. Crap. I hate roaches!*

"Dave, you go that way, and I'll look over here," Blondie called not far from me.

Behind me, I felt a gap in the fence that I could slip through, and I did.

I stayed crouched beside the fence in the shadow of a large bush. The crunching of gravel nearby induced me to hold my breath. I saw a shadow fall between the two dumpsters nearest my hiding place. Blondie, too large to get between the two dumpsters without moving them, leaned over as far as he could to peer behind them. I remained as still as a statue.

Dave hollered from farther away in the compound. "FRENCHIE, JIMMIE'S DEAD! SHE KILLED JIMMIE!"

Frenchie uttered a low growl and ran off toward the yelling.

When I heard him moving on, I slipped away into the brush and the shadows. After a few moments, I heard him yell, "Where's Jeri? Find her. Now! And kill Jeffries if you find her. I don't care how you do it."

I could still hear the two men yelling back and forth to each other as they started looking for me again.

I ran toward the front of the compound, thinking I was on the outside, but instead I had slipped into some kind of a locked area within the compound. It held trailers, motorcycles, and ATVs.

I ducked into the shadow of a motorcycle that was parked up against a big bush when I saw Blondie, now known as Frenchie, slinking by the gate. He rattled the gate to make sure it was locked and moved on. When he was out of site, I climbed the outer fence and jumped down on the other side, outside the entire compound, into the vacant field.

Without stopping, I took off across the weeded lot in a flat-out run toward the street on the other side. The sound of me climbing the fence brought Frenchie back, and he didn't like the fact I was getting away.

I made it about halfway across the field when the shooting started and I heard a bullet whiz by my left ear. I hit the dirt, rolled on my back, and pulled off three rounds in the general direction of the compound. I heard Frenchie scream once and then there was silence. I didn't wait around. I got up and continued running, crouched low, toward the road.

Morgan pulled up beside me as I reached the sidewalk. He leaned over and pushed the front passenger door open, and I jumped in. We drove away.

"You okay, Jeffries?" Morgan asked.

"None the worse for wear. How are both of you?" I looked over the back of the seat at Jeri.

"I'm fine," Jeri answered.

She was pale as a ghost and shivering. I guessed she was in shock. "Did they hurt you, Jeri?"

"No, I'm fine. I was scared for you when Morgan told me you were in there with those ... those beasts, and I'm really worried about Riley."

"You know Riley. He'll be okay, Jeri." Morgan was matter-of-fact about it.

I gave Morgan the address I memorized before leaving the office. While Morgan headed in that direction I radioed Hector that we were on our way there.

The radio squelched and we received, "ten-four," from Hector.

We pulled into the driveway of a small single-family home on a quiet residential street and waited a moment. The garage door began to open and Morgan pulled inside. The headlights illuminated Hector as he pushed the button to close the door behind us and Morgan turned off the engine.

"Where are we?" Jeri asked while getting out of the car.

"We're in a safe house in Idaho Falls. Jim will call when he gets things wrapped up at the house of horrors."

"House of horrors?"

Hector, dressed impeccably as usual, was standing at the door from the garage into the house waiting for us to enter. I walked in first followed by Jeri and then Morgan.

"We'll tell you when we get settled." I glanced over my shoulder at Jeri with a smile.

"Everyone alright?" Hector asked.

Jeri walked from the kitchen into the living room and, sitting on the edge of the sofa, put her hands to her face and started sobbing.

"Yeah." Morgan clapped Hector on the shoulder.

I sat down beside Jeri and took her in my arms. I held her and let her weep. She had been through a terrible ordeal, and I completely understood the need to cry.

When her sobbing subsided, I asked if she'd been hurt in any way. She said it wasn't too bad. They kept her gagged and tied up but they would give her water every few hours.

"Where's Riley? I really need to know he's okay." She turned pleading eyes on me. "They said they were going to kill him."

Morgan squatted down in front of her and took her hands. He was a bloody, swollen mess and Jeri gasped at seeing him in the light.

"Jeri, I owe Riley my life. He saved me in El Salvador, and I will go to the ends of the earth to make sure he's alright. You can count on that."

Jeri nodded.

"Riley's a smart guy and we both know he knows how to handle himself. He had a transmitter implanted in his shoulder, just like Jeffries and me. We know where he was when we lost his signal.

"We believe he smashed it at the scene to let us know he was okay and doing his own investigation. We'll find him ... or he'll find us. We're certain he is alright and working on this case. You're both going to be fine."

Jeri stared at Morgan, her eyes full of anguish. She nodded in understanding and acceptance. "I hope so, Morgan. I can't live without him."

**********

$A$s Morgan stood, he groaned and wrapped his arms around his ribs.

"What's wrong, Morgan?" I asked.

Jeri rose from the couch, her hands on his arms. "Morgan, you're hurt. We have to get you to a hospital."

"I'm fine, Jeri. We can't go to the hospital right now, anyway." He headed for the bathroom.

Hector came into the living room with a tall glass of water for Jeri. "Is there anything I can do?"

Jeri sat back down and took the water. "Just bring my husband home in one piece, please." She offered a thin, tight smile, tears welling in her eyes again.

"We're doing everything we can. Right now it's more important that we keep you safe so Riley can do what Riley does best. He'll be here by your side soon enough."

I continued to sit with her to acknowledge and comfort her fears.

Morgan called out to me from the open bathroom door. "Jeffries!" He sounded frustrated and out of breath.

He had his shirt off and wide ace bandages in his hand. He held those out to me.

"Will you help me bind my ribs for now? I'm not sure, but I think I might have a broken rib or two. It sure hurts like it."

Morgan had already cleaned the blood from his face. He had a nasty cut high on his right cheekbone, a swollen left eye, and a split lip. Ugly abrasions on both wrists where the metal cuffs kept him strung up like a side of beef were washed and wrapped with bandages. His torso was almost one giant bruise.

"Where'd you get these?" I asked, indicating the bandages.

Hector gave a low whistle as he looked in on us. Jeri, who followed Hector, started sobbing again.

"Here, in the emergency kit. Every safe house has a complete field kit."

"Do you want me to call Dr. Bell?" Hector asked as he put his arms around Jeri and patted her on the back. "You might have some internal bleeding."

"Nah! Not unless Jeri needs him. There's nothing he can do for broken ribs, and I've bandaged the rest. We've got too much to do right now. I'll be fine."

Jeri shook her head and muttered she didn't need a doctor.

We got Morgan's rib cage wrapped as tight as possible. He pulled his t-shirt on over his head, and we walked into the kitchen.

"What do we have to eat?" Morgan asked.

"Sit down and let me fix you a sandwich, Morgan." Jeri led him to the table. "I'll fix one for everyone; I'm hungry, too."

Morgan sat at the table with Hector, and I helped Jeri. We ate in silence, each wrapped up in our own thoughts.

Morgan swallowed the last bite of his sandwich and took a drink of water.

"Hey Hector, is Jim still cleaning up at the house?"

"He has a team there mopping up, but Jim's at the office getting ready to start interrogations."

Morgan told Jeri he wanted her to stay with Hector while we went to the office to help Jim with the interviews. After some discussion she agreed.

I grabbed the keys off the counter where Morgan had tossed them. We left the same way we came in, but Morgan got behind the wheel before I could and reached his hand out for the keys. I dumped them in his palm as I buckled up.

"Don't like my driving, Morgan?"

"It scares the crap out of me." He grinned.

"Chauvinist," I muttered under my breath as he backed out of the garage.

"Wild driver," he spit back.

"Huh? What was that, Morgan?"

"Oh, nothing." He looked over at me with a silly grin.

I backhanded his shoulder. "Oh, shut up and drive!" He grimaced and we both laughed. It was a nice break to the tension that had been building up.

At the office, there wasn't much we could do to help Jim and he sent us back to the safe house to get some rest.

**********

**I** leaned back into the couch next to Jeri and dozed off while we waited for Jim to show up. The sun came up slanting rays of light through the window blinds. I woke. Jeri was curled up at the other end of the couch with a blanket thrown over her and a loud snoring emanated from across the room where Morgan slept in a recliner. I threw the light blanket that had been laid over me onto the armrest, rose and slipped away.

Walking into the kitchen to get a cup of coffee, I saw Hector sitting at the table. He was jacketless with his shoulder holster on still cradling his Kimber 1911 .45 ACP duty weapon. He was reading the paper.

"Morning," he said when I walked into the kitchen. "Coffee's fresh."

"Morning. Don't you ever sleep?"

"Not a lot." He shrugged.

"Hmm," I said. "Heard anything from Jim or Riley?"

"Jim will be here in about an hour. It took them all night to process the scene and interrogate everyone they detained."

"Hmph." I poured myself a cup of coffee. "Was Canfield alive?"

---

"Didn't say."

"What about the storage unit compound? What did they find there?"

"Didn't say. Jim will fill us in when he gets here."

"What's up?" Morgan stepped into the kitchen and stretched with a wide yawn. He grimaced at the soreness in his body.

"Looking for food, Morgan. Is there any breakfast food around here, Hector?"

"Fridge is stocked ... cabinets too. Jim said he's bringing donuts. Does that count as breakfast food?"

"Not hardly!" I opened the refrigerator and took out a dozen eggs, a pound of bacon, a bunch of green onions, some grape tomatoes, and a small block of cheddar cheese.

"I'll cook up some breakfast for everyone."

Morgan walked up beside me at the stove and found a frying pan in the side cabinet. "Want any help?"

"Sure. Start the bacon, will ya? I'm going to the bathroom to freshen up. I'll fix the toast and eggs when I get back."

When I came back to the kitchen, the table was set and Jeri was across from Hector. She was working the crossword puzzle in the morning paper; Hector had moved on to the sports section. Morgan was transferring the last of the bacon from the pan to a plate lined with paper towels. I diced up the green onions and grape tomatoes, cracked the whole dozen eggs into a large bowl and whipped them up to a froth.

While I diced up the ingredients and whipped up the eggs, Morgan started making toast. I added the diced ingredients to the whipped egg mixture, reduced the bacon fat in the frying pan, and poured the egg mixture in. I stirred until the eggs were fully cooked and fluffy.

Morgan finished buttering the last piece of toast and carried the stacked plate to the table while I grated some of the cheese into a bowl. The bacon was already waiting on the table.

After I spooned scrambled eggs onto each of our plates, I placed the skillet with the rest of the eggs back on the stove.

Jim walked in the front door carrying a box of donuts. "Smells great in here; is there any left?"

I grabbed another plate from the cabinet and piled on the last of the scrambled eggs. I brought it to the table and handed it to Jim.

"Have a seat. We were just about to eat."

Breakfast was quiet until everyone finished eating. Jim looked at Jeri and told her Riley was off the grid. He gave her the same rundown Morgan did.

He inform her the two goons were found dead in the bed of the pickup Riley was driving—a broken neck on one of them and bullets in the other. Their van was missing, probably taken by Riley. Since Morgan and I were met by only two men, Jim didn't have any reason to believe Riley was taken alive or killed.

Jim believed Riley was in his Special Forces mode, out for blood to avenge Jeri's kidnapping. They were hoping he would use common sense and stay within the boundaries of the law, but he assured Jeri they would do everything they could to help him.

"Special Forces mode? I thought he was in the Marines." I turned to Morgan.

"He was. He was recruited from the Marines into the Special Forces. Until he went to Special Forces, we were in the same unit.

"His Special Forces team later rescued me and some other guys who had been taken captive by the El Salvadoran FMLN. We were beaten and starved for days before his unit came through and cleaned out that location rescuing me and five other men who were still alive.

"We've been best friends and brothers ever since our Marine days, but when he saved my life and those of my men..." The corner of Morgan's mouth rose in a half smile.

"Whoa, I had no idea."

Jim cleared his throat and told us ADA Canfield was dead and hanging from the rafters in the basement. Morgan and I explained to him what happened and that it was in self-defense.

"Then why did you string him up and put a gag in his mouth?"

"To slow down his goons from following us if they found him before we got away."

I interrupted Morgan. "We took the cuff keys so they would have to work to get him down."

"Right," Morgan butted back in. "Nobody wants to see their dead leader hanging from the rafters."

"Okay I guess. Seems like a waste of time to me, but you got away."

"What about Mary? Did you find her at the house?"

"No. She must have left before we raided the place."

"I did hear her say something about an engagement she had to get to. No sign of Tabatha?"

Jim shook his head. He went on to tell us they didn't find anyone at the storage compound. The unit where Jeri had been held was open; the chair and ropes used to restrain her were still there.

Forensics did a complete sweep and found fingerprints matching Freidrick French, Jimmie Duncan, and Dave Plinkerton—all three known felons.

"You heard them yell that Jimmie was dead?" Jim asked me pointedly.

"Yes, Dave yelled that to Frenchie just before I made my escape."

"They took his body with them. We found blood by the open unit and the fence near where you escaped. You must have caught Frenchie with one of your rounds."

"Seriously, I can't say I'm sorry. I hope the S.O.B. dies from lead poisoning. I'm figuring Morgan dropped Jimmie. I'm not even sure he knows he killed the guy."

"I didn't kill him, just knocked him out." Morgan glared at Jim, daring him to argue.

"He was stabbed." Jim squinted at Morgan.

Morgan raised his eyebrows and stared at Jim. "I didn't stab him and neither did Jeffries."

Jim nodded.

"So, it looks like ADA Canfield, who is the son of The Mongoose, was in cahoots with Mayor Dempsey too." Jim shook his head. "Did either of you hear anything incriminating the mayor?"

Morgan shook his head while he shoveled the last bit of scrambled eggs into his mouth.

Remembering something I heard, I turned to Jim and opened my mouth to speak. He jumped up from the table and pointed at me. "I want to talk to you alone. Follow me."

*"What the heck did I do?"* I wondered.

---

I followed him out to the car and got in the passenger seat when he opened the door for me. When he got in on the driver's side, he turned to me. "You saw or heard something, didn't you? What was it?"

"I didn't realize the significance at the time and with everything else it slipped my mind until you asked. When I slipped into the hallway at the house—before going down to the basement, I heard some guy say, 'Benjie, Benjie, calm down. We'll keep you out of this.'

"Another guy said in a very calm but threatening tone of voice, 'It's Bentley. My name is Bentley, and I had better be kept out of this or heads will roll. See to it.' I didn't place the name at the time."

"You're sure?"

"Jim, I swear! I thought I recognized Bentley's voice from the news in Albuquerque, but I couldn't place it. Bentley and Canfield were making a name for themselves and it's been national news. I had other, more pressing things on my mind at the moment. They were beating the crap out of Morgan, and I needed to get him away.

"Okay, I believe you. I never really liked the guy or trusted him ... a story for another time and place."

We put our heads together and came up with a plan to flush the truth out of Mayor Dempsey.

**********

"**J**effries, you can't walk into his office and confront him. He'll kill you.

"Look, Morgan. You know I can handle myself. I have the highest attainable degrees in several of the martial arts. I can disarm someone before they know what hit them. He's not going to get the drop on me. I'll be okay. I have to do this for Riley. We have to end this so he can come home, and I'm the only one who can do this part. I'm the one who heard the exchange at the house. I can get him to confess."

"What good will that do? You'll be searched for a wire so any confession will be your word against his, and he knows that. His goons will disarm you before you go into his office."

"I know. I'm not going armed. I don't *need* it. No matter what you think about martial arts, I *am* a weapon."

Morgan held me by the shoulders. "I know you're good at hand-to-hand but you're not super-woman. You can't stop a speeding bullet."

"I'll be fine. I'm meeting him in his office in broad daylight with plenty of witnesses. They can't all be on his payroll. He won't do anything. He'll want to, but he won't. He has to keep the act up for the voters." I sighed and shook my head.

Morgan leaned in to me and said in a heated whisper, "Look, Riley's already out there on his own doing God knows what. I don't need you going rogue, too. At least confer with Jim about your plan?"

"No! I told you." I pushed away from Morgan. "We talked and I don't like his plan. This is the only way. He wants to bug the office, but it could take weeks or months to get anything on him. Trust me, will you?"

"I don't suppose I have a choice. I know how you are." He glanced over his shoulder then back to me. "Okay, but I'm going too."

"No! You're not. I'm going alone. I'm only telling you in case something does go wrong. You can notify Jim."

"I don't like it."

"You don't have to. Promise me you won't say anything to *anyone* until I've had time to carry out my plan. No one, you hear? Promise me!"

"I promise," he replied with reluctance. "What do you want me to tell Jim when he notices you're gone?"

"Tell him ... tell him..." I shrugged. "Tell him you don't know."

Morgan shook his head. "Do you still have the blade and the cuff key tucked inside the back seam of your waist-band?"

"Yes, but I dug out the tracking device this morning in the shower. If I go missing it's up to you to let Jim know where to start looking."

"Be careful, Jeffries."

"I will. Distract Jim and Hector while I slip out of here."

I left the house unnoticed and made it to the bus stop at the corner. I had filched some cash from Morgan's wallet before leaving and made it to a Walmart where I purchased some "office attire": a dress, a pair of heels, a pair of stockings, some cheap earrings, a matching necklace, one of those small purse-sized sewing kits for repair, make-up, and a very large handbag.

After checking out, I asked the cashier if she could cut the tags off of everything so I could change in the bathroom. I told her I had a job interview and didn't have time to go home to change. She was very helpful cutting off all the tags and placing them in the bag with my other purchases.

Once I was changed, I put the receipts and my other clothes and shoes in the handbag. I left the store and waited at the bus stop for the next local transit bus to take me to the Greyhound station. Once there, I bought a ticket to Boise and waited. I was in luck; the next bus would be pulling out at two, only thirty minutes away. I picked up a newspaper sitting on a chair and opened it up, pretending to read while I watched my surroundings.

*So far, so good.*

Once on the road, I relaxed a little. It was going to take me about seven hours to get to Boise, and then I'd have to find a room for the night. I leaned back into the seat and closed my eyes as the bus hit the outskirts of town.

I found a Motel 6 after I got off the bus. In my room, I hung up my new clothes, already prepared for the next day. I set the alarm for five o'clock in the morning, showered, and slipped naked in between the sheets.

I tried to fall asleep but my plans kept running through my head, demanding scrutiny to see if I needed to alter any of them. If nothing else, it helped me prepare for the day ahead.

Sleep eluded me until some time in the wee hours of the morning. When the alarm went off at five, I groaned.

*I swear I'm going to sleep for a week when this is over.*

Showered and dressed, I grabbed my bag and checked out. I walked next door to the pancake house and ordered a Denver omelet and coffee. I didn't waste a lot of time eating; I wanted to make sure I was at the mayor's office when he arrived. As soon as I finished eating, I called a taxi to deliver me to the devil's lair.

The cabbie dropped me off in front of a small diner across the street from the mayor's office. I went in, took a table by the window, and ordered coffee. While enjoying my second cup of joe, I watched the street out front. At seven thirty, I paid the waitress and told her I would be leaving soon.

At eight o'clock sharp the mayor came down the sidewalk from the parking garage and was approaching the front of his building. I got up from the table and grabbed my purse.

I ran across the street to meet him. The traffic was light. I walked into the building before the door closed behind him.

"Hello, Mr. Mayor. Beautiful morning, don't you think?"

He turned around with a warm smile on his face, but when he recognized me, he scowled and looked around the lobby.

"Well, well, well. Yes, it is Miss ...?" he said loud enough for everyone to hear. He smiled like a wolf.

"Jeffries. Mariah Jeffries. I need to talk to you about a little situation in which your name was brought up yesterday."

"Yes. Mariah! Of course! Let's go to my office." He put his arm around my shoulders and pulled me close.

I walked with him without saying a word. We went through his outer office and passed a secretary sitting at a desk. She looked up in surprise. She didn't say anything when he opened the door to his inner office and flung me into the room. The front edge of his desk halted my momentum. I stood up and straightened my clothes.

He slammed the door closed and frisked me. He dumped out my large purse to check for weapons and recording devices.

"I'm surprised to see you here. So how did you get my name?" he hissed and turned locking the door. "You know you won't get out of here alive."

I kneeled with absolute calm to put my things back in the purse.

"My friends know I'm here." I stood and looked him in the eye. "You know ... my FBI friends and the cops. If you get rid of me, you're sunk."

"You think you have it all figured out, don't you Miss 'I'm an expert at everything'?" He waved his arms and wiggled his fingers. "Well, you don't." He leaned forward and got in my face. "My godfather ... you've heard of him ... James Franklin, The Mongoose?"

I nodded.

"Well, he got me to this position and nobody gets in his way without paying dearly. Our organization is far-reaching and you will not escape this time.

"Oh, and don't worry about your friends either. It may take some time, but Morgan's days are numbered, and we already have Riley. His sweet little wife will never see him again."

I was surprised when he said he had Riley, but if I showed it, he didn't respond. The rest of it I expected. In fact, I wanted him to tell me morc. I needed to find out just how far-reaching this organization really was. I walked over to the leather sofa against the wall and sat.

"You don't believe me?"

I stared at him. He growled.

He walked to his desk, turned the phone around, and dialed a number.

"She's here. ... *Yes*, you idiot. She's in my office. Send Pete and Larry ... in uniform ... IMMEDIATELY!"

"It sucks when you have idiots working for you, doesn't it?" I asked with a smirk.

"Shut up!" He glared at me a moment and started pacing back and forth in front of his desk. He stopped, eyed me, went behind his desk, and sat in the swivel chair. He wrote something on a legal pad, looked me up and down, wrote a few more things on the pad, and stood from his chair.

"Don't move." He left his office, closing the door behind him. I heard the click of the lock seating itself and glanced around the office, but I didn't move. He came back into the room about five minutes later, walked around to the back of his desk, sat back down in the swivel chair, and watched me.

Apparently, "immediately" doesn't have the same meaning in thug language as it does for the rest of us. The mayor and I sat for an hour, staring each other down and sharing a ridiculous conversation about the merits of crime before two uniforms showed up.

The mayor cancelled all appointments through his secretary and refused all calls while we waited.

"Actually, we weren't sure you were involved. Thanks for clearing that question up for us."

"Why did you come here? You were free, Morgan was free—you and Morgan got Jeri. Why didn't you and Morgan go home and leave it alone?"

"The goons from your godfather's organization abducted me and brought me here. Besides, we're not going to abandon Riley. Until we have him back, this is never going away, and neither is Morgan or me."

He turned very civil then and gave a heavy sigh. "We can make you dead real easy, Jeffries. And it will look like an accident."

"My friends know I'm here. They watched me come into the office, and they're watching for me to leave."

"LIAR!" he shouted and jumped up from his chair. He sighed again and sat back down.

"They don't know you're here, and they're not watching. We know ... and my guys would spot them if they were.

"We will devise our plan to work around whatever the situation is anyway. Anything is possible for us ... no big deal."

We sat in silence a moment before I responded.

"So, The Mongoose is your godfather, huh? Is that godfather as in head of the mob, or a real, christened godfather in the church?"

"He's my godfather from church, and he took his oath to heart. Even when you guys had him locked up, he kept in touch, coaching and guiding me every step of the way. Not only me but his other sons as well."

"How many other sons does he have involved in the organization? We know about Canfield."

"Canfield is his bastard son."

"Was! You mean was his bastard son, right?"

He glared at me. "He has two sons who carry his name in Denver. Since they're so closely related to him and carry his last name, they're not in the organization proper. They have helped him from time to time, however.

"The rest are godsons and goddaughters except for Mary, who you already had the pleasure of meeting. She's Canfield's sister. We're all very loyal to Franklin, you see."

"Who are they?"

"I'm not telling you!"

"Well, you're gonna kill me anyway, right? So, what's the problem?"

"None of your business." Bentley glared at me.

"True! I'm just shooting the breeze while we wait for your idiots to show up. No big deal to me." I paused. "So, your godfather helped you get into office?"

"More or less. He's been grooming me for public office since I was a young lad."

"What kind of strings did he pull to get you into this position?"

"None, really," he said with pride, preening like a peacock behind his desk. "I've kept my nose clean and worked hard. I ran a clean campaign on a clean ticket and won fair and square. He coached me, that's all. He's a brilliant strategist."

"But your godfather is going to use your position to his own advantage. Is that how it works?"

"If something comes up that I can help him with, I will. He's a good guy. You could always come and work for us, you know. That way we wouldn't have to kill you. It would be a shame to kill such a comely, capable woman. Of course, you would have to prove your loyalty to us first."

"A good guy? Really? He orders the murder of people and runs drugs and firearms all over the country from what I understand. Maybe even outside the country for all I know. How is that a good guy?"

"You just don't understand. What he's trying to do is create social and political reform. He believes everyone has the right to bear arms. No one should have to register for them or get approval from the government to purchase one. The government doesn't need to know what the citizens have. Drugs and alcohol shouldn't be regulated either. It interferes with free trade."

"What about all the thieving, robberies, murders, and rape your godfather orders?

"Really, we're just a group of people who believe in survival of the fittest. People like us believe in taking what we want and taking care of our own. If someone opposed to us isn't strong enough to defend themselves *or* is *unwilling* to, like a lot of the mandy-pandy citizens today that want to sit around and let the government take care of them, then tough. They get what they deserve ... *nothing.* They won't survive; only the strong and determined will."

"You're crazy!"

"Jeffries, survival of the fittest and smartest is still alive and well. It's as natural as birds eating worms. It makes the earth go round. It's what civilization is built on and has been going on for millennia. Humans think they can stop that, but they can't.

"You think the government is your friend?" He laughed. "They're the fittest. They're the ones who are smart enough to get elected. Everyone already knows you can't believe anything the politicians say, but they get elected anyway, because they're smart. They line their pockets while in office. They use their power and influence to better themselves and their causes.

"Stop being so blind and open your eyes. Come join us and you will become one of the most powerful women in this country. You have the looks, the education, and the background. What do you say?"

"You're serious, aren't you?"

"Look, what you call criminals are just people making their way in this world. We're not bad people, really we're not. But we're not going to let someone else's ideals restrict us from the positions in the world that we know we deserve.

"We're going to work our way up into the Governments of this country and change things from within. We're going to take what we need, what we know we deserve, and what we want … as long as we're fit enough, strong enough, and *smart enough*." He tapped himself at his temple with his right index finger.

"Nothing you regular people—the uninspired, the lazy, the sheep of the world—do will ever change that. There's no place in this world really for the mentally ill, the handicapped.

"Oh … we'll use them to our advantage. We'll espouse how we want to help them, provide for them, and accept them as equals. You've got to be smart enough to know that's only to get the sheeple of the country to vote for us and follow us."

We bantered around this ridiculous notion of how saintly criminals are until the secretary announced Pete and Larry. Bentley moved to the door, and they were let into the office.

The two guys were dressed in city police uniforms that appeared authentic but sloppy ... real sloppy. I recognized them as the two men who were standing out on the front porch of the house where Morgan was held.

"What do you want, boss?" the six foot tall, bald guy asked.

"We're going for a little ride. You and Larry follow in the squad car and keep an eye out for anyone following us." With that, he stood and held his hand out to me like a perfect gentleman. I took his hand and stood, sliding my hand into the crook of his arm. I smiled. He placed his other hand over mine, squeezing tight.

"Don't try anything and leave the bag," he whispered to me as I leaned to pick it up. We exited the building to the alley. The two goons got into their car which was parked outside the back door. They waited for the mayor and me to walk to the parking garage next door. Once we were on the road, they fell in behind us. We drove about twenty blocks and pulled into a barbeque slop house parking lot.

"BBQ Heaven? I didn't know we had time for lunch." I gave Bentley an 'Oh My' look when he opened my door. We walked into the restaurant with his arm around my shoulders. He slid his hand to the small of my back and kept it there all the way to the back of the dining room and into another room behind curtains. Once the four of us were in the back room, Bentley closed the door.

"Stand guard," he told the two goons. He grabbed my upper right arm and jerked me through another doorway and down a long and narrow flight of metal steps.

"Oh, great. Gonna take me to the basement of this dump to kill me?"

"You want to join us?" I told him no. "Then shut up and move."

At the bottom we turned left and entered what appeared to be some kind of utility tunnel. He jerked me to a stop after about twenty-five feet. We stood in front of a metal ladder that was bolted against the wall. It began at my waist and ascended into the black unknown above.

"Climb!" he barked.

"What's up there? If you're going to kill me, why not just do it twenty-five feet back there where we started? What's your game, Dempsey?"

He slapped me hard across the face. I could taste blood from my split lip. "I can't kill you in my office, and people saw us go into the barbeque joint. Sally was waiting in the restaurant with clothes to match yours. Once we left the back room, she went into the room and changed. When she looked enough like you, she left with Pete and Larry just in case anyone is questioned about what they saw when the feds look for you."

I reached up and grabbed the sides of the ladder, pulling myself up and putting my right foot on the first rung. Pretending to lose my grip with my left hand, I swung around and kicked Bentley square in the face with my left foot. I broke his nose just for good measure and hopefully marred his good looks a little bit. I grabbed the rung above my head and scrambled up the ladder before he could grab my leg and pull me back down.

Bentley emitted a loud groan and cursed me.

"You're going to pay for that. You just broke my nose!"

I looked down, and in the faint glow of the lights in the tunnel I saw him grab a handkerchief from his back pocket. He wiped the blood from his face before grabbing the ladder and following me. The ladder ended at a metal landing, which I climbed onto and waited.

When Dempsey reached the landing, he tried to punch me, but I blocked him and shoved him back. He almost fell through the opening to the platform. He grabbed the railing and steadied himself.

With his right hand, he pulled out some keys from his pocket shooting darts of menace at me with his eyes. He unlocked the metal door still holding the handkerchief to his bleeding nose with his left hand. He pushed the door in to open.

It was a small utility closet, and he shoved me up against the wall when I stepped inside. He pinned me with his right forearm across my neck and kicked the door closed. He threw the keys on the floor.

He turned me around and pushed me up against the wall face-first and grabbed my hair with his right hand. He wrenched my head back, his left forearm pressed hard across the back of my shoulders, keeping me pinned. He pressed his body up hard against my back.

His minty, moist breath was on the side of my face when he whispered, "I'm going to have a little fun with you before I kill you."

I pushed back and maneuvered out of his clutches, hitting him in the side of the neck with my elbow, interrupting blood flow to his brain and taking him to his knees. Before he could get to his feet, I punched him hard where the back of his skull connects to his spine. A maneuver like that has to be done skillfully or it can snap the neck. In this case it pinched the nerve running from his brain to his spine rendering him paralyzed and unconscious for a few minutes.

I checked the hall beyond the only other door to the room. No one was around. I locked both doors to the room before I unzipped my dress and extracted the vial of Scopolamine that had been sewn into my bra where the cups meet between my breasts. Then I pulled out the syringe needle that had been stitched to the underside of the left cup of my underwire bra. The syringe was extracted from the heel of my left shoe that I had hollowed out the night before in the hotel room. The plunger came from the heel of my right shoe. I put the syringe together, extracted enough of the barbiturate for Bentley's estimated weight and injected him.

The barbiturate Scopolamine acts on the central nervous system making it easier to extract information; however, questions have to be very pointed, or the information extracted could be scattered and useless.

Another advantage to scopolamine is that it will not only wipe out Mayor Dempsey's memory of the session, but anything previous to it as well. Bentley won't remember the situation leading up to his memory loss when this is over, much less the information he gives me, which is to my advantage.

I figured my time was limited before someone came looking for us, so as soon as I redressed I started slapping Bentley awake. I discovered he does not in fact have Riley and that Franklin has three sons in Denver working in various fields. Franklin, Jr. owns a construction company, Bryan Franklin owns a jewelry store chain, and Bobby Franklin owns a string of barbeque restaurants called "BBQ Heaven." Canfield was Franklin's illegitimate son that he kept in touch with and groomed for his position, and Mary is another of Franklin's illegitimate children with the same mother as Canfield.

I learned that the organization is vast, but not as vast as he wanted me to believe. I got the names of Bentley's associates from underling thugs to crooked officials including some of the local and state law enforcement.

I was also able to extract some crucial information that would enable us to get the incriminating information we needed to convict him and many of the other officials involved. Best of all, I believe I got what we needed to convict Franklin. We just had to get the books that listed the entire organization and activities since The Mongoose was eighteen years old and climbing up the chain. Supposedly the books contained dates and times of every killing he had committed or ordered and all illegal activities to include money laundering, jewel smuggling, arms running, and drug activity. I even learned of a prostitution ring that he had on the side.

"Who did you send to kill the two men at the farm after I escaped?"

"Pete and Larry went. I told them there couldn't be any witnesses, so they killed them. Killed them, they killed them both."

"Where's Tabatha?"

"She went back to her mother, the Madame of the prostitution ring. She's Franklin's on-again, off-again girlfriend."

"So Tabatha is Franklin's illegitimate daughter, too?"

"Yes ... yes, ... yes, her too."

I grabbed Dempsey's keys and left him where he was under the influence of the Scopolamine and exited through the second door, which opened to a wide hallway with numbered doors on either side in measured intervals. Turning the corner at the end of the hall, I realized I was in a large hotel. I saw a group of six people; probably conventioneers or something, and I slipped in behind the group and exited the building with them. At the curb while they were waiting for their cab, I slipped away.

I walked as quickly as I could down the sidewalk, looking behind for any sign of pursuit and crossed the street at the corner. I wanted to get as far away as I could before they found Dempsey, but I knew I couldn't keep walking down the street. It would be too easy to spot me.

I ducked into an insurance office and told the secretary my purse with my phone and all my cash had been stolen. She let me use her phone, and I called Jim who was standing by waiting for me to contact him.

"We have your location and are around the corner. Stay in the office if you can and watch for a white Ford Expedition. Hector will be driving."

When I saw the Expedition coming down the opposite side of the street, I left the office and stopped for traffic to clear so I could cross to him. I looked down the sidewalk to my right and saw Pete and Larry running toward me.

The traffic was too heavy to cross without killing myself, so I took off down the sidewalk. I ran hoping Hector would see what was going on and take pursuit.

The heels were a real problem to run in, so I kicked them off and ran in my stocking feet. I took the next corner at full speed and then ducked down the alley to try to get back to Hector.

Pete and Larry were pretty fast on their feet, but Larry had a bit of a beer gut, and Pete began to outpace him. Since I run every day, I was able to put some distance even between me and Pete until I came up against an eight-foot-tall chain-link fence that blocked the entire alley exit.

I tried the back door to the buildings on either side of me. They were locked. Pete caught up to me and tried to grab me, but I was able to spin away from him. I went at him with kicks, chops, and punches. He was a decent adversary, both of us getting in a couple good strikes and punches. I was blocking more of his strikes than he was of mine. It was making him mad and the madder he got the sloppier he got.

I had the advantage with my experience in Jujitsu and Aikido. I dropped and swept his feet, and he fell hard but before getting back up, he pulled a knife. Larry caught up to us and grabbed me from behind. Pete started toward me holding the knife out—intent to kill me. He had a very cruel and perverted look of pleasure on his face.

"You're not worth the effort to bring in alive."

As he drew back his arm to strike, a crossbow bolt hit him in the back piercing his heart, and traveling through his body. It bounced off the wall of the building behind us. If the angle of the shot were just a little different, it would have gone through Pete and hit me, too.

Larry, stunned, let go of me and started looking around for the shooter. I took advantage of his confusion and threw him to the ground. I had him in a hold just as the cavalry showed up. Hector was first to pull into the alley, and Morgan and Jim came running in on foot behind the vehicle, guns drawn. Behind them came a couple more FBI agents in their cars and the local cops.

I was sitting on Larry's back and rubbing my feet when Morgan and Jim caught up to me.

"You okay?" Jim asked, and I nodded in the affirmative. "What happened to him?" He indicated Pete.

"Our masked rescuer?" I shrugged. "I'm not sure. Larry here," I patted the back of his head so his face smashed into the pavement a couple of times, "was holding me while Pete was coming at me with a knife. I was pretty sure I could get out of the hold and avoid being knifed—I've been in situations like that before and always won—but before I could move, this bolt came whizzing in, passed through Pete's black heart, and hit the building over there." I pointed to the bolt lying on the pavement by the wall.

Larry was grunting and making muffled pleas to be released.

One of the FBI guys went over and photographed the bolt, Pete's body, his knife that had fallen out of his hand when he was hit, me sitting on good ole Larry, and anything else he found interesting. While he was performing that task, two other agents were blocking off the local cops from the scene and explaining this was a federal case.

I spied Riley coming around the corner of the building by the news vans and start walking our way. He was dressed in a black t-shirt and black jeans. He had his shoulder holster on, holding his Kimber, an assault knife sheathed on his hip and the sheath tied to his thigh, and a wicked-looking crossbow slung over his shoulder. His badge was displayed prominently on a cord around his neck, swinging with each stride.

I jumped up and ran to him as he came through the last block of FBI agents, and I threw my arms around him, hugging him tight.

"You're alive. I've been so worried about you. I'm so glad you're alright." I blabbered a lot of other stuff out of happiness to see him alive and ... well ... and from the adrenaline rush from the recent events.

Laughing, he released me. "I'm fine. I've been keeping an eye on you and Morgan. Jim did say I was in charge of you guys, you know."

Morgan came up and clapped Riley on the shoulder and gave him a big "guy" hug. Jim came and shook his hand.

"Let's leave this mess to forensics to clean up and go to the office."

We turned to leave the alley as one of the agents escorted a handcuffed Larry to the waiting vehicle.

Jim took us to the Boise office, which was bigger than the one in Idaho Falls. We gathered around a small round table in a small private meeting room but before we could get started, Riley asked for food.

"I'm starving. Is there anything around here to eat?"

"We can order carry out. Tell me what you want, and I'll have the secretary call it in."

"A big juicy steak with all the fixings would be great, but if that's asking too much, whatever is quick and easy. I've been living off fast food and MRE's ever since I went dark." Riley grabbed a napkin and wiped the sweat from his bald scalp.

"I'll call it in. There are drinks in the kitchenette, so get something if you want, and then let's go over everything. I want to hear from you first, Riley, then Morgan and Jeffries." Jim inquired if Morgan and I were hungry too. We declined.

"Get me some water, will ya?" Morgan asked as he sat down at the table and started jotting down notes on a legal pad.

Riley, Jim, and I went to the little kitchen and I got a bottle of water for Morgan and one for myself. Riley got a Diet Coke and pounced on some day-old donuts that were on the counter. Jim must live on coffee, because that's all I've ever seen him consume, with the exception of yesterday's breakfast.

Back in the meeting room Jim told Riley to start from his disappearance at the meet site.

"Fill the others in on what happened out there."

********

"When I went to the rendezvous in the assigned pickup, I had a little time to kill, so I pulled off onto N 130th East and parked. I ran to the rendezvous site to reconnoiter the area, and the van was there with Mutt and Jeff standing out behind it shooting the breeze.

"I overheard Mutt say he wasn't going to take any chances with me. When I showed up, he was going to blow me away and then tell the boss I resisted. That was all I needed to hear since it meant they already had plans to kill Jeri no matter what, or she was already dead.

"Either way, they were not going to take me. I jogged back to my truck and headed toward them.

"I was doing about thirty when I approached the guys. Once they were fully in view, I floored it and turned into them. As the truck got up beside the two guys, who jumped out of the way, I rolled out of the truck on the driver's side letting the truck plow into the ditch.

"In the confusion, Mutt and Jeff ran to the pickup to grab me—or shoot me is more like it. I came up behind them, grabbed Jeff by the head and snapped his neck. As Mutt was bringing his gun up to shoot, I kicked it out of his hand and shot him with Jeff's gun. I threw both bodies into the back of the pickup."

Riley acted out his story in detailed animation, and I couldn't help but laugh.

"Hey, it wasn't funny. I could have been hurt." He feigned insult, and I smirked.

"I didn't want the team to follow me. I knew the kidnappers had Jeri, and they weren't going to release her to anyone. I also figured they had the two of you as well." He cut his eyes to me and Morgan, "I was going to do everything I could to get the three of you safely away, so I took their van and headed to your rendezvous, Jeffries."

"So you're the guy who helped me get away? It didn't look like you. Why didn't you say something? We could have worked together."

"It wasn't me. Your truck was there, but you were gone and the van was driving off as I got there. I figured they had you trussed up in the van. I pulled a U inside the gates and hung back, following.

"The van led me straight to a Walmart, and I watched as you got out and started hoofing it toward the office.

I realized you were alright which made me happy. I stayed back and watched you make it to the office before I left and went back to your pickup. That's where I found the two guys you knocked out and tethered to the truck." He raised his hand in a 'high-five' to me. "Good work, Jeffries. How did you do it?"

"I'm embarrassed I didn't see you tailing me. I'll have to be more careful in the future." I shook my head with a grimace on my face. Morgan laughed.

"It wasn't entirely me that took care of those two goons. Some dude all in black whacked the guy handcuffing me and knocked him out. I didn't know what was going on, so I hightailed it outta there on foot. I'd sure like to know who it was that helped me out.

"Anyway, I hid at the side of the building and watched as he snuck around the back and hit the other guy over the head. Then he took off. I think he left the area on a motorcycle. He took the guns too ... they were both missing. I can't believe it was just a random mugger. Too coincidental, don't you think?"

"I know who it was." All eyes turned to Jim.

"It was Kenny Rhode. We picked him up at the house. He was recruited from your department by the NSA. They discovered this crime organization who was stealing the identity of people, filing false income tax returns, and using the money to buy arms and narcotics. It was the identity theft part of their operation that got the NSA involved, and Kenny volunteered to go undercover. That's not their usual MO, but between them, the ATF, IRS, FBI—which I was not privy to— and DEA, they put together a very small and highly specialized unit.

"Two guys were selected to go undercover: Kenny and a DEA agent named Raymond Cortez."

"Wow!" I said. "Morgan, you were right ... well, sort of."

"We owe the guy, then," said Riley. "I'd like to meet him. Anyway, when I got to the house where they took Morgan, the team was there mopping up. I got Jim to the side and let him know what I was up to, and he filled me in on what was going on. We felt I would be a better asset if I stayed out of sight and out of play as far as everyone else was concerned. Jim gave me a radio to keep in touch with him and keep me posted on the events.

"I followed you and Morgan to the storage units and made sure Morgan and Jeri got out safe. Thanks, by the way, for what you both did to get Jeri free.

"No problem," Morgan said as I muttered, "You're welcome."

Riley nodded. "Then I went back to help you out, Jeffries. I took out Jimmie when he came at me with a knife. You nearly got me with one of your wild rounds, but it was enough to distract Frenchie. I slipped up behind him and knocked his feet out from under him. He lost his gun but pulled a big bowie knife from his belt and came at me. We struggled for a bit.

"I tried to disarm him instead of kill him, but he moved just right and with the forward momentum I had, I jammed his knife into his gut. He yelled real loud and fell to the ground. I didn't think it was a mortal wound."

"We've checked out all the local hospitals and clinics but haven't found him yet," Jim said.

Riley nodded and continued, "Dave was a lot easier to take care of. He was already woozy from a couple blows to the head, and I found him staggering around. With him being so dazed and confused and Frenchie bleeding from the gut, I figured they were no longer a threat for the moment, so I left.

"I pocketed Jimmie's and Frenchie's bowie knives and stowed them in the van for fingerprint evidence. Then I went to a buddy's house and 'borrowed' his son's Nissan." He raised his hands and used the first two fingers of each hand to indicate quotation marks when he said "borrowed." I smiled at him again.

"It's a junker that his high school kid uses to run around in, and I knew he wouldn't mind. I left a note on the door letting him know I was in desperate need and not to call the cops. I also noted he could find the car in the morning down the street from my house with the keys under my front door mat.

"I grabbed the knives, stowed them in the trunk, and drove home. I needed weapons. I parked down the street but in sight of the front of my house. I surveyed the area and didn't see anything suspicious. I didn't think it was being watched.

To be on the safe side though, I slipped down the alley to the backyard. I let myself in the back door to the garage, which let me into the kitchen. I grabbed my Kimber. I'd left it at the house when I picked up my sniper rifle, and I grabbed my assault knife. I donned the holster and strapped on the sheath with the knife. As I was heading out, I decided I should take my crossbow in case I needed a more silent and distance precision weapon, so I went back in and got it. Then I headed out in Jeri's Volkswagen.

"I contacted Jim to get an update and see where I was needed. He told me about your trip up here to Boise and he wanted me here in advance to watch for you."

"Wait ... what?! You guys knew about this?" Morgan asked incredulous.

"Yes, it was all planned," Jim said. "I suspected someone in our office is working for The Mongoose, so I had to make it look like Jeffries was going on her own. We didn't suspect you, Morgan, but I knew if you thought it was real and the snitch was watching and feeding his organization info, they would believe she was going rogue. I needed it to be authentic.

"I was right. They do have a man inside, but Jeffries wasn't able to extract that information. It's possible Bentley doesn't know who it is."

"Oh, okay ... but I don't like being kept out of the loop. I could have played along too, ya know." Morgan glanced at me with hurt in his eyes.

"I'm sorry I lied to you Morgan. I didn't want to, but you're the closest person to me. If you thought I was really on my own—"

"Get your ego out of the way, Morgan." Riley interrupted. "You know it was the right move to make. You've worked undercover before.

"Jim and I met down the street from the safe house. He handed off the sniper rifle to me, and I gave him the two bowie knives I confiscated. I got to Boise and set up on the rooftop next to that little diner you were in Jeffries. I was also rigged with an earpiece and could hear your conversation like Jim.

"Talk to yourself often, do you?" Riley's eyes were twinkling.

"You're enjoying this way too much, Riley!" I felt the heat of embarrassment rise to my face.

"I was going to hang outside and wait for you to come out, but I knew you had walked into the lion's den. After thirty minutes, I decided to go in even though I could hear you two talking. I didn't like what I was hearing so..." He shrugged.

"I ducked into a utility closet across the hall from the mayor's outer office and watched. I saw Larry and Pete show up in those bad cop uniforms. When the four of you came out of the office and exited the rear of the building ... I followed.

"I walked into the restaurant about twelve minutes after you guys went in. Just before I walked in, a woman came out dressed a lot like you. I cased the joint but none of you were there, so I figured you were behind the curtained area.

"I took a table and ordered a diet Coke. I walked to the curtain and found a locked door. The waitress came running up to me saying it was a storage room and for employees only. I apologized to her and she showed me to the bathroom. I went back to my table and listened to your conversation.

"When you said he was taking you to the basement, I threw a five on the table and left. I went around to the back of the building but there were no rear or side exits and no windows. I sat on the place for awhile and listened to your comments. I didn't like the fact that I couldn't get to you without kicking down doors.

"When I heard you say you were twenty-five feet from the restaurant, I headed north. I heard your conversation with Dempsey after you injected him and knew when you were leaving. I heard you say something to that group of people about what a nice hotel it was, and I knew I went in the wrong direction. I turned and headed south.

"I saw the two stooges run out of the building and up the street looking for someone, so I followed and saw when they spotted you.

"Having cased the whole neighborhood earlier, I knew that alley was a dead end. I couldn't get around the block to come into the alley behind you in time to be of any help, so I came in the other direction and got there just in time to strategically place that bolt through Pete's heart from the other side of the fence. Then the team came charging down the alley.

"So basically ... I saved your bacon." He gave me a wide grin.

"I would say, 'thank ya kindly' but the truth of the matter is, I had it under control. Thanks anyway, pal. I'm glad you were there just in case." I held his gaze with my eyes and winked. He nodded back.

Morgan sat at the table in a pout for being left out of the loop.

**********

"**M**organ. Why don't you fill us in on the investigation prior to hearing from Jeffries? Maybe we can fill in more of the blanks." Jim gave Morgan a nod.

Getting his chance to be the center of attention, Morgan perked up. He's such a ham.

"From the beginning again?"

"Yes. Let's see if we can put together more of the pieces since we have more information."

"Well, we, the department, were first notified Mariah was missing when her secretary, Norah, called us. She explained that Mariah left with a young client and her parents to go to the bus station. Norah didn't know why except that it had something to do with the child.

"She advised us that Dr. Jeffries never returned to the office that day, and when Norah arrived at work the following morning, the whole office had been ransacked."

"Now I know what they were looking for. It was..."

"Hold that thought, Jeffries. Let's get Morgan's rundown of events. Then you can fill us in on any blank spots that you have information for. Go ahead, Morgan." Jim nodded for Morgan to continue.

"As I was saying, uniform was first notified of the break-in, and they called the burglary unit to investigate. During the questioning of Norah, they determined you were missing, and my division was called." Morgan addressed this statement to me then turned to Jim.

"Since my wife, Molly, and I go way back with Jeffries—we are practically like family—we each have a key to her house just as she has a key to ours. I was first on the scene at her place and let myself in with my key. I found no trace that she had been home. Her dog, Paisley, was ecstatic to see me and was out of water. With the dog mess in the kitchen where Paisley is kept when left alone, it was obvious she hadn't been outside in at least twenty-four hours. After checking the house, I gave Paisley some water, let her outside, and cleaned up the mess in the kitchen."

"Thanks, Morgan." At the mention of Paisley tears sprang to my eyes.

"No problem. Since the house hadn't been breached, I called Molly to come collect the half dead house-plants and Paisley until we could determine what happened to Jeffries and where she was.

"Back at the station, I interviewed Norah myself. She gave a complete physical description of the three people that Jeffries left with. When I asked for the registration paperwork they filled out, she said it was missing but she still had it scanned into her computer. I told her I would come by the office later for a copy of those papers and to do my own investigation of the break-in.

"I turned Norah over to our sketch artist and got copies of the reports that had been filed so far in the burglary and the disappearance. Back at my desk, I started going through them and taking notes for my own records.

"At two, I went back to Jeffries's office and found Norah there. She printed out the information for me, and I pocketed it while I checked the place out for anything that might have been missed.

"The burglars entered through the back door after using a blow-torch to cut through the dead-bolted security door. Once they got through that, it was quick and easy to pry the backdoor open.

"It looked like they hit Jeffries's office first." He turned to me. "Your desk is pretty much destroyed. Sorry!" Morgan looked at me with a pout and shrugged his shoulders.

"Well, great! I loved that antique desk."

"I know. The two drawers that you had locked were pried open, but the rest of the damage just looked random and malicious.

"They pulled all the books off the shelves and tossed them on the floor. I'm not sure if they were looking for something in the books or something behind the books on the shelves, but apparently they didn't find what they were looking for.

"They moved through the office, pulling things out of the bookshelves and file cabinets. The kitchenette and bathroom bins and cabinets were dumped, and they dumped every drawer in the place. The only thing they didn't bother were the computers, so we suspect they were searching for something tangible and not electronic.

"I left there and drove back to my office to get the composite drawings of the family and my camera. I went over the registration documents Norah gave me, made copies for the files, and pocketed the originals. Then I drove out to the residential address listed on the registration forms and found a vacant field in a new subdivision. I canvassed the sparse neighborhood. So far there are only four homes built, and two of those four were occupied.

"I talked to the construction workers who were building two other homes in the subdivision, and they never heard of the people listed on the client forms and hadn't seen anything unusual. I showed them the composite drawings, and they didn't recognize any of them.

"A very short, very rotund lady of the house answered the door to the first occupied home I went to. Her husband was at work and the children at school, so I was going to have to go back. She informed me she never heard of those people or seen anything untoward in the neighborhood. She didn't recognize anyone in the drawings either.

"No one answered the door at the other occupied house, so I sat on it until an unmarked unit could sit and watch for someone to come home.

"I was at Dr. Jeffries office doing another walk-through and taking pictures to make sure I didn't miss anything when the call came in that the second family had arrived home.

"When I showed up, a black man answered the door dressed in a suit and tie. He had the television remote in his left hand. I asked him about the family we were looking for, and he advised he hadn't heard of them. He did remember seeing something odd about two weeks prior.

"When I asked him to tell me about it, he gestured me inside. "'Come on in, and I'll tell you about it." He told me *it* struck him as pretty odd, 'but then this is a new subdivision and a lot of people are looking at the lots and the new construction.'

"I followed the gentleman, Mr. Theodore Trenton, into the living room and sat on the edge of the leather overstuffed chair he indicated. He removed his suit jacket and neatly folded it in half and laid it over the back of another chair, loosened his tie and sat on the couch before he muted the baseball game on his 55-inch hi-def flat-screen TV mounted on the wall above an elaborate sound system. I was envious of the set up he had." Morgan grinned and shook his head.

"Is that information relevant, Morgan?" Jim cocked an eyebrow Morgan's way.

"No, but it was impressive." Morgan chuckled and continued.

"He said he'd been home, sick with the flu, and went to the kitchen to fix a bowl of homemade chicken soup. While the soup was heating in the microwave, he looked out to the back yard. He was thinking about the landscaping they wanted to do ... visualizing it in his head.

"Their new fence had been put up the week before, and he noticed the back gate was standing open. His fever had broken and he was feeling a lot better, just drained, so he went out to the back gate and looked out on the field behind his house and to either side.

"The address to the vacant lot that was given by our family was right next door to this guy. He said he saw a man who met Eric's description walking around the lot, kicking over stones, and squatting a couple different times to take sample plugs of dirt.

"The man had a pair of binoculars hung around his neck. Before leaving the lot, he held the binoculars up to his eyes and made a slow 360-degree turn. The last direction he faced was toward Mr. Trenton.

"Mr. Trenton waved to him when the binoculars were turned his way, and the guy lowered them and walked away without any kind of acknowledgement. He seemed like he was in a hurry to leave.

"I asked Mr. Trenton to show me where he was when he saw this man. We walked into the dining room, and we went out to the back gate. He showed me where he was standing outside the gate and pointed out where the man he saw was standing when he was using the binoculars. I traipsed over to the spot, and Mr. Trenton verified I was about in the same place.

"When I showed him the composite drawings, he said the guy he saw could have been Eric, but he didn't recognize anyone else.

"We talked about the Arizona Diamondbacks and the Texas Rangers, his job as a computer programmer and tech director for his company, and motorcycles which are his passion until his family arrived. They didn't have any further information. I thanked them for their time and left.

"I walked across the street to the first occupied house and was able to talk to the man of the house and their teenage son. Neither of them could give me any additional information.

"I was curious about the actions of the guy with the binoculars, so I went to my trunk and got my own binoculars out and walked over to the vacant lot. I did a pretty thorough search and found a couple of small holes where soil samples appeared to have been taken. I stood in about the area Mr. Trenton said the guy had been standing and checked everything out in a 360-degree radius with my binoculars. I didn't see a thing of interest and couldn't figure out what he was looking for, or at for that matter.

"From there, I went to the courthouse and looked at the land deeds to see who the developer was and went to their offices. I discovered from the county assessor that the lot had been purchased by a Calvin Josephson. They gave me the name and address of the contractor who will be building Josephson's new house as well as Josephson's current phone number and address.

"The contractor, Matt Claunch, who matched Eric's description fairly well, told me Josephson was a little bit quirky and wanted a complete soil sample before he agreed to build. He was worried about sink-holes, insect infestations, and other such concerns. He also wanted the house situated on the lot far to the back with a long drive. He did not want any kind of obstruction to the view of the mountains from his study that would be on the second floor. That was why he had the binoculars out.

"I asked him why he didn't acknowledge Mr. Trenton's wave, and he said he never saw it. He just saw a man standing at the back of his fence watching, and since he was finished collecting his soil samples and checking the radius of the land, he left.

"I left Mr. Claunch's office and headed back to my own. It was quitting time, but because this was Jeffries, I couldn't give it up for the day.

"I typed out complete notes on everything up to that point and made sure every 'i' was dotted and every 't' crossed. I didn't want anything slipping through the cracks on this.

"It was ten thirty by the time I got home that evening and Mia, my fifteen-year-old daughter—" he nodded toward Jim since Riley and I already knew about her, "and Molly, my wife, were on the couch in the den crying and consoling each other. They were both worried about you." Morgan gave me a nod.

"I'm sorry I worried y'all."

"We know. It wasn't your fault, but you're like a sister to Molly and me and an aunt to the kids. Anyway, as soon as I walked in the house the girls ran to me, and Max, short for Maximus," he directed his son's name to Jim, "came out of his room to see if you were found and if you were okay."

He smiled at me. "Of course Paisley was right there, sniffing at my feet and legs.

"First thing the next morning, I checked out this Josephson fellow and he was clean as a whistle—not even any traffic violations. I gave him a call and made an appointment to come by and visit him at eleven that morning at his office.

"He certainly is an odd duck. He's about fifty-two years old, five feet five inches, and as round as a medicine ball. He was bald right down the middle of the top of his head, not even any comb-over hairs in the middle, but the sides and back of his head were dark brown, thick, and curly. He wore coke-bottle glasses in tortoise shell frames and although he's a divorce attorney, he was dressed in knee-length cargo shorts, a very loud Hawaiian button-down shirt, and a pair of Crocs with white knee-high socks.

"It was the funniest darned thing I'd seen in a long time, especially when he sat down behind his huge ornate desk in this *beautifully* decorated office.

"His speech was very slow and precise, enunciating each word clearly and carefully. I wondered if he had some kind of speech impediment that he had overcome, or maybe he was a mild stroke victim that had to concentrate on his speech.

"Whatever the case, it was frustrating waiting for the answers to my questions to be spoken.

"He explained that he had just gotten remarried to a thirty-four-year-old woman whose divorce he had worked. They had spent a lot of time together working up the divorce and getting all the documentation together to get her a huge settlement.

"When the divorce was finalized, and she was set up very comfortably for the rest of her life, she called him and asked him to dinner so she could properly thank him for all the work he had done. They started dating and three months later were married.

"It was her idea to buy the lot and build a big new house that was theirs and not hers from another marriage or his from another marriage.

"I asked for her demographics, and he cheerily gave them to me. He was *very* proud of her age and even volunteered her measurements. Her name was Mary, and as he described her further, I realized she resembled the lady from the fake family. I hoped I had finally found a lead in this case.

"When I asked him for his wife's former married name, he said, 'Now wait just a minute, here. You don't think for one minute that my little angel cakes had anything to do with this ...' he waved his hands in the air while he continued, '... this psychologist that's gone missing. Do you? Is that why you're asking?'

"He was getting agitated until I told him it was routine information I needed in order to make a thorough investigation.

"'If she's not involved—'

"'Oh, I assure you she's not. Not my honey bunch.'

"'As I was saying, the information I collect will only clear her *if* she's not involved and found to be a person of interest.'

"He started to interrupt me, and I raised my hand and my voice for him to stop. I said, 'I'm not saying she *is* involved. I'm saying in case someone finds her to be a person of interest.'

"'But how could she be found a person of interest? She doesn't know that psychologist.'

"'The problem, Mr. Josephson, is that the description you're giving me is very close to one of our suspects. That's all, and since the evidence has brought *you* into the picture, it will also require that I interview *her*. Just to clear her. You understand?'

"'Right ... right, I see. Of course ... that makes sense. So, do you have pictures of this woman that you're looking for? I can ease your mind right away.'

"I pulled the composite drawings out of my jacket pocket. 'It's a composite drawing.'

"'Oh, well then, there you have it!' he said, holding the drawing in his left hand and slapping it with the back of his right hand. He looked up from the drawing and said, 'This is just what one person thought she looked like. Sure, it looks a little bit like my Mary, but that's all—just a coincidence.

"'Anyway, to answer your question, her former married name was De Angelo. She had been trapped in a loveless marriage for years to Romeo De Angelo. He was a very notorious safe cracker back in the day. He married my little sweet cheeks when she was sixteen—met her in Philadelphia and whisked her away from her home and family to New Mexico.

"'They didn't know what happened to her or where she was for years—actually reported her as kidnapped, but the police never found anything and wrote her off as a runaway. She didn't get along with her family, and that was the major basis for their assumption.

"This De Angelo was part of a group of bank robbers that worked all over the southwest: Texas, New Mexico, Arizona, and Oklahoma. The gang was busted back in the seventies right here in Albuquerque, and he served fifteen years in a federal pen. Mary met him after he got out, and they settled in Hobbs. He wasn't even supposed to be out of the state when he met my gal in Philadelphia.

"Mary lived in fear of De Angelo because of his bad temper and his ability to have one of his old cronies make her disappear. He's old and sick now, and a lot of the old gang are dead or in old folks homes. Mary finally stood up to him and told him she was divorcing him.

"He screamed and threatened her, but because he was a con, he couldn't own a business or guns or buy a house. So, everything they accumulated over the years was legally in her name, and he didn't have a leg to stand on as far as monetary threat went.

"He had a lot of money from his bank-robbing days secreted away and after they married, he opened a bar and a pawn shop under her name. He appointed his son from a previous marriage as the manager of the bar. Mary ran the pawn shop. Everything was in Mary's name, and she was a good money manager. And smart, too—she hid money away for herself, knowing she might need it to run one day.

"'They, well ... he was behind it ... used the two businesses to launder his old ill-gotten money, and he was also running guns and dealing drugs without Mary's knowledge. "'She found out about that after we started working on the divorce.

"'That was how we were finally able to secure her divorce. It took a lot of time and work, but we got the goods on his illegal activities, and she told him she would turn him in if he didn't give her the divorce without a fight.

"She also told him her attorney—that would be me—had set it up so if anything happened to either one of us, the information would go to the feds. Of course, we didn't. I never even saw all the evidence she has on him; she has it locked away in a safety deposit box. I've tried to convince her it is safer for her to let me have it, but she insists that I'm safer if I don't know where it is.'

"'I see. So where is Mary now? I do need to interview her for my reports because she resembles the woman in the composite drawing.'

"'Yeah, but only a little bit. That drawing doesn't really look that much like my Mary.'

"'I know, I know. I still need to interview her.'

"'She's out of the country with a couple of her cousins she recently reconnected with.'

"'Where?'

"'Well, they're travelling. She's in Cancun right now. Then they're going to Fiji, Italy, Spain, Germany, Ireland, and then Australia. I don't know in what order, of course. They're just enjoying themselves and getting reacquainted after all these years. I gave her my credit card since we haven't gotten her money from the divorce yet.'

"'When did she leave on this trip?'

"'Last week, on Sunday.'

"'Okay. When will she be back?' I asked him.

"'Oh, whenever. There's no rush. She's a very wealthy woman now and doesn't have any responsibilities. I'm planning on meeting them in Spain next month after I wrap up some of my pending cases.'

"After a few more queries, I thanked him for his time. It was one thirty by the time I got out of there, and I headed back to the office to type up my report on the interview. I checked the NCIC database on this De Angelo fellow, and there was quite an extensive résumé on him. Most of what Josephson told me about him matched up with the intel.

"Then I looked up Mary De Angelo. Now that was some interesting reading. Nothing of what Josephson told me matched up with the intel I was getting on her.

"She had been reported as a runaway, true enough, but she ran away from a group home for wayward girls in Chicago. Her last name was Hollister, Mary Hollister, before she married De Angelo. I called and talked to the head mistress of this group home, and she said she would have to dig the files out on her from the archives and call me back.

"While I was waiting, I did a little research on their businesses in Hobbs. Sure enough, Mary was listed as the owner of the two businesses that Josephson told me about. I drew up an affidavit and called Judge Harvey to let him know I was bringing it over to get a subpoena for Mary's business records, bank records, and divorce records."

"How is Judge Harvey?" I asked.

"He's getting old and tired. I don't know why he hasn't retired. He did tell me how much he admires and respects you and that he was praying we find you well and unharmed. He said he's added you to his church prayer list so the whole church is praying for you."

I nodded and Morgan turned back to Jim.

"I called the Hobbs P.D. and talked to one of their detectives, letting him know I was transmitting the subpoena for them to execute. I also filled them in on the case and asked them to interview De Angelo for me. Craig, the detective I talked to, was happy to help and said he would get back to me as soon as he could.

"I hadn't eaten all day except for some coffee and a piece of toast before I left the house that morning. I was running on empty. I typed up my reports on the day's investigation and headed home. I walked in the front door at six p.m., in time for dinner with the family.

"We were relaxing in the living room, reminiscing and sharing memories of time spent with Jeffries that we all had. The kids and Molly were really upset and worried, and this kind of helped them get over some of the anxiety. I was worried too, but I had to keep up a strong front telling them I was getting closer to finding you. I hoped it was true.

"At nine thirty, Craig called me at home and told me De Angelo was gone.

"I asked him what he meant, *"Gone?"*.

"'Gone. He told his neighbor he was going camping and fishing up in Montana and that he would be unreachable for the summer. He closed up his house and drove off in his brand new Ford F-350 and fifth-wheel trailer.

"'I thought he was in an old folk's home, or something.'

"'Not hardly. He's seventy-three and in very good physical condition. He's well known by the department, but hasn't been in trouble for years.'

"'I see,' I said.

"Craig told me he checked with the Ford dealership, and they produced the paperwork on the sale of the pickup. De Angelo paid cash. He hadn't tracked down the fifth wheel purchase yet. He said he had the docs I subpoenaed, and he's having them couriered to me along with the financial papers from the Ford dealership. 'You'll have them by ten tomorrow morning,' is what he told me.

"'Great! Thanks, Craig.' I hung up.

"With this information I went to bed with a heavy heart. I didn't feel any closer to finding Jeffries than when I first learned she was missing, but it was starting to look pretty bleak for her. I had a strong suspicion this

Mary character was in some way involved, maybe De Angelo, too.

"I had trouble getting to sleep. I had about two hours of deep sleep before Jeffries's call came in."

"Thanks, Morgan," Jim said. "We just got the documents from the Hobbs detective in our Idaho office this morning. With the info from Hobbs, I wouldn't be surprised if De Angelo is involved. I've got our Montana agents checking for any trace of him. They've put out a BOLO for him and are checking surveillance video all across the southern entrances to the state trying to get a lead on him. My guess ... they're not going to find anything, but we've gotta try.

"I've got this stinking suspicion he's with Mary—wherever that may be. Morgan, did you get a feel for whether this Josephson fellow is involved, or is he just a dupe used by Mary and De Angelo?"

"I think he believed everything was on the up and up. I'm with you, though. I think De Angelo is with Mary, or they are planning on meeting up somewhere."

**********

"So, Jeffries, what do you have to add to any of this information?" Jim asked me.

"Well, first of all, did you guys find the tunnel that Dempsey used to take me to the hotel?"

"We did. He was picked up. Do you remember anything else from when you first met Mary, Eric, and Tabatha?"

"No, I told you everything about that. You guys know everything since then, except what my office was searched for."

"What do you think it was?" Morgan asked.

"Well, remember that police-involved shooting about three months ago where Officer Sanders was killed?"

"Yeah, what about it?"

"Kyle Trent was the surviving officer. He killed the two guys that had engaged them in the shoot-out. Since the incident, he had been suffering from PTSD, and I had been counseling him for the department.

"He and Sean Sanders were following these two guys near the scene of a home-invasion robbery in the foothills subdivision. The scene of the robbery was already being handled by a couple of other officers. When they drove by to see if they could be of any assistance, they spotted these two guys walking down the street about four blocks away. They followed them two more blocks.

"The two guys started looking over their shoulders, acting nervous, until they broke out and ran, one of them cutting across the street and between two houses. Sean got out of the car and started after him while Kyle stopped the other guy and questioned him. The guy dropped a backpack he'd been carrying and pulled a knife on Kyle. There was a struggle and Kyle got the knife away from him, but the guy broke and ran across the street and between the same two houses behind Sean and the first guy. Kyle took pursuit, and when he rounded the corner, the guy he struggled with beamed him across the shoulder and chest with a two-by-four, knocking him to the ground. He rolled out of the way before he could be hit again and pulled his weapon. He saw a gun pointed at him, and he rolled again, avoiding getting hit by the first round and then fired his weapon hitting the guy in his right shoulder first and center mass with the second shot. The guy's second round grazed Kyle in the left side of his head above his ear.

"Kyle heard more gunfire in the backyard of that house, so he ran back there. He found Sean and the first guy in a standoff pointing their guns at each other. Kyle drew on the suspect and told him to drop the gun, but Sean fired a wild round as he fell to the ground. The perp fired another round at Sean, hitting him in the right thigh as he was falling.

"Kyle shot and killed the guy. He checked Sean, who was dead on the scene. The first round that hit him went through his neck, severing his artery, and he was bleeding out when Kyle got there. He hadn't realized Sean had already been hit at the time. All of this is in the police reports.

"Anyway, back-up showed up and Kyle was transported to the hospital to check out his wound. An officer named Dave Hites was reported to have driven Kyle's unit back to the station, since *he* was transported to the hospital by ambulance. Later he asked Dave about the backpack that the suspect had dropped ..."

"Who did?" Riley asked.

"Kyle did, but according to Kyle, Dave said there wasn't any backpack and he was acting weird about it. Kyle went to his sergeant and reported it because he had noted the backpack in his reports, and his sergeant dismissed it saying someone else must have carried it off.

"Kyle was convinced the backpack was retrieved by Dave and contained the loot from the home invasion. He started investigating Dave on his time off. One day, when he knew the family was going out of town on a weekend trip to Ruidoso, he broke into Dave's home and found the backpack stuffed in the garage behind some boxes.

"He was shocked when he looked inside but knew he couldn't go to the station with it, because it was an illegal search and seizure … a burglary, in fact."

"What did he find in the backpack?" Morgan asked.

"Well, besides the two revolvers and some cash and jewelry they got from the residence they robbed, he found a burner cell phone. He checked the numbers on it and found only one—eight calls from a single number and six calls to it, spanning three days. There were two voice messages and three text messages."

"What did they say, the voice mails and texts?" Jim asked.

"He didn't tell me. He brought the phone to me to hang on to until he figured out what to do. He said it was very incriminating and referred to some personnel at the department who were involved.

"He was scared and begged me not to listen to it or read the texts ... just to keep it safe for him. He was really freaked out, and I figured it wouldn't hurt to hold it for him while I counseled him to contact the FBI if he felt he couldn't notify anyone in his own department. I just about had him convinced to do that when I was kidnapped."

"Where did you keep it? Was it in one of the locked drawers of your desk?" Morgan asked.

"No, I put it in the wall safe behind the big picture of the Sandia Mountains ... the one on the wall across from my desk. Was it broken into also? My safe?"

"We didn't know about a safe. I don't remember if the picture was still there, but I didn't see a wall safe. I didn't look for one either. Norah didn't say anything about a safe."

"Norah doesn't know about it. I had it installed last year when I did the remodel on the office, and I kept quiet about it. It's possible it was never discovered. I hope it wasn't."

"Jeffries ... the evening after you went missing ... Kyle Trent was found dead. His patrol unit was found at the abandoned drive-in movie theater. It's patrolled, you know ... to run off the parkers that would use it ... since it's marked as private property. When the grounds were investigated, they found his body.

"He'd been tortured inside the old concession stand, strung up from the rafters and shocked with some sort of electrical device. It's remote enough so no one could hear him screaming. The last I heard, the M.E. thought it was a modified cattle prod. He had burns all over his body, and he was put out of his misery with a bullet to the head."

"Oh my God, no." Mariah closed her eyes and shook her head. "No, no, no ... they must have figured out he got the phone and forced the information out of him about what he did with it."

"Did you only have the phone or the other evidence, also?" Jim was leaning forward in his chair, elbows on the table.

"Just the phone. He said he left the backpack and then went over his sergeant's head and talked to his captain about the backpack that went missing. He didn't admit to breaking into Dave's house, just said he knew it was missing and that Dave was acting weird.

"His captain supposedly talked to Internal Affairs, who was going to do an investigation,

but he never heard any more about it …
standard operating procedure." I shrugged.

There was a long silence in the room as we all
contemplated the loss of a good man's life—a
fellow officer—and the implications it might
have on this case.

"Okay." Jim clapped his hands and then
rubbed them together.

"I think we're done here. We've got the
information we need to mop up this ring.
The information you got from Dempsey has
been sent to our Denver office. They'll have
the agent inside the organization try to
acquire the ledgers. If not, we'll use other
means.

"There's nothing left here for you two to do.
Mariah, let us know if you still have that cell
phone and if any of it pertains to this case.
There's a good chance it will."

Morgan and I went back to Idaho Falls with
Riley. We stopped and picked up Jeri from
the safe house before going to their home.
We spent the night with Jeri and Riley and
then flew out the next day. Jeri and Riley
had become very precious to me, and we
vowed to keep in touch.

**********

# V

It was six o'clock in the evening when we touched down in Albuquerque. Molly and the kids had been released from protective custody the night before, and it was a grand reunion when I walked into their house with Morgan. Molly, of course, rushed to Morgan and hesitated taking him in her arms. She investigated what she could of his wounds from the beating he took, before he grew impatient and wrapped her in a fierce hug and kissed her with passion. When finished, she came and embraced me. The kids, Max and Mia, came running down the stairs when they heard my voice and threw themselves at me, bear hugging me. Paisley was jumping all over the place—my legs, the chairs in the room, and the couch—trying to get close to me ... get in my arms. She was so happy she yipped in joyous squeals. After all the hugs, I was able to pick her up and hold her.

Molly had dinner prepared for us and insisted I stay and eat with them. She and the children had all kinds of questions about everything that transpired. Morgan and I filled them in on everything we could disclose without compromising the case.

Molly wanted to know how Morgan got beat up so bad. We told her about Jeri's abduction. She and Mia wept. Max's face turned red with anger. Morgan cut the rest of the explanation to the briefest of facts to spare his family any further upset.

Molly picked up my car from my office when they first learned of my abduction. They left it parked in their driveway, so Morgan and Molly helped me carry out my revived houseplants that Molly saved, Paisley and her bed, food, and toys, and a plate of leftovers from the evening's dinner. Molly and Mia had already gone to my place that afternoon and cleaned the house thoroughly. They stocked my kitchen with enough groceries to get me by for a few days and put fresh linens on my bed.

I hugged Molly one last time, and she went back into the house so Morgan and I could talk in private.

"Do you want me to go to the office with you tonight to check the wall safe?"

"No. If it's gone, it can wait until tomorrow to be reported. You need to be with your family and I'm ready to go home and sleep for a week. Are you reporting to work tomorrow?"

"Tomorrow is Sunday, but I'm going in anyways for a little bit. I have to wrap up the reports on this case." He hugged me. "You sleep in, and I'll try to keep Molly and Mia from calling you for as long as possible." He released me and I patted him on the shoulder.

"I'll call you guys tomorrow evening if not sooner. Okay?"

"Sounds good. Sweet dreams." He gave me a chaste kiss on the cheek, saw me into my car and the seatbelt fastened, and stepped back while I backed out of the drive.

I was tempted to drive to the office to check the safe, but I was exhausted and ready to get home. Once home, I put the leftovers Jeri sent with me into the fridge, let Paisley out in the backyard, and unloaded the rest of the stuff from my car.

Paisley came in and we played while I told her how much I missed her. She jumped all over the place and around me with glee. There's nothing in the world like dog joy.

I took a quick shower; towel dried my hair and climbed into my own bed with fresh, clean sheets. It was like falling into a cloud, or embracing an old friend. It felt safe and comfortable. Within minutes, Paisley was curled up beside me, and I drifted off into a sound sleep.

My sleep was peaceful and deep, and I woke at noon the next day feeling completely rested. I was ready to get back into my normal routine so the first order of business was my 'morning' run. I could tell Paisley missed the regular activity also; she was excited to get harnessed up and out the door.

I was still a little jumpy, so I kept watch for anyone following or tracking my progress. I didn't notice *anything* or *anyone* suspicious. By the time I got back home, I felt a lot better about the whole situation being taken care of.

I fixed lunch from last night's leftovers and put together the ingredients for green chili stew in the crock-pot for dinner. I thought about going to the office to see what there was for mail, but I decided to take a nap instead. Paisley was happy to be with me no matter where we were. I slept until five o'clock in the evening with Paisley faithfully by my side.

I was restless when I got up and decided to take Paisley to the dog park for a laid-back jog. The stew smelled delicious but it wasn't quite ready to eat, so I grabbed an apple to munch on the way to the park.

Later that evening I fixed myself a bowl of stew and ate in front of the television. After eating and cleaning up, I picked up a book that I'd been reading. I tried but couldn't concentrate and decided to spend some time meditating before going to bed.

Monday dawned beautiful, and I was finally feeling refreshed. I took Paisley for our daily run at sunrise and thought about the last week. There was something about the whole kidnapping thing that kept nagging at the back of my mind—something I couldn't bring forward into my consciousness. I had this feeling that, because I was so focused on my own escape and survival, and then rescuing Jeri and Morgan, I didn't register something important I heard or saw. Maybe it was something about Kyle Trent that I was forgetting, but I couldn't bring it forth.

When we got home, I heated up the last of Molly's leftovers for breakfast, showered, dressed, and took Paisley with me to the office. I couldn't bear to be away from her for even a few hours.

Norah, my ever-faithful secretary and assistant, had cleaned up the mess in the office. Her husband made repairs and hung a new security door. My beautiful antique desk was damaged almost beyond repair. It will never be the beauty it once was, but as I looked it over, I thought it could be salvaged into something useful by a woodworker with more creative juice than I possessed. I had a friend that might be interested in looking at it.

I closed the door to my office and took out my old fingerprint kit and a pair of latex gloves I brought from home. I dusted the picture frame of the Sandia Mountains for prints first. It had been wiped clean. No problem; my cleaning service could have done that. I took the picture down and dusted the face of my safe. The pit of my stomach dropped—it too had been wiped clean. I used the combination and opened the safe, finding the cell phone inside.

*This is good. Maybe they couldn't crack the safe.*

The first thing I touched was the phone. I found the battery and SIM card were missing.

*Now that's strange. Why would they take the SIM card and battery but leave the phone?*

I dusted the phone and lifted the partials I found before I bagged it. I went back to the wall safe and checked the rest of the contents. Everything was there: my passport, insurance policies, my will and advanced directive, some extra credit cards, and some cash. Nothing was missing. I dusted everything for prints, lifted and labeled them, and put everything in a plastic bag. Lastly, I dusted the lip and interior of the safe and lifted the prints and partials I found there.

I called Morgan at the station.

"Detective Sergeant Sellers."

"Hi, Morgan. It's Jeffries."

"How ya doing?" He sounded jovial.

"Much better, and you?"

"Good. So, was the safe compromised?"

"It appears so. I dusted the face before I opened it." I sighed. "It had been wiped clean. Then I worked the combination and opened the safe. Everything was there—"

"The phone?"

"Yes, but the battery and SIM card are missing."

"Really?"

"Yeah. Why would they take the battery and SIM card but leave the phone? Why not take the whole thing?"

"I don't know. That doesn't make much sense." There was a long pause between us. "Are you sure—"

"Yes. It was intact when I put it in the safe."

"You're sure!"

"Yes."

He grunted, puzzled.

"I'm calling Jim," I told him, "to let him know, but I've got an uneasy feeling about this. I dusted the phone, the rest of the contents, and the inside of the safe for prints. I found a lot of prints but I suspect most, if not all of them, will be mine. I'm bringing them for you to run."

"Okay. Doesn't sound very hopeful."

"Morgan, they didn't take any of the cash I had in my safe."

"You keep cash in that safe? How much?"

"Not a lot, five hundred dollars, but they didn't touch it. Isn't that weird?"

"Well, huh..." He paused, giving it some thought. "Maybe if nothing in the safe looked disturbed, you wouldn't think the safe had been compromised. If the safe hadn't been compromised, the battery and SIM card couldn't have been in the phone when you put it in there."

"Maybe ... okay. I'll be there soon with the prints."

On the way to the station, I was stopped behind a dump truck at a red light. When the light turned green, I followed the truck into the intersection. Before I could get through the intersection the truck stopped, leaving me right dab in the middle of cross traffic. I looked right and the vehicles were all stopped for their red light. I looked left, and I saw a speeding car approaching. I could tell it wasn't going to stop for traffic, and I was trapped in its path. I swung out into the oncoming traffic lane and hit the gas to get out of the way. Fortunately for me, the oncoming traffic had already cleared the intersection. The car behind me saw what was coming and remained at the light.

A traffic cop sitting at the corner went in pursuit of the speeding car. I went around the dump truck and the stalled car in front of him and continued to the station.

I was rattled and shaking like a leaf in the wind—whether from fear or from rage I wasn't sure.

Once at the Police Station, I told Morgan about the traffic incident. He contacted dispatch to see what was going on. He said he wanted to make sure it wasn't an elaborate set-up to kill me.

Dispatch advised Morgan the officer got the driver stopped and was told there was a mechanical problem with the car. In actuality the floor mat had slid up onto the accelerator and the driver hadn't realized it. Out of desperation after blowing the light and barely missing me, he turned the ignition off and was able to stop. He was a high school kid on his lunch break, and he was rattled.

The officer who arrived to check on the stalled car learned the driver had run out of gas. The vehicle was pushed into a parking lot, and the driver was waiting for a friend to bring gas.

"Wow, after all we've been through, I was sure it was another attempt on my life. I feel better knowing it was a coincidental string of events."

"Yeah, I'm glad no one was hurt. It seems like the whole kidnapping scheme is finished. Keep an eye out to be safe, and let me know if anything else weird happens."

"You know I will. Here are the prints I lifted, and the cell phone. Since Kyle's dead, how do you want to handle this information?"

"Send the phone to Jim. The FBI is handling this now. If there are dirty cops in the department, I don't want them knowing where the phone is. I'll let you know if we get any hits on the prints."

"Thanks. What are you doing for lunch?"

"Haven't thought about it. Since you're downtown, do you want to go to the bistro and have a sandwich?"

"Yes." I gave him a big smile. "I was hoping you would suggest that."

Morgan left the prints on his desk and rose. "Give me a sec. I'll be right back."

I sat in Morgan's office and watched the hustle and bustle of the detective department. I missed the challenges and adrenaline rushes of an exciting case. I don't get that with my current job.

At the bistro we sat outside, with Paisley at my feet, and enjoyed our sandwiches.

Back at my office, I locked the phone in my safe along with copies of the prints I lifted. I went through the mail on my desk. Norah cancelled my appointments for the next two days, so I went home with Paisley.

I changed into my running clothes and took Paisley out for a run. We were headed to the dog park taking the same route we took the day of my abduction. As if that wasn't enough to set my nerves on end, I was still jumpy from the morning's events, so I kept a keen eye out for anything out of the ordinary.

By the time I finished my run around the track, I was feeling pretty euphoric, and we started our jog home.

Halfway down the hill, I saw a runner approaching me from the opposite direction. He was jogging and broke into a sprint as some runners do for interval training. He started waving his arms for me to get out of his way and he was yelling, but I couldn't make out what he was saying.

When he reached me, he wrapped his arms around me and dove into the yard to my left. As we hit the ground, a car went past, jumped the curb, and crashed into the light pole on the corner. Paisley, having been on a short leash, was jerked out of the path of the vehicle when I was thrown to the ground. I checked the guy to make sure he was unharmed, checked Paisley, who was all over me, and then pulled my cell phone out of my back pocket. I called Morgan while the runner went to see if he could help the driver of the car. The people of the neighborhood who were home at the time, were all coming out of their houses to see what was going on.

"How's the driver?" I asked while the runner was pulling an elderly gentleman out of the front seat. There were no passengers.

"He's not breathing," the guy said and started doing CPR. I knelt down and assisted until the ambulance arrived. They worked on the driver and transported him to the hospital. We gave an accounting of the incident to the officers who arrived on the scene.

"What's your name?" Officer Bart McCleary asked the runner.

"Steve Farmer. I'm an EMT and this is one of my days off. It appears the old guy was driving down the street when he had some kind of episode or seizure. I witnessed the car veering to the right, bounce off the curb, and start in our direction, picking up speed. I tried to warn the lady to get out of the way, but she didn't understand. When I reached her at the last minute, I grabbed her and dove out of the way."

Steve gave his contact information to the officer, who then turned to me.

"Hi, Jeffries. You're a disaster magnet today."

"Not funny, McCleary. It's turning into a traumatic day for me."

Morgan pulled up and walked over to me. "You alright?"

"Yes, a little rattled is all."

"Hey there, Paisley. Are you okay, girl?" Morgan bent to pet Paisley but she jumped into his arms instead. "Poor thing. You're shivering!"

I took Paisley from Morgan, and he brushed the white dog hair off his suit with his hands.

"I don't have anything to add, McCleary. I didn't see anything until after I was thrown to the ground. Poor old man. I hope he makes it."

"I'll follow up for the report. Maybe you should stay home the rest of the day and hide out until this curse is lifted." He snickered, then sobered. "I'm real glad you're back home from that kidnapping ordeal. We were all worried about you."

"Thanks. I'm glad it's over, too."

I turned away and muttered under my breath. "...if it really is. Maybe I *should* stay home and hide out."

"What's that?" McCleary asked.

"Oh, nothing. I'm fine."

"Why don't I give you a ride home?" Morgan suggested.

"Thanks. I'll take it." I thanked Steve for saving my life and got his contact information. I wanted to do something for him in thanks.  He risked his life to save mine.

"Do you really think all these were just coincidental?" I looked across the seat to Morgan.  "It's so odd.  I'm really feeling targeted, Morgan."

"It does seem odd, but so far, everything checks out as independent incidences.  I'll follow up with the old man's situation and let you know." He paused as he approached the turn to my street.  "Do you want to stay at our house tonight?"

"No, I'll lock up.  We'll be okay, won't we girl?" I scratched Paisley's neck.  "I locked up my weapons in my fireproof gun locker, but I think I'll start carrying that Five-seveN you sold me.  I would feel safer."

Paisley licked my hands as I talked.  "I need something at the office anyway, since my grandfather's Colt Python was stolen."

No sooner than getting that out of my mouth we turned the corner toward my house and there was an explosion.  Flames shot out of the windows and roof of my home.  Morgan's car rocked violently and Paisley yelped and started climbing over my shoulder and on top of my head.

"That's no accident!" I murmured under my breath. I grabbed Paisley and pulled her back into my lap holding her tight.

"No, that's no accident," Morgan repeated while bits and pieces of my house rained down all around us.

"Get down. Don't let anyone see you." Morgan sped past my house and pulled over at the far end of the next block.

"I'm going to check on things. Stay out of site and don't get on the phone or radio." He pulled a snub nosed .38 out of his boot and handed it to me. "Use this if you need to. If they think you blew up in the explosion, you'll be a lot safer."

**********

Morgan radioed dispatch and reported the explosion. Within seconds, we heard the sirens from the fire department which was only a mile from my neighborhood. The neighbors who were home were running out of their houses.

Morgan got out of the car and walked to the crowd congregating across the street from my demolished and burning home. Crouched in the floorboard of the car, I started to cry and Paisley whimpered and licked my hands and face.

Melissa, a widowed mother of three who owns the home everyone was in front of, was sobbing—her two youngest children clutching at her.

The firemen were still working on extinguishing the fire and the police taking statements for their reports when Morgan started back toward the car. Before he reached it, McCleary, who was the first officer on the scene, called Morgan back. They talked a moment, and then Morgan came back to the car, got in, and started it up. I began to push myself up.

"Stay down so no one sees you."

Morgan eased away from the curb and drove away from the neighborhood while I remained ducked down in the floorboard with Paisley.

"Do they think I'm dead?"

"They're not sure. One of your neighbors saw you come home earlier. No one seems to have seen you leave for your run. No one saw you sitting in the car when the house exploded. Your neighbor, Melissa, is very distraught over the thought of you being dead."

"Yeah, she and I have gotten pretty close since her husband died last year. She's a sweetheart."

I started to get up out of the floorboard, and Morgan put his hand on my head.

"Stay down I said. I'll let you know when you can get up. I told McCleary I just dropped you and Paisley off at the house before it blew." He paused.

"I want to make an announcement to the press that you were killed in the explosion, but I don't have the authority to do that."

"The FBI would."

"I know. I've got a call in to Jim to see if he could arrange it. Another thing—McCleary said they picked up a guy a few blocks from your house. He didn't have any ID on him, and he kept walking back and forth up and down the same block trying to see what was going on. When Nicholson stopped him for questioning the guy asked, 'Was that woman killed? The woman who lived in the house that blew up, was she killed?' Nicholson is taking him downtown for interrogation."

That was it. I broke down and started crying again ... no, not crying—I was bawling my eyes out, the sobs guttural. Morgan reached over and patted me on the head.

"It's going to be okay. You're alright and that's what matters most right now. Come on. We'll figure this out. For now, I'm taking you to my house. We'll figure out the rest later."

"But my safe," I blubbered. "Maybe there's other stuff that can be salvaged. I can't just leave it there to be gone through by strangers." At this point, I was no longer rational.

"Jeffries, don't worry about that. I've already got it covered for you. The fire department will be there for a while to watch for hot spots, and the department called the FBI. They are sending a team over. I'm also going to have a unit sit on it until morning in case anyone comes around."

"But Morgan—"

"No. You have to stay out of sight."

"But—"

"To make sure your office is secure, we're sending a bomb squad over there to check it out, but I need you in a safe place now. You've been through a lot in just one day, not to mention the past week."

I wiped my eyes. "I'll be putting Molly and the kids at risk if I go to your house. Take me to a motel for the night, and I'll figure out what to do tomorrow."

"No, I..." Morgan slammed on the brakes and I hit my head on the glove box. Poor Paisley was shivering; she was so frightened I could feel her heart thumping in her chest.

"Sorry. A dog ran out in front of me. You okay?"

"Yes." I rubbed my head. The absurdity of it all hit me, and I broke out in hysterical laughs.

"I'm taking you to my house for now. I'll keep you posted on the developments."

"Take me to the station with you, Morgan," I said between guffaws. "I'll stay out of sight, but I want to be there so I can get immediate updates."

"Jeffries, you're in shock. You need to calm down."

It took a few minutes for me to get my laughter under control. "You're going to be busy and may not get back to me right away. Please, Morgan. Take me to the station."

He thought for a moment. "You've got to remember it's believed there are dirty cops involved in this." His cell phone rang and he answered.

"Hi, Molly ... Yeah, I just came from there. I'm on my way home and will be there in just a sec. ... CALM DOWN, OKAY?" Morgan was abrupt and angry. I'm sure his tone worried Molly. "I'm sorry. I'm on my way."

Morgan pulled into his garage and closed the door behind us before he let me get up off the floorboard. Molly was waiting at the door to the laundry room, wringing a dish towel. She sobbed as soon as she saw me.

"Mariah. Mariah. Thank God you're okay." She wrapped her arms around my neck when I got close enough and hugged me, Paisley crushed between us. "I'm so sorry about your home. I'm just so, so thankful you and Paisley weren't there."

"Me too, Molly." I started crying again. I was beginning to feel like a pathetic coward with all the crying but this was too much for me after the last week I've had.

We walked into the house with Molly's arm around my waist. She led me into the living room. After a moment, I dried my eyes and Molly and I started talking about the day's events.

"Why does this keep happening to me?" I asked no one in particular. "I'm so tired of it."

Molly kept her arm around me and told me everything would be okay.

Morgan took a call on his cell phone. When he hung up he said, "Got a matchup on the prints from the safe."

"Who?" I asked wiping my eyes.

"Ricky 'Big Ears' Saldivar, Bjarne King, and Benny Para."

Morgan's cell phone rang again, and he answered it. "Morgan." He stepped into the kitchen. I followed.

"Hi, Jim. ... Yes, blew her house to smithereens. ... No. She's shook up but unharmed. We're at my house right now, and she's going to keep out of sight." He turned an eye on me, eyebrow raised. "I want to give the news media a statement saying she was killed in the bombing. ... Okay! Right, the New Mexico guy has to do it. ... Good. I'll let her know. I want to put my family in a safe house again too. This is getting out of hand. ... No, not directly, but if it has anything to do with the kidnapping, and I think it does, then I'm at risk, and consequently my family is also. ... I understand. Slim Potter? ... Okay, we'll stay here until he arrives. Oh, Jim ... we got a match on the partials from her safe. Yep, see you then. Thanks, Jim. ... Right. Bye."

"The FBI is taking over the investigation," Morgan told us. "Jim is friends with the Albuquerque lead agent and was expecting my call. They have an agent in the interrogation room with the suspect now, and another agent, Slim Potter, is on his way here to take us to a safe house. He also has an investigative team at your house right now, and he's going to announce to the news media that you are believed dead."

"And what about you? You're going to the safe house with us, right?" I gave him a glare.

"I'm going back to the station to help on the case."

"You just said the FBI is taking it over, and you're—"

"I'm not working on it directly. Jim's flying in to head this investigation because it might be related to the last one. I'll be working with Jim and his team."

"You can do that from the safe house."

Morgan sighed. "I know. I just don't want to trust this to anyone else. I need to be involved in the investigation."

"Don't you think I feel the same way? It's not in my nature to sit back and let others take all the risk ... or be kept out of the loop. Jim won't do that. He knows us and our capabilities. He'll run everything by us, I know he will."

"We'll see. He did say he wants me at the safe house too in light of everything.

"Morgan." Molly stepped between me and Morgan. She put her hands flat on his chest. "Please go to the safe house with us. We need you there. I need you with me and the kids. Let the FBI handle this. *Please!*"

Morgan put his arms around Molly. She wrapped her arms around his waist and laid her cheek on his chest.

"I know, babe," he murmured. "I know. I'll go with you when Slim gets here, and I'll talk to Jim before I go anywhere. Okay?"

Molly, sobbing into Morgan's shoulder, nodded as Morgan continued to hold her. She pushed back and looked into his eyes.

"I'm so tired of this. The kids are overwrought, and we need it to end. We just need to know that you and Mariah are safe and that we can get on with our lives."

"I know baby. We're going to get to the bottom of this. You'll see. I promise we'll all come through this safe and sound."

Mia came down the stairs, Max following. "What's wrong now?" Paisley ran to her and jumped on her legs. Mia bent down and picked the little dog up.

"There's been an incident," Morgan said. "Go back to your rooms for now. I'll fill you in when we know more."

The kids looked at me and I nodded, shooing them back upstairs.

**********

$\mathbf{F}$BI Agent Slim Potter was a tall, slender man with a full head of greying, dark brown hair. He came to the house disguised as a repair man. Morgan checked his credentials and let him in, introducing him to everyone after having called the kids downstairs.

"Dressed kinda casual for an FBI agent, aren't you?" I glared at him with skepticism.

"Yes, Mariah, I am. Here are my credentials." He handed me his identification badge, driver's license, and his shield.

"Standish Potter. I can see why you go by Slim." I was rude, trying to provoke him to slip up. I didn't trust him. I didn't trust anyone, so I was snide. I handed the IDs back to him.

I realized I was behaving like a trapped animal, snarling and growling. I sighed.

"I'm sorry. I'm pretty jumpy right now and I don't want to take any chances."

"I understand. I've been studying your case."

He cleared his throat and turned to Morgan.

"I have a utility van out front marked 'ACE PLUMBING.' I understand Mariah is presumed dead and we want to keep her that way."

He turned an eye on me. "For the time being, I mean."

Morgan grinned and nodded. "That's correct."

"I suggest I back the van into the garage. She can enter through the back doors, you and your family too. This way no one sees any of you leaving with me. We'll do the same once we get to the safe house.

"Each of you can take a couple changes of clothes and your personal toiletries. Nothing else—*NO* electronics! We'll provide everything else for you while you're in hiding."

"Sounds good to—" Morgan began when Mia interrupted in a whiney voice. "I thought this was all over with. Now what?"

"I'll explain everything to you in a minute. Max, you and Mia go pack a small bag."

Morgan turned back to Slim. "I'll go move my car out of the garage so you can back in."

"No electronics," Slim directed to Mia and Max. "Not even a cell phone, kids."

Mia stamped her foot. "Daddy, really? That's not fair!"

Morgan turned from the garage door. "Listen, you cannot contact anyone for the safety of us all. Just leave all your electronics here. They'll be here when you get home."

"Can I take my gaming laptop?" asked Max.

"No! No electronics."

"What are we supposed to do while we're locked up again? It's not fair." Mia stomped her foot.

"We'll discuss that in the van. Go pack, and I'm going to search your bags so don't try to sneak anything in." Morgan turned and went into the garage.

Mia growled and stomped off to her room. "I hate you!" she yelled down the stairs. Max smacked the wall with the side of his fist, hung his head, and went upstairs.

Once we were loaded into the van, Morgan filled the kids in on the bombing. Max turned to me and told me he was sorry for being mad. "I'm glad you weren't blown up at the house."

Mia was holding Paisley and giving the rest of us the silent treatment.

I understood the children being upset, but they needed to understand they were in danger too. We were trying to keep them safe while this situation is figured out and cleared up.

**********

# VI

The FBI was very generous with the facilities they provided us for a safe house. We were all assigned our own bedroom. There was a Wii system with lots of games set up in the living room and lots of board games and jigsaw puzzles to keep the kids occupied—no internet connection or wifi, but something to occupy the occupants.

The kids started playing a bowling game on the Wii when Jim arrived. Morgan and I met him in the kitchen while Molly stayed with the kids in the living room.

"Well, the explosion and resulting fire didn't leave us much in the way of evidence. From what the bomb squad could tell, there was a bomb in your bedroom and another in the garage or on your car. We did collect your safes, Mariah, and we have them in a secure location."

"Oh, good. I forgot about the little fire box. So it was still intact, along with my gun safe?"

"Yes. Of course we didn't open either one to see if there was any damage inside. I'll take you to check them out at a later time.

"Right now, I need you to stay here and out of sight. We also had a bomb squad go through your office. We didn't find any type of incendiary devices. Norah believes you perished in the explosion, so your office is locked up for now. We will keep surveillance on it in case anyone comes poking around.

"Do you have any questions for me—any family members you're worried about learning of your supposed death?"

"My mom's in a memory care facility for Alzheimer, but my uncles, John, Dan, and Richard, on my dad's side keep in touch with me. They'll be real upset if they hear about this."

"Those are the two retired career cops down in Texas?"

"Yes, Dan is retired FBI, and Richard is from the Dallas Police Department. John is a martial arts instructor. Can we let them know on the down-low that I'm safe—just working a case?"

"I'm not sure we can, but I will send an agent to talk to them and get an assessment of how safe it would be to let them know. Anyone else?"

I shook my head. "A few cousins and a couple close friends. I know we can't let them know. I'm most worried about my uncles. My mother's older sister passed away last year. It was only the two of them. I don't have any siblings."

"Okay. I'll let you know what we decide about the uncles.

"Morgan," Jim turned to Morgan, "we will keep surveillance on your house for any suspicious activity, as well."

"Thank you, Jim," I said, and Morgan followed with, "Yeah, thanks."

"No problem. I'm really sorry about all this. I thought we had the situation under control in Idaho. Obviously, this is bigger than we realized and The Mongoose is still at it. He's really got it in for you, Mariah. Any idea why?"

"No. None." I shook my head.

"Oh, and I realize you don't have anything, so make a list of what you need in the way of clothing and toiletries to get you by. Include sizes, and I'll give the list to one of our female agents to make the purchases for you."

"Sure, I'll have a list for you before you leave."

"What about the suspect?" asked Morgan.

"He started talking when we told him what the charges would be and what he was facing in prison time. His name is Bjarne King, a gang member. He just got out of the pen last month. He was incarcerated for tossing Molotov cocktails into a rival's car passing him on the street—also for throwing some in the windows of another gang member's house. He said he's afraid of going back to prison, so he seems to be cooperating. We just have to validate the information he's giving us.

"He said his cousin had a friend who needed someone to do a job for him. He met with this anonymous person at Pedro's Sports Bar over on the west side, and he gave us a description, but he didn't have a name.

"We're following that lead. He also said he was paid five thousand dollars up front and if he was successful, he was supposed to meet this client back there tomorrow to get the rest of the payoff ... another ten grand."

"Wow, they really want me dead!"

"We don't' know yet if he's telling the truth. We're bringing in his cousin for questioning. We'll get this tracked down."

"His was one of the prints that we found on Mariah's safe. The other two are Saldivar and Benny Para. What can we do to help?" asked Morgan.

"Nothing. I want you guys to stay out of sight and out of the way. Especially you, Mariah."

"Come on, Jim. We were a big help in Idaho," Morgan said.

"Yes you were, and I got my ass handed to me for letting you two participate in the investigation. If you want to do FBI investigations, then you have to apply and get hired, go to Quantico for training, and be assigned to an office. That's how it works."

"Are you serious? You can't keep me here!"

"Morgan, if you refuse our protection then you and your family are free to leave. If we catch you interfering in our investigation, you will be prosecuted. That's on the record. Off the record I liked the work you two did. I wish I could use you, but I can't. It's that simple. I can't."

"Okay, I understand," Morgan conceded. "Is Riley going to be here to help?"

"After the ordeal Jeri had been through, Riley took some time off to take her on a vacation. We're trying to reach him to keep him updated since we believe this is related."

"I'll feel better when I know you've reached him and can report they're both safe," I interjected into the conversation.

"Me too. We'll get hold of him, and I'll let you both know once we do."

"Thank you," Morgan and I said at the same time.

Jim talked to Slim and checked on Morgan's family. Before he left, I gave him the list of things I needed for myself and Paisley. He said he would have an agent make the purchases and bring them by later that day.

We started to settle in. I helped Molly fix spaghetti and a large salad for dinner. We ate in the living room in front of the TV while we watched a video, of which there were several to choose from.

As we were getting ready for bed, Agent Joy Love showed up with new clothes and toiletries for me and supplies for Paisley. She relieved Slim for the night and sat visiting with me and Morgan about the case since my kidnapping. Molly and the kids went to bed so we could talk. We weren't going over any strategies; I think she was curious, asking random questions.

We learned she graduated from Quantico at the top of her class five years ago but this was the first time she was assigned a case of this magnitude. She wanted to learn as much as possible about it. She told us she also talked to Jim and got a lot of information from him on what procedures were followed (and not followed) to this point. She wasn't very forthcoming with information to us.

"Jim said he will keep you guys updated. He doesn't want any of us to say anything. He's afraid the information would get skewed and create unnecessary stress for the two of you." She relayed that information after we pressed her.

"Oh, and Mariah, he wanted me to tell you your uncles were notified about the case, and they are sworn to secrecy. They were relieved to hear you are okay, and they are looking forward to hearing from you when this is over with."

"Thank you, Joy. I really appreciate that."

**********

**"T**his is ridiculous!" Morgan and I stood at the back fence discussing the situation. It had been a week and still nothing was wrapped up.

Jim hadn't been able to reach Riley and Jeri, and two days ago Jim was called back to the Boise office. Riley being missing in action alone was enough of a concern to Morgan and me, but Jim being suddenly and mysteriously called back to Boise was an altogether different concern.

We hadn't received any updates on anything since Jim left. We'd been keeping Molly and the kids out of as much of the intel we were getting (which was slim at best) to avoid upsetting them any more than necessary. The wait was wearing on us all.

The Sellers family was worried about Riley and Jeri, as was I. Since Morgan and Riley were so close, Morgan's family had naturally spent time with them—vacationing together and visiting each other's homes when possible. They were like family.

Agent Love, who seemed sympathetic to our case, stayed with us frequently as part of the guard detail. I got her aside on several occasions, but she said she couldn't share any information with us—not on Jim, his current activities, or on Riley and Jeri. The new head of the investigation had instructed all the agents not to share investigation information with me or Morgan.

Agent Love did let slip that Bjarne King's cousin turned out to be a gang member and not a cousin at all. His name was Freddie Naegle, and the guy he led the FBI to—the guy who supposedly ordered the bombing of my house—was found executed in his apartment.

My bombed-out house didn't offer up much in the way of evidence either. They did find the sources of the explosion and the type of incendiary devices used, but so far it hadn't offered up a lead. Morgan and I were beyond frustrated.

"I don't care what Jim said. We can't just sit around and do nothing anymore. If I slip out and disappear, I don't believe they would put my family out and at risk."

"I agree, but you're not leaving without m—"

"Fttt, Mariah," we heard coming from the other side of the fence. Morgan and I both ducked down and drew our weapons.

Jim had taken me to check on my safes before he left for Boise and everything was intact. I grabbed the Five-seveN Morgan sold me, along with the gear, and Morgan brought his new Five-seveN when we came to the safe house.

I was grieved when my grandfather's Colt Python was taken in the burglary of my office. I was hoping when everything got cleared up, that particular piece would be recovered.

"Mariah, it's us, Uncle Dan and Uncle Richard," came to us from the other side of the fence. I holstered my weapon and stood up about the time Slim came out the door.

"Hey, Morgan, Jim's on the horn—" He drew his gun and ran, crouched, to the fence. "What's up?" he whispered.

Morgan stood and holstered his gun. "Oh, we heard something, but I think it was a couple cats fighting."

I brushed my hair off my shoulder. "Something thumped on the trash can, and we thought someone was prowling around."

Slim stood and holstered his gun. He glanced around the yard and peered over the fence while Morgan continued.

"Then we heard two toms snarling. I think you scared them off when you opened the door."

"Why don't both of you go inside. I'll check the perimeter."

"I'll help you," I said.

"Nothing's there—the cats ran off. I'm going in to take Jim's call." Morgan walked away.

Slim and I went out the back fence. I told Slim to go left. I went right, hoping my uncles were well out of sight. Slim and I crossed each other's paths at the front of the house and proceeded around the house, meeting again at the backyard. We went into the yard, latching the gate, and checked the perimeter of the yard itself before Slim met me at the back door.

"Let's go back in."

"I'll stay out here for a little bit. I'm getting claustrophobic in that house, and the weather's perfect right now. I'll be in in a little bit."

"Fine. Keep an eye out and holler if you see or hear anything."

"Will do. Tell Morgan I said good night."

"Yep."

I waited about five minutes, walking around the yard and looking up at the beautiful

Albuquerque night sky making sure Slim was satisfied everything was cool. Then I moseyed over to the back fence and leaned my back against the gate, looking up at the stars.

"The FBI told us you were in trouble. Since we haven't heard anything in a week, we decided to come help," Uncle Dan whispered from the other side of the gate. I jumped when he first started talking. These guys were good. I was listening for them and didn't hear them come back to the fence.

I turned facing the gate, and crossed my arms across the top of it. I continued looking up at the stars.

"Morgan and I were just talking about that. We're tired of waiting for someone to resolve this matter, and we're ready to take it into our own hands."

"We're here to help. Where do you want to meet?"

The door to the house opened and closed, and I heard someone approaching me from behind. I looked over my shoulder and saw it was Morgan.

"Hi Morgan. What'd Jim have to say?"

"Not much yet. He said they got all the ledgers and notebooks on The Mongoose's activities. It will put The Mongoose away for the rest of his life. They are running coordinated search and arrest warrants on the whole organization at five o'clock Mountain Time tomorrow morning. They'll be making arrests in Denver, of course, and other locations in Colorado, Idaho, Utah, Oklahoma, Texas, New Mexico, Arizona, and Southern California.

"Dempsey didn't have the full scope of the organization. No one did. The Mongoose kept all aspects of his organization compartmentalized. That's why he has been so difficult to get evidence on."

"So, do they now know who's behind the attacks here in Albuquerque?"

"No. He said none of the information implicated The Mongoose or anyone else they had on the radar for this. They don't know who is involved in the recent attacks."

I snorted and shook my head. "It *has* to be him, Morgan."

"I know. Where are the uncles?"

"We're right here and heard everything," Uncle Richard whispered.

"I'm getting out of here. Jeffries, are you in?"

"Is the Pope Catholic? I'd rather die trying than sit here and wait for someone to kill me."

"We've got a car across the street from the north end of the alley, parked in front of a house. We'll wait for you."

"Jeffries, go with them. I'll slip out behind you."

I eased the gate open and it emitted a loud squeal. I ducked down and left with my uncles. Morgan stood in the open gate. As my uncles and I passed the edge of the yard, I heard the back door open and Slim asking Morgan what was going on.

"And where'd Jeffries go?"

"Jeffries went in about five minutes ago. She said she was going to bed."

"I didn't see Jeffries come in. She went to bed you say?"

"Yes, she did. Those cats came back, and I was running them off. I want to see if there is a source of food right here that keeps bringing them back. They kept me awake half the night fighting last night."

"I was on alert most of the night, too because of the noise. What'd you find?"

"Some spilled trash. I'll clean it up and be in shortly. I want to make sure they don't come back."

"Good! Don't be too long." Slim retreated back into the house.

**********

Morgan stepped into the alley and closed the gate, latching it behind him. He ducked up and down so it would look like he was picking up trash if Slim was watching. After a few fake pick-ups, he made a final duck and ran to the car.

Uncle Dan drove to an old rent-by-the-week motel where they had a small rented suite. We barely got the door closed when I turned and hugged Uncle Dan and Uncle Richard so tight I thought I would crack their ribs. I was beyond happy to see them.

"You guys look wonderful. I see you're still working out every day," I patted Uncle Richard on the chest. "How's Uncle John doing?"

"He's good. We don't have a choice about working out, you know. John sees to that." Uncle Dan chuckled.

The door opened and in walked Uncle John. I ran to him and threw my arms around him. "Oh my God!" I exclaimed. "You're here too?"

"Where else would I be? My favorite student needed my help, so I came." He hugged me back and whispered in my ear, "I've missed you, kiddo."

"I've missed you too." Tears of joy sprang to my eyes and I strained to control them.

We visited for a while and got caught up on their lives and especially this case. We decided to sleep before brainstorming.

While Uncle Dan and Uncle Richard were rescuing us, Uncle John was shopping so we wouldn't have to go out and risk being seen by anyone. We knew the FBI, as well as my attackers, would be looking for us.

Uncle Dan and Uncle Richard shared one of the queen beds in one room. Uncle John and Morgan shared the bed in the other room. I slept on the small couch in the sitting area.

The next morning, Uncle Dan and I were looking over some maps and discussing what to do next. Uncle Richard was sitting on the bed, tying his shoes, and Uncle John was in the bathroom when Morgan called from the kitchenette.

"Jeffries, you want coffee?"

"Yes, please," I answered.

"Sure," called Uncle Richard.

"Thanks, but I have some," replied Uncle Dan, and Uncle John opened the bathroom door and asked, "Somebody call me?"

We all busted out laughing. Morgan slapped his forehead with the palm of his right hand and rolled his eyes.

"Oh, great, this is gonna be fun!"

"Oh, I see," said Uncle John. "To eliminate confusion, let's call each other by our first names. Morgan, that means you have to refer to Mariah as Mariah, and not Jeffries. I know you've always called her Jeffries, but we're all used to going by our last name at work. You think you can do that?"

"Sure, I wasn't thinking, that's all."

"You can call me 'Oh Great One ... or Master John, for short if that helps."

"I'll be sure to remember that, Oh Great One." Morgan grinned and made a sweeping bow to Uncle John. Everyone laughed again.

"Okay, who wants coffee, and I'll pour it up."

"We need to do our exercises first. Come on, everyone." Uncle John herded everyone where he wanted them as we all groaned playfully.

We practiced our stances, punches, and kicks as best we could in the limited space. Morgan, who studied under me, kept up with the uncles, though he wasn't as fluid. Uncle John corrected him and made suggestions for better fluidity in his movements.

After thirty minutes, Uncle John bowed to us.

"That's enough. Now for that coffee..."

Over coffee there were some arguments about what should be done next—Uncle John, the control freak older brother versus Uncle Dan, retired FBI. They don't always see eye to eye.

Another trait of Uncle John's is his intuitiveness. It's uncanny, and I planned to utilize that during this investigation.

Uncle Dan receives information in his dreams which advanced him in the FBI by helping him in investigations. He's what I call a dream clairvoyant.

Uncle Richard is practically a mind reader. The way he reads people and situations is uncanny. He can sense their feelings and motives—an empath.

I am intuitive. I also have some empathic abilities that Uncle John worked with me to develop further. I didn't keep up with the meditations like I needed to, so that ability remained stunted.

My intuition, however; is one reason I was so surprised I got sideswiped and kidnapped. Normally I would have seen it coming and been able to avoid the whole thing. Okay, okay, I admit it ... I have a strange family.

John fixed bacon and eggs for everyone. We ate and cleaned up before Dan sat at the little table with a yellow legal pad. "Let's go over everything we know so far.

"Mariah, tell me whatever stands out as most relevant about the kidnapping."

I went over the entire kidnapping, my escape, and rescue so as not to miss anything no matter how trivial it might have seemed. After the long narrative, Dan put the pen down and shook his hand to relax the muscles.

"Let's take a break while I rest my hand."

Dan uses a unique shorthand that is fast and thorough. Unfortunately it's his own, and no one else knows how to use it or read it. It was faster to take the break than to have someone else pick up the pen.

We chatted and joked around for a while. The uncles, all of whom visit my mom routinely, filled me in on her condition. Her Alzheimer is worse, and she no longer knows them. She mostly sits and stares into space.

Uncle John said he didn't think she was long for this world, and that made me sad. I was more determined than ever to clear this case so I could go visit her before she died.

Dan went back to the little table and picked up the pad and pen. "Now tell me about Mariah's office burglary, Morgan. Start from when you first got notification. Tell me every detail you remember."

Morgan gave him a complete rundown of everything he remembered. Dan and Richard would occasionally ask questions that seemed irrelevant, and Morgan would close his eyes to view the scene in his mind before giving them an answer. Most of the time his answer was confident, a few times he told them what he thought, but he wasn't sure.

Dan flipped to a clean page. "Let's make a list of everything you remember pertaining to the burglary of your office. Tell me everything about your office that you can think of once you returned, except the wall safe. We'll get to that next."

I told him about the office. "Norah had cleaned up the mess, and her husband made repairs."

"What was broken?"

"The back door was broken into, my antique desk was destroyed. I got it from my mom's dad. It was his grandfather's before him."

"What kind of damage did it sustain?" asked Uncle Dan.

"The two locked drawers were pried open, splintering the front of the drawers. The contents—mostly files on current cases, some personal effects, and Grandpa's Colt Python—were all taken. I'm sorry about your dad's gun."

"Don't worry about it. Let's focus on details right now. Go on."

"The drawers were then smashed into pieces. The center drawer was pulled out and dumped but not destroyed, the other drawers were dumped and the bottoms kicked out. They took something sharp and cut deep grooves and scratches in the top. It looks like they used a small ax and cut holes in the sides and front panel, also. It's really messed up."

"So," said Dan. "What evidence from your office burglary did you and Morgan get to see?"

Morgan and I gave him a rundown of everything that was collected and what we knew while Dan took notes. Every once in a while, John or Richard would ask clarifying questions. When I told of the phone in my safe and the missing battery and SIM card, Uncle Dan's head jerked up, and he gave me a sharp look.

"Are you sure they were in the phone when you locked it up?"

"Yes, I'm positive. I took prints off the phone, and Morgan ran them." When I told him who the prints came back on, and that they were the ones picked up for the bombing, Uncle Richard interrupted, "Bjarne King and Ricky Saldivar? Are you sure?"

"Yes," Morgan answered. "Matched them up in the NCIC data base. Why?"

"Bjarne King was a cop in Dallas. I was his training officer and washed him out. He lied in his interviews and on his application about never being in trouble with the law.

"When he was a teenager, he and a friend, Freddie Naegle, were arrested for armed robbery of an Allsup's store in Fort Worth. They were fourteen and fifteen years old respectively—juveniles, so the records were sealed.

"During training, he let slip a few things that didn't add up. I called your Uncle Dan and had him investigate it on the side.

"His mother sent him to California to live with an uncle after that incident. He had a number of brushes with the local law enforcement in southern California and was arrested a couple of times. He either paid fines or served a little time in the local clink, but none of that was on his application when he applied."

"I remember that," said Dan. "The public defender's department set them both up on the Pretrial Diversion Program for the juvie charges, and the later, California charges were as adults. I never heard any more about it after that."

"Me neither," said Richard. "They must have kept their noses clean or at least grown some brains so they didn't get caught ... until they moved up here."

"And Ricky Saldivar lived in Albuquerque. He was busted once for his part in a home-invasion burglary of a prominent business man. They left the man and his wife gagged and tied in their home, and the couple wasn't found until the daughter came home the next morning from a sleepover she was attending. Saldivar was the safe cracker and served five years for that crime."

I shook my head.

We had the TV tuned into the local news and the volume turned down. As Uncle Dan finished telling about Saldivar, John reached over and turned the volume up. We all turned to watch the breaking news report.

Morgan's and my pictures were on the screen and the reporter was saying we were wanted for kidnapping District Judge Harvey.

Outside the steps of the courthouse, the reporter turned to Judge Harvey's legal assistant and asked him what he saw.

"Detective Sellers came to the judge's chambers. He had a woman with him, about five-ten, shoulder-length red hair. She looked slender and fit. The judge said, 'Hi, Mariah,' and hugged her. He ushered them into his office before closing the door."

The reporter held up a picture of Morgan and asked, "Is this the detective that came by?"

"Yes, that's him."

The reporter faced the camera, holding up the picture of Morgan for the viewers to see.

"This is Detective Morgan Sellers of the Albuquerque Police Department."

She turned back to the legal assistant and showed him another picture.

"And is this the woman that was with Detective Sellers?"

"Yes. That's the woman the judge called Mariah."

The reporter turned again to face the camera showing a picture of me.

"This is Mariah Jeffries, a prominent forensic psychologist who was believed killed in the explosion of her home a week ago."

"What happened next?" She turned and asked the assistant.

"Well, then I heard some yelling. The detective was shouting, 'You will help us!' and the judge said, 'No. It's illegal.' He asked the detective what happened to him.

"There was a crash and the door opened. The detective had his arm around the judge's shoulders, and the lady, Mariah, was right behind the judge. The detective told me they were going to lunch and would have the judge back in about an hour.

"I started to say something, but the judge told me not to worry about it. He said he

---

would be back after lunch. It was obvious he trusted the Detective and felt safe with him.

"That was it. He never came back. I went into the office after they left and a chair was knocked over, a picture on the wall was hanging crooked, and a lamp was shattered all over the rug."

"Do you have any idea what they were arguing about?" the reporter asked.

"No."

"Thank you." The reporter walked over to one of the court clerks and asked her what she saw and heard.

"Not much really. Detective Sellers and the judge were walking out of the courthouse. Detective Sellers had his arm around the judge's shoulders, and he was whispering something to the judge."

"Did you hear what he was saying?"

"No! He was whispering. I didn't hear anything."

"Was there anyone else with them … a lady perhaps?"

"I didn't notice. I just saw Detective Sellers and the judge."

"And you know Detective Sellers on sight?"

"I've seen him around the courthouse. I don't know him personally, but it looked like him."

The reporter showed her my picture and the clerk said, "I saw her come out behind them, but I didn't know they were together."

"How did the judge look?"

"Angry, but otherwise fine."

Before turning back to face the camera, the reporter dismissed the clerk with a 'thank you.'

"Please be on the lookout for Judge Harvey, Detective Morgan Sellers, and Dr. Mariah Jeffries. It has come to light that Detective Sellers and Dr. Jeffries are wanted by the FBI for impersonating FBI agents in another state. They are believed to have committed several murders there. It has also been determined that the explosion of Dr. Jeffries' home was due to a meth lab in her home. The FBI believes this crime rampage is the result of a drug deal gone wrong. Their accomplice, FBI Agent Jim Benton in Idaho, has been arrested. We will keep you posted."

I was shell-shocked. I couldn't wrap my head around that news report. Morgan, who had been standing next to the couch, slumped down onto the edge and put his head in his hands.

"My God," he muttered.

He looked up at Uncle Dan. "What is going on? Is this standard operating procedure for the *FBI*?"

"You know it's not, Morgan. I don't know *what* is going on, but we *will* get to the bottom of this. You two are going to have to stay in this room during the day. We can all do whatever investigations we have to do after dark. If there is something that has to be done during the day, John, Richard, or I can do it."

"This is unbelievable." Morgan stood and kicked the trash can next to the small refrigerator. "WHAT about my *family*?"

"I can't imagine the FBI will allow anything to happen to them."

"Can you imagine them framing me and Mariah for kidnapping and murder? Huh?! Yeah, they'll protect my family if they're not all corrupt and involved in this farce. For all I know, it's the FBI who has been after me and Jeff ... ah, Mariah."

"There is no doubt someone in the organization here is on the take, but not all of them are crooked. We'll figure it out."

**********

$W$e spent the rest of the day giving Dan more details about the case. We batted around different theories and strategies.

The next morning, Uncle John went out to buy some burner phones. When he returned, he called Norah, my secretary.

"Hello?" she answered the ringing phone.

"Norah Riddle?"

"Yes, this is Norah."

"Hi, this is John Jeffries, Mariah's uncle."

"Oh, Mr. Jeffries! I'm so sorry for your loss." Norah began to cry. "Is there something I can do for you? Anything? I loved Dr. Jeffries, and I'm devastated she is gone. Now they're saying she's involved in kidnapping a judge. They're saying she's a murderer and drug dealer. It's crazy. I know her. She would never do the things they're accusing her of."

"Yes, I know. We are saddened and grieved by her death, but to answer your question, I'm here in town to take care of her affairs. I'd like to meet with you and talk about her last days. Would you be willing to meet me for lunch?"

"Yes, of course. When and where do you want to meet?"

"How about La Fiesta at eleven thirty?"

"Yes, that would be great. I look forward to meeting you, Mr. Jeffries. Mariah spoke often and with so much love about her uncles. She loved you very much."

"Thank you, Norah. Call me John, and I'll see you at eleven thirty."

When John met with Norah, he showed her a yellow legal pad with a written note at the top.

*Just shake your head yes or no to these questions while I talk to you. Do you understand?*

When she nodded, he wrote a question.

*Are you being followed or monitored by anyone that you know of, such as the FBI?*

She indicated no.

After further questions, John was convinced he could talk freely with Norah.

Uncle Dan and Uncle Richard were outside watching for anyone following her. They didn't see anything suspicious and let John know in his covert tactical earpiece.

I told my uncles Norah could be trusted and if she knew she was being monitored, she would tell them. Of course, she would have no way of knowing if she was under surreptitious surveillance and that's where Uncle John's intuition came in.

Uncle John told her what was really going on and asked if she was willing to help us. I was certain she would say yes.

We needed the phone that Kyle Trent gave me. We also needed the prints I lifted, all of which were locked away in my office. Norah was our best chance to get those items.

Morgan and I paced a groove in the carpet of the motel room until the uncles returned.

"Well?" I barely gave them time to get in the door before asking.

"Norah was very confused because first she was told you and Paisley perished in the bombing. The recent news reports indicate you're alive and a murdering drug lord." Uncle John sat on the couch and sighed. He crossed his legs.

"She's relieved to learn you are alive and that we are on the case. You were right, Mariah.

She knew you hadn't done the things reported on the news. She had no doubt about that. She's more than happy to help.

"She is going to your office this afternoon. It's being watched by the FBI. If they stop her from entering, she will tell them she needs to get her personal effects she kept inside. I hope they will let her in without hovering, so she can get to your safe. I gave her the combination and told her to grab everything in it.

"I'm meeting her at the library tomorrow at ten. She will have her children with her in case she is followed. When she comes down the reference aisle I will be there at the end of the row, reading the titles. She will place the safe items in a large manila envelope on a shelf about halfway down the row, grab a book, and leave. I will retrieve the package and put it in my briefcase and stay in the isle a good ten minutes longer. Dan has already cased the place and there are no security cameras in that area, but I don't want anyone to see me exit behind her."

"So, now we sit and wait," I said. "What are you going to do with the phone and prints once you get them?"

"We are going to send the prints to a trusted friend of mine at the Boston Police

Department." Dan sat at the table and rubbed his index finger around a water ring.

"He'll have those prints rerun to make sure you and Morgan weren't misled about the origins. With them being run from an outside department, we can avoid the FBI getting wind of our investigation. We can't go forward until we have that information.

"I contacted another close friend of mine in the FBI at the Salt Lake City office to inquire about Jim. He nosed around and learned that Jim is being held for aiding and abetting in a felonious crime. My contact is going to see if he can talk to Jim and get more information but there are no guarantees. Since this is a huge cover up of some sort, Jim may be highly guarded and not allowed visitors."

"Has anyone heard anything about Riley? He was involved in the Idaho Falls stuff. Is he wanted also?" asked Morgan.

"I asked my FBI contact, and he hasn't heard anything about Agent Riley, but he's looking into it."

"Okay. What now?" I sat at the table and tapped my fingers on top.

"We sit and wait. Who wants to play a friendly game of Texas hold 'em?" Dan raised his eyebrows and grinned.

We pulled up chairs and sat at the little table. Dan and I faced each other across the table. John and Morgan sat opposite each other. Uncle John laid a box of colored toothpicks on the table and pulled a deck of cards from his pocket.

Uncle Richard declined the offer to play and told us he was going out for fresh air. Dan shuffled the cards, Morgan cut them, and the game was on.

The next morning, Dan left and got us McDonald's breakfasts before the uncles left to meet Norah. John was meeting her, while Dan and Richard were the lookouts. Morgan and I lounged around the room and watched the news. We were no longer the headline, so I convinced Morgan to meditate with me until the uncles returned.

No one said anything when the uncles got back to the room. Richard unpacked a bunch of high-tech computer equipment that had been sitting in cases against the wall and set it up. Richard is the tech guru of the group. He could have easily been a corporate techie or a computer hacker, but he loved police work.

Once he got it hooked up, John pulled the cell phone and copies of the fingerprints from the envelope.  He handed the prints to Richard and the envelope with the rest of the contents to me.  Richard scanned the prints into the computer.  He logged into a secure site, opened a secure email, and uploaded the prints to send to Uncle Dan's contacts.

John laid the phone, sans battery and SIM card on the desk next to Richard's keyboard.

"We need to get out of here sooner than later."  Dan ran his hands through his hair.  "The FBI is looking for you two, and it's only a matter of time before they get to this motel.  Any suggestions?"

"We've got camping equipment."  Uncle John squinched his eyes in thought.  "What we don't have, I can go get.  We can hide out in the mountains and run our investigations from there."

"No, that won't work.  Besides, I don't want to camp out for God knows how long."  I shot a glare at Uncle John for suggesting such a thing.

"We need someone's house to stay in.  My friend, Jerry, is a realtor; he actually buys houses and fixes them up and then flips them.  I could call him and see if he has a place we could camp in until this is over."

"Mariah, honey, the more people who know where we are, the greater the risk of being caught before this can be resolved."  Uncle Richard gave me a look of pity.

"I *know* that, and Jerry *can* be trusted.  He cares about me, he really does.  We dated for a while and have settled into a really good friendship.  Let me contact him, please."

Dan and Richard looked at each other and then at John.  "What do you think, John?  Are you getting any kind of vibe about this?"

John sighed.  "It's not clear.  I would have to meet him to get a better sense of things."

"Then you call him like you did Norah.  Tell him you came to town to wrap up my affairs and would like to meet him since I spoke of him to you."

John watched me while he thought about it.

"Come on.  I know Jerry.  He's safe!  We have to get out of here.  We all agree on that."

"Okay," John conceded.

Dan nodded at Richard.  "Can we scramble a call from the burner phone through the computer so it won't be traced?"

"Sure."

Richard did some technical stuff and nodded at John.

"What's the number and full name?" John asked me, and I told him. Uncle John dialed the phone.

"Jerry Fowler? ... Uhum, hi, Jerry. This is John Jeffries. I'm Mariah's uncle, and I'm in town wrapping up some business for her since her death. ... What's that? ... Really! I haven't heard that. You would think the FBI would notify her next of kin that she's not dead after all. ... What? ... She's a fugitive?" Uncle John barked a bitter laugh.

"For what? ... Murder! ... And kidnapping? Are you kidding? That's impossible. Not Mariah. ... Yes, I see. Of course you don't believe it. No one who knows Mariah would believe such bunk..." John cleared his throat. "From what Mariah told me, she cared about you very much, and—"

I slugged Uncle John in the upper right arm. He glanced my way, and I shook my head whispering, "as a friend!"

"Uh, well, as a close friend, you know. She always talked about what a good guy you are. ... Oh yes. She did. ... I was wondering if I could meet with you for lunch and get some information about her last month or so. ... "

Uncle John nodded. "Could you help me piece together the last of her life? ... Of course, one thirty at Picasso's would be fine. ... Sounds delicious. What's the address, and I'll GPS it? ... Great. See you this afternoon. And Jerry, thank you. I look forward to meeting you. ... Bye."

I sighed and clapped my hands. "Yay, I know he'll be able to help us."

"We'll see, Mariah. Don't get too excited until I meet with him."

"I know, but it will work out."

When John got back from meeting with Jerry, he told us he didn't have a real good feeling about Jerry's character which concerned him, but Jerry did seem sincere in his affection and concern for me.

Jerry told Uncle John he didn't believe I was involved in the murders or the kidnapping, but he believed I was still alive somewhere. After talking to him for a while, Uncle John finally confided in Jerry and told him what was going on. Jerry said he would be more than happy to help us out.

He said he had a house he bought six months ago and just finished renovations on. He was about to put it on the market, but he would allow us to stay there until this mess was resolved.

We started packing up and getting ready to go to the address Jerry gave Uncle John. We were going after sundown so there would be fewer people out and about to witness us showing up. John said Jerry would meet us there to discuss our needs and what else, if anything, he could do to help us.

When we arrived at the house, located on a busy street two blocks from downtown, Jerry was standing in the driveway. He directed us past the side of the house to the garage in the back corner of the yard. Dan drove down the driveway, and Jerry walked to the single-car garage and pulled the door open. He pulled the door closed behind us and met me when I stepped out of the car. We embraced, and I thanked him for believing in me and helping us.

"Anything for you, Mariah. I'm happy to help. Here, let me help you carry your gear into the house." He grabbed some of our things and opened the small door leading into the fenced backyard.

The rest of us grabbed everything else and followed him down a narrow, flower-lined path to the back of the house. Jerry unlocked the door and pushed it open. We followed him through the large kitchen and into the small living room at the front of the house. We put our gear on the floor next to the wall, and Jerry showed us through the house.

It was a two-story and had a narrow stairway to the second floor where there were four very small bedrooms and one bathroom. It looked like it was built in the late nineteen-forties or early fifties. I claimed the bedroom closest to the bathroom at the top of the stairs, Morgan took the one at the end of the hall, and Uncle John took the one across from Morgan. Uncle Richard and Uncle Dan took the last one (the largest) across from my room.

There wasn't any furniture or appliances except a built in electric range and microwave. We had electricity and running water. With the camping equipment Uncle John picked up, we were going to be comfortable and able to stay under the radar.

I lugged my sleeping bag and the few changes of clothes Uncle John bought me up to my room, while the others did the same. Jerry brought opaque plastic sheeting to put up over the new blinds in the windows since there were no curtains. There wasn't a fridge, so Jerry said he would bring us fresh ice once a day to keep any perishables—not that we had much or planned on cooking big meals, but it would be nice to have eggs in the morning and keep some lunch meat on ice.

Uncle Richard set up the electronics in the living room on a camp table, and after Jerry left, we sat on the floor and started making plans. Uncle Richard checked his secure email and found a response to the fingerprints he uploaded to Dan's friend in the Boston Police Department.

Low and behold, we were lied to ... sort of. The contact advised there were two sets of fingerprints, not three. One set belonged to Ricky Saldivar, a safe cracker, hence the handle "Big Ears". He could hear the tumblers of a safe move like nobody's business.

"Here's the big surprise, and our link to solving this thing: the other set of prints in your safe belong to an Albuquerque detective named Newton Marshall. He's..."

"That low life, sniveling, sneak!" Morgan seethed. "He kept nosing around the case when I was investigating the kidnapping and office burglary. After we got back from Idaho, he continued to ask me what happened there. I actually caught him reading one of my reports before I filed it." Morgan slammed his fist on the carpeted floor beside him. "I thought he was being nosey because he wanted in on the investigation—seeing that it was a big, high-profile case—to put on his résumé. He was always like that. Now I know why he was really snooping around so much."

"I was going to say he's our first lead and we are definitely going to follow up on it."

"Oh! You're right about that, and I'm going to be the one to take him down."

"Just back off, Morgan." Uncle Dan glared at him. "We are going to follow up on it, but we have to be smart about it, not go off half-cocked. If we get caught, you two are going down the pike, Richard, John, and me along with you."

Morgan took a deep breath. I could see the muscles in his jaw clenching. "You're right. Just like I told Riley when Jeri was kidnapped—gotta think like cops. But I'm really mad right now."

"We understand." Uncle Dan nodded. "When your brother in uniform is found out to be dirty, it's a huge betrayal. He'll get his, I promise! Here's how I think we should play this—"

Richard interrupted. "Just got another email from your FBI contact. Still no word on Riley, but he was able to get in and talk to Jim. He writes, *Jim is doing fine, just mad as* an old wet hen. He's being held in solitary confinement to keep him safe from the other inmates. He doesn't know who in the FBI is on the take, but he has a few ideas, the first being DEA Agent Raymond Cortez who was working undercover on The Mongoose case.

"Jim said when Cortez's name first came up in the investigation, he had a check run on the guy. He recently had some pretty large deposits posted in his bank account. After The Mongoose's ring was broken up and arrests were made, Cortez was reassigned to Albuquerque.

"The other person he thinks could be involved is FBI Agent Nylla Palmer. She's an agent here in New Mexico who went to see him in the slammer in Idaho under some guise of following up on Mariah's kidnapping case. He said she had a lot of questions, some of them pertaining to his arrest as an accomplice to the killings in Idaho and a lot of questions about the investigation in Idaho itself. She wanted to know what he learned about The Mongoose's crime organization. He said some of the things she was asking were pretty suspicious. Hope this helps you guys out. Let me know if I can be of any further assistance."

Richard looked up from his screen to the rest of us and whistled.

We discussed different ideas on how to proceed until two in the morning. Before we turned in for some shut-eye, Richard sent off an email to Dan's contacts in the Boston Police Department and the FBI.

**********

$\mathbf{D}$an and I were the first two up the next morning. We fixed some coffee and Dan told me he had a couple notable dreams the night before—one about some man tying me up and another about a woman entering a building with Morgan.

"Did you see the woman's face? Who was she?"

"No. She was helping Morgan break into a house."

"Hmmm, interesting. What did she look like?"

"It's not important. I wanted to talk to you about the other dream."

"Some guy tying me up? Maybe you were getting a glimpse of my abduction. I was tied up then."

"No. I don't think so. What I saw in my dream was the back of a man and you tied to a chair in front of him, facing away with your head hanging down as if you were unconscious. You weren't tied to a chair, were you?"

I shook my head. "Not that I remember."

"He was bent over and tying your hands behind the chair, or untying them. I couldn't tell for sure."

"Did you get a sense of who it was or how I got there?"

"I'm not sure, but I got a look at the profile, and it made me think of Jerry."

"Oh, Uncle Dan. He would never hurt me. It couldn't have been him."

"It was more than a dream. It felt real. You watch yourself around that guy. I think we should find another place to hide out."

"Don't be ridiculous. Maybe someone else tied me up and he found me and was untying me. You don't know Jerry like I do."

"John got bad vibes from him regarding his character and now this dream. I'm concerned."

"I think your subconscious is responding to Uncle John's spoken concern. It's nothing. We're fine here."

"You be careful and watch your back around him."

"I will, Uncle Dan." I kissed him on the cheek. "What about—"

"Morning." Uncle John came in for some coffee. "What's on the schedule for today?"

"Too early to tell yet," Dan responded.

"I'm going in the backyard to exercise. Want to join me?" Uncle John arched an eyebrow in my direction. It wasn't a question.

Uncle Dan and I went out to the backyard with Uncle John and started our workout.

Everyone was up and about by eight in the morning. Richard checked his secure email.

"Good news. We got a response from the FBI contact. Here's what he found out." He waved us to the computer to read the email.

"Good. We can work with that." Dan grinned after reading it. "Let's get ready. John, after breakfast, I want you to go to the store and get something Morgan and Mariah can use for disguises. I want them to be able to move around a little more freely. What's for breakfast?"

I fixed bacon, egg, and cheese burritos for everyone. Dan was pretty quiet during breakfast, working out the day's plan in his head. When we were finished eating and before John went out the door to get our disguises, Dan told John to rent us two more vehicles.

"Will do. Any particular kind?"

"No. Something inconspicuous but nice ... something businessmen would drive ... company-type cars I guess."

"Sure thing. I'll be back."

While Uncle John was gone to get disguise supplies, Uncle Dan filled us in on his plan. We drew up contingencies with all the little details that we could think of and waited for Uncle John to get back. Once he returned, we went over the plans with him and then went upstairs to get ready.

I couldn't believe the get-up Uncle John bought me. I had a padded push-up bra that transformed my C-cup breasts to DDs, a low-cut, v-neck stretch top, fairly tight black leather pants, and a pair of boots. He bought me cheap make-up and told me not to be afraid to overdo it a little bit ... or a lot, and to top off the whole look, he gave me a long blond, curly wig and large dark sunglasses.

I asked him why he bought me such an outlandish outfit if he wanted me to be incognito.

"Anyone who's on the run would not be calling attention to themselves with a getup like that." He smiled.

Morgan had a fake mustache, a brown button-down, heavy cotton work shirt, a pair of Carharts, a pair of work boots, a ball cap, and dark sunglasses. When John and Dan came downstairs, they were dressed in three-piece suits, and both were carrying briefcases. Richard was in his regular clothes.

We piled into the car with Morgan driving and headed to the Hertz rental office, where the two vehicles were waiting for us. Morgan dropped the uncles off at the office to pick up the rentals, one for John and Dan the other for Richard. Morgan left the Hertz parking lot and went downtown. He dropped me off at a gift store on the corner.

"I'll be back in about an hour to pick you up. Will that be enough time?"

"If she's in the office, yes. If not ..." I shrugged and smiled. I closed the car door, walked into the gift shop, and pretended to shop for about five minutes. I left the gift shop and meandered down the block to an old college friend's office. A twenty-something, Hispanic female sat at the front desk typing away on her computer. The phone rang and she answered, "Jewel

Diamond's office. How may I help you? ...
Yes Mr. Collins. One moment, please." She
pressed the intercom and announced the call.
I heard Jewel say, "Okay."

The receptionist turned her smile on me.

"How may I help you?"

"Hi, I would like to see Jewel if she's
available." I smacked my gum and tugged
one of the curls out straight without
unseating the wig.

"I'm sorry. I don't have anyone down for an
appointment at this time. Did she schedule
you herself?"

"No, I don't have an appointment," I smiled.
"I'm an old college friend and I'm in town for
a day or two. I just wanted to catch up with
her. Would you tell her Roofus is here?"

"Yes, Ms. Roofus. Just as soon as she gets
off the phone ... oh, she just hung up." The
receptionist pressed the intercom again.

"Ms. Diamond, there's a Ms. Roofus—"

"Roofus, just Roofus," I corrected her.

She nodded and continued, "Uh, Roofus is
here to see you." Before she let go of the

intercom button, Jewel came busting out of her office door.

Jewel is a five-foot-three, lithe blonde with average good looks and above-average intelligence. We were dorm roommates throughout our college years, both graduating with our bachelor's in psychology together. I took my bachelor's degree and joined the force while Jewel continued at school, getting her Psy.D. She practiced for a few years but got bored with it and decided to use her knowledge in the more interesting, and sometimes exciting world of private investigating.

We've kept in touch through the years and often got together when she wasn't working a case—for dinner and drinks, a movie, and different social events for which we had no dates. She was my maid of honor when I married the love of my life, Paul, and she was by my side when I put the love of my life to rest at Sunset Memorial Park.

Paul graduated from college a year before me and enlisted as an officer in the navy. We were married a year later after I graduated. Because the death of my father was still so raw, I wasn't ready to give up my maiden name and take the name of Carlton. He was a fighter pilot, and due to a malfunction with his plane during training operations, he was killed in a fiery crash five years later.

"Roofus, Roooofus, how ARRREEE you?" She rushed to me with open arms and hugged me tight. "It's been so long since I've seen or heard from you, I thought you were *dead*, or in *jail*."

"Ha ha, Cracker. You know me. ... If I'm not almost dead, I'm almost in jail." We both laughed.

I got the nickname Roofus one night when we went to a frat party with some other friends my sophomore year. It was right after my boyfriend dumped me for a cheerleader. I started drinking and got pretty drunk. In the course of some kind of diatribe, I expressed what a dog this cheerleader was and started barking at the moon.

Jewel was from Mississippi. Her best friend in high school was a beautiful girl named LaVie who had the smoothest, creamiest, chocolate colored skin you ever saw, and the voice of an angel. LaVie later went to Nashville to try and get a recording contract. She hooked up with a group of musicians, formed a band, and they have been playing the circuit as an opening act for some of the better-known artists and groups ever since ... and making a name for themselves.

LaVie and Jewel were together all the time in high school, and their friends referred to them as Ebony and Ivory, but in private, LaVie called Jewel 'Cracker'. Jewel divulged this bit of information to me in our dorm room on a night neither of us could sleep. After that night, every time Jewel called me Roofus, I called her Cracker. We became known as Roofus and Cracker to many of our college friends, but few of them knew what those nicknames originated from.

"Come into my office, my dear, and tell me EEEVRYYYTHINNNNG you have been up to since I last saw you." She marched me into her office closing the door behind us. As soon as we were behind closed doors, she hissed, "What is going on? I've been sick with worry about you." She hugged me hard and pushed me away. "Let's talk."

We sat facing each other, and I gave her a quick rundown of recent events. She shook her head.

"That's terrible. What can I do to help?"

"It could be dangerous. Are you sure you're willing to get involved?"

"Anything for you, hon. You know that."

"There's a DEA agent, an FBI agent, and an Albuquerque homicide detective who we believe may be involved. We can take care of the Albuquerque detective, but we need some help with the other two. It's going to be risky, but do you think you can help?"

"Oh, pish posh. Risky is my middle name. Of course I'll help. What do you want me to do, sweetie?"

"We need to get into their homes to see if we can find any incriminating information. That's where you come in. I know you're familiar with alarm and surveillance systems, and we want you to help us scope the places out and break in."

"Your uncles are here helping out?"

"Yes and they're good, but we can accomplish it faster with a little more help. Time is against us right now."

"Sounds like fun. When do we begin?"

"Jerry is letting us stay at one of the projects he was about to put on the market. Here's the address. Meet us there tonight around ten."

"I'll be there with rings on my fingers and bells on my toes, sweetie." She gave me a big grin.

"Come on, Cracker. Leave the rings and bells at home." I lowered my voice. "We need stealth." We both laughed.

"Mind if I include my partner, Norela? She's a genius and has impeccable contacts. Her father is retired Secret Service and consults now on corporate security all over the world. She knows things that will stun and amaze you about security, surveillance, and personal protection."

"Norela? What's her last name and where did you find her?"

"Norela Morales. Her father is a descendant of one of the original families in what is now Guadalupe County. They've been around since before the state was admitted into the Union. I wouldn't have partnered with her if I hadn't checked her out thoroughly. Mariah, she's above reproach, and she can really help us."

"But, will she be willing to take the risks with us?"

"I'm sure she will and I trust her implicitly."

"Okay, I trust your judgment. If you believe she's safe, bring her in. Tell her if this goes sideways, we could all end up in jail."

"I'll make sure she knows about the risks before I bring her in."

"Thanks. I gotta go, but I'll see you tonight. Watch your back and make sure you're not followed."

She gave me a look that said *Really? Me followed?* "You know better than that, Roofus!"

We hugged, and she opened the door with a flourish. "It was wonderful seeing you again. Don't be a stranger."

Morgan was pulling up in front of the gift store when I arrived.

"How'd it go?" he asked while I was fastening my seat belt.

"Great. She's in. How'd it go with you?"

Morgan held up a plastic baggie with a battery and SIM card inside.

"Really!? He had it?"

"Yep, in his sock drawer. I can't wait to get to the house and see what was so important he killed over it." Morgan pulled into traffic and headed back to our hideout.

**********

While I was talking to Jewel, Morgan broke into Detective Marshall's home to search for evidence. Richard stood lookout for him. When Morgan came out of the house without incident, Richard went back to our hideout and waited for Morgan to pick me up and return to the house with whatever was found.

Morgan handed the baggie with the battery and SIM Card to Richard who put the phone together. He checked the called numbers, of which there was only one, and he ran that number to see who it belonged to. Sure enough it belonged to Detective Marshall. There were two voice messages, which were Marshall's voice, according to Morgan.

*"You will do it, or you will be arrested. I have the evidence and can put you away for a very long time."* That was the first message. The second message was two days later, in which Marshall said, *"Meet me in the park on Alameda at three o'clock. Bring it with you."*

"Whose house was this phone originally taken from?" Morgan asked.

"An artist named Wade Andersen. His wife's name is LaRue. She's a real estate broker."

"What kind of artist?" asked Richard.

"Just a local painter. He does portraits for a lot of the upper echelon and has sold a few landscapes and still lifes he painted. Nothing big-time, I don't think."

"I think we need to visit this guy. Is it possible his wife was the dupe?"

"We don't know what Marshall was demanding or who was using this phone, so it's hard to say."

John and Dan returned. They went to Santa Fe to stake out the offices of the DEA, which were in the same federal building as the FBI offices. They were trying to track down Cortez and Nylla Palmer.

"We can't find any trace of Cortez. Are you sure he's in Albuquerque?" Dan asked Richard.

"That's what your contact with the FBI said. Maybe he had it wrong."

"No, Curt doesn't make mistakes like that. Check all recent hotel registrations in the area and if you can, check on any recent apartment rentals." He sat at the computer table next to Richard. "I wonder if Albuquerque was his home base and he already rents or owns a place here. See what you can find out, will ya Richard?"

"I'm on it."

"We did find Nylla Palmer's place. It's in a wooded neighborhood on the east side, up in the foothills, so it shouldn't be too much of a problem to watch and get in and out of undetected.

"Mariah, how about your P.I. friend? Is she in?"

"She's in, and she's bringing her partner, Norela Morales. Before you blow up, Uncle Dan, Jewel swears Norela can be trusted and that she has skills and knowledge that will help us."

"Mariah, what—"

John placed his hand on Dan's shoulder. "It is okay, Dan. This Norela is going to be a big asset, and she's not going to jeopardize us or the case."

"Why do you always assume I'm going to blow up?" Dan was looking at me. "I was going to say I already told you about my dreams last night—one of which was about a young blond woman who I remember to be your friend, Jewel, walking into the house here with a short and well-built—muscular really— woman with long black hair. Then I dreamed this other woman was helping Morgan get into a house. I already told you I had a dream about a woman helping us."

"You didn't tell me about Jewel or that the other woman was with Jewel." I sighed in frustration. "I'm sorry, Uncle Dan. I know how protective you are, and I assumed you would be upset with me for bringing her on the case without your approval. You didn't tell me the part about the woman showing up with Jewel, or give me the description of the other woman."

"You said "dreams", as in more than one. What else did you dream?" Richard turned from me to Dan.

"I trust you and your abilities. When I get upset about someone changing the plans, it's because I have a lot more experience than most of you do." Dan directed his comment to me.

"Okay."

Turning to Richard, he replied, "It doesn't matter about the other dream. It was about Mariah, and we already discussed it."

Richard shrugged a shoulder and turned back to his computer.

We filled John and Dan in on the voice messages before we checked the text messages.

The first one was sent to Marshall and read; *I can't do what you're requesting. I won't.*

The second one was sent to Marshall the following day and read; *Okay, give me two days. It will take at least that long.*

The third one was a response from Marshall, saying; *You've got until three p.m. two days from now. I'll let you know where to meet me. Don't be late!*

"Not much help." Richard's forehead furrowed.

"Nope, but at least we know what's on it, and we know who was using it. Now to find out why," Dan said.

We fixed bologna and cheese sandwiches for a late lunch and batted around some ideas on how to proceed.

Dan rose from his chair. "I'm going to take a nap. Wake me in an hour."

"That sounds good to me." I yawned and stretched my arms and back before following Dan up the stairs.

I had trouble getting to sleep, tossing and turning in my sleeping bag with all kinds of thoughts rushing through my head. At last I drifted off and slept for about thirty minutes before laughter from below woke me. I got up, freshened up in the bathroom, and headed downstairs where Morgan and Richard were telling jokes.

John was in the backyard again practicing the movements of his arts. I stepped out the screen door to get some fresh air.

"Come and join me, Mariah. You need to work your muscles every day you know, and this morning was a short workout."

I stepped up to John's side and fell into the graceful movements of Tai Chi Chuan. It felt good to get lost in the movements and meditation involved. After an hour, we broke for a late dinner consisting of Campbell's chicken noodle soup and grilled cheese sandwiches.

Jewel and Norela arrived as I finished cleaning up the kitchen and fixing a fresh pot of coffee. The uncles had met Jewel years ago, but they hadn't seen each other in ages. I made introductions all around and welcomed Norela, telling her we were glad to have her help.

Norela was short and compact, with well-defined muscles. She had on a short-sleeved, scoop-necked T-shirt that was tied under her breasts. Her midsection was bare to just below her navel where a pair of skin-tight jean shorts began, showing off her six-pack abs. Her hair was ebony black, shiny, long, and straight. After introductions, we settled down to work.

Richard found an address on Cortez. He had an old family ranch between Santa Fe and Albuquerque. Being isolated, it was going to be a little harder to conduct surveillance without being seen.

We decided to split up. Jewel, Uncle Dan and I would check out Cortez's place. Morgan, Uncle John, and Norela would watch Agent Nylla Palmer's place. Being in the foothills, they would have a lot more cover there.

Dan gave everyone his 'evil eye'. "Be careful. Nylla's place should be easier to watch, but she may have loyal neighbors who watch out for her. According to the information Richard found, Cortez doesn't have any family at his place, so if he leaves, we don't have to worry so much about another person coming home unexpectedly, and it's isolated enough we shouldn't have to worry about neighbors."

John cleared his throat. "Morgan, what are we going to do about Marshall?"

"You leave Marshall to me. He'll get his."

"Okay, let's get an early start before they leave home for work." Dan turned to Jewel. "Jewel, you tail Cortez when he leaves his place. Once he leaves, Mariah and I will see if there's a way in."

Richard started handing out burner phones to everyone.

"Let's use these to keep in touch. Keep them on silent so we're not discovered by a ring or buzz. Text if you can. These are all equipped with voice texting, so it will be a lot easier as long as you're in a position where you can speak."

"Jewel, if you and Norela have personal cell phones on you, please remove the batteries and leave them here like the rest of us have done.

"Mariah, use the same get-up you used when you went to see Jewel."

"My own clothes will be much more comfortable and less conspicuous, and that wig is ridiculous. It will only draw attention to me. I'll pull my hair up and wear a ball cap."

Dan looked at me, opened his mouth, and then closed it. "You're right."

He turned to Morgan.

"Wear your disguise, Morgan. Richard, stay here for monitoring. We're leaving in an hour so let's get ready."

Norela went out to their car and retrieved a duffle bag. When she returned, she and Jewel followed me up to my room to get ready. Norela pulled out a black knit long-sleeved T-shirt. She braided her hair and twisted it into a bun at the back of her head. Shedding her shorts, she pulled on a pair of black skin-tight wranglers and the dark t-shirt. She threw her discarded clothes and tennis shoes into the duffle, pulled out a pair of hiking boots, and laced them up over her pant legs. She strapped on a shoulder holster with a Taurus 1911 .45 ACP pistol and donned a dark green, light-weight windbreaker. She reached back into her little bag of tricks and pulled out another shoulder holster and tossed it to Jewel along with another dark green windbreaker.

Jewel had been carrying that Desert Eagle 1911 G Model .45 ever since she got into the P.I. business. She had me take her out and teach her how to break it down, clean it, handle it, and shoot it. We did a lot of target practice together over the years, and she's quite a marksman now.

I, of course, had my Five-seveN already in the shoulder holster and strapped on. I braided my hair pinning the ends up under the braid and topped it with a camouflage ball cap. I grabbed a zip-up, black hoodie, and we headed downstairs.

When we were ready to leave, Dan tossed me the keys to the Chevy, but Jewel stopped us. "Let's take my car. It's registered to my little brother, who's attending the university. I set it up that way so I would have something that, if the tags were run, wouldn't come right back to me.

"Since we'll be out in the open, if someone calls on a parked or abandoned car on the side of the highway, it will take the cops and Cortez, a while to figure out it belongs to a P.I. instead of a college kid who lives in a dorm on campus."

"Good thinking!" Dan said with a smile.

We got to the entrance gate of Cortez's ranch at about two in the morning. With night-vision binoculars, we could see a black, crew-cab Toyota Tundra that was pulled up in the circle drive in front of the house about 300 yards from the highway.

It was a ranch-style stucco that looked to be about 1800 square feet. We continued up the highway, driving 40 miles per hour to see the scope of the ranch along that stretch.

The fencing along the drive to the house started at the main house and ran along both sides of the drive all the way to the highway. In front of the fencing on both sides was a column of junipers. From the corner of the drive at the highway, and for two and a half miles in either direction along the highway, the fencing continued.

There was a sign hanging over the entrance to the ranch that read, "Diamond Back Ranch," and it had a cattle guard as you entered the drive. A large gate on the left side of the drive, forty feet from the house allowed access to the land, the barns, and the out-buildings. Inside the fencing to the north of the drive, we could see a large number of cattle spread out the whole two and a half miles up the highway and going as far back from the highway as we could see.

We drove up the highway a mile beyond the edge of the ranch and then turned around and drove back down to scope it out once more. About a half mile south of the drive, Jewel turned her headlights off and pulled over to the side of the road. Dan and I got out, and Jewel drove on down the highway where she would find a place to pull off and wait for Cortez to leave.

Dan and I went to the drive and started down the row of trees toward the house—Dan on one side of the drive, me on the other using the trees for cover. About halfway down the drive, a couple of dogs started barking and growling. From the moonlight, we could see them standing in front of the pickup, looking down the drive. They looked like blue heelers, but I couldn't be certain.

"Don't move" Dan whispered as he hid behind one of the trees. I froze behind a tree on the other side of the drive. We heard a soft whistle and someone called, "Here boys. What's out there, huh?"

Squatted down behind the tree, I peeked around and saw a tall Hispanic man walk out from behind the truck, bare chested and wearing a pair of jeans. He knelt down between the two dogs. He was holding a rifle with his right hand, butt on his knee and reached out and scratched the ears of the dog on his left. After the barking subsided and the man, Cortez I thought, went back inside, Dan motioned for me to retreat, which we did with caution.

A few soft growls drifted to us on the breeze as we retreated, but the dogs didn't bark again, and they didn't come down the drive after us. I was glad of that.

We went down the highway and met up with Jewel, who was waiting.

"Dogs, at least two of them," Dan said as we got into the car. "Some guy came out with a rifle when the dogs started barking and growling, but they didn't come down the drive. They're well trained to guard the house."

"Cortez?" asked Jewel.

"We believe so, but it was too dark to tell for sure. Mariah and I are going to hide in that bunch of Sycamore trees inside the fence on the south side of the drive until Cortez leaves. We'll text you when he leaves and let you know in what direction he goes."

"Okay, I'll be waiting. What about the dogs?"

"I've got some small raw steaks loaded with a few sedatives that I can slip them if I have to. It won't hurt them ... just put them to sleep for a while.

"I think we can get to the grove of trees without being detected. If we approach from this side, and the breeze continues to blow from the north, we'll be alright. They may smell us, but it will be far enough off that I don't think they'll send up an alarm. If they do, we'll bug out."

"Be careful," Jewel said as we slipped out of the car and climbed through the barbed-wire fence. We made our way to the small grove of deciduous trees without incident. There were several cows lying about under the trees, and although they raised their heads and watched us as we climbed a tree, they didn't move or make a sound.

There was enough foliage to keep us concealed, and I was able to find a nice large branch to sit on and brace my back against the trunk. I looked across to the tree Dan was in and saw he had done the same thing. We settled in for a long stake out but about an hour later, lights came on in the house.

From our position in the trees, we could make out the front of the house with binoculars and at five ten, the front door opened and a man called the dogs.

"Here, boys." There was a whistle and then "Duke, Rocco, come here." I saw one of the dogs crawl out from under the truck and lope around to the front door. I heard the man, who must have been squatted down on the other side of the truck, speak to the dogs. "Good boys. Come on in. I've got your breakfast ready." The man stood and walked into the house with both dogs following. The door closed.

At six thirty-five the same man, Cortez, dressed in a dark grey suit came out of the house pulling the door closed behind him. He climbed into his truck and retrieved his hat, a dark grey Stetson, from the hat rack. He squared it on his head and put on a pair of sun-glasses before starting the truck. We watched as he drove down the drive and turned right towards Santa Fe.

Dan spoke into his phone saying the subject had flown the coop and was headed to the capital. He pushed a button to send the text message to Jewel, and we watched as she drove by to get in sight of Cortez's truck. We waited until she texted back saying she had Cortez in sight and they were heading into the city.

Some of the cows below us had stood up and were starting to mill around when Dan and I climbed down from our perch.

"What do you want to do?" I asked.

"I say we approach the house and see what we can find. Be careful where you step or you'll track cow dung into the house."

I nodded.

"We'll knock on the front door and if someone answers, we'll tell them we broke down on the highway and ask to use their phone. Zip up your jacket to conceal your gun, and tuck your cell phone out of sight. If there's no answer, we'll see if there's a window or something we can get into."

"Uncle Dan, we should wait for Jewel. She can detect if there's any surveillance or alarms."

"She's following Cortez and won't come back until Cortez does. Besides, I can detect the same things. Trust me, kiddo!"

"Okay, let's go, then."

We walked across the field to the fence lining the drive and climbed through. We watched and listened for the dogs as we walked up the drive with caution. Duke and Rocco didn't greet us, so we figured they must be in the house. When we got to the front door, we rang the doorbell and waited. The dogs barked inside but there were no other sounds.

While standing there, a cherry-red Dodge Ram pickup came up the drive, and my heart jumped into my throat. Dan turned around to watch. When it pulled up and parked, he smiled and waved before stepping off the porch.

A weathered old man got out of the truck and asked, "Can I help you, folks? This is private property."

"Howdy, sir. I know it's private property—we saw the post—but, you see, our car broke down on the highway, and we were wondering if we could use your phone?" Dan gave him an engaging smile.

The old gentleman had salt-and-pepper hair, mostly salt, and an impressive grey handlebar mustache. He put his left hand in his jeans pocket and scratched his cheek with his right.

"Welp, that's curious. I didn't see no car broke down on the road."

"You didn't? What direction did you come from?" asked Dan.

"Up north. Where were you headed?"

"We're from Lubbock, Texas and spent the night in Albuquerque last night. We're headed to Santa Fe for some sightseeing. We hear that Old Town is a great place to visit."

"Yep, yep. It is. Welp, why don't I drive you to your car and see if I can get you started?"

"I don't think it will help unless you have a new timing belt. I'm a mechanic by trade, and I found the broken belt. If I can call my sister in Santa Fe, she'll call her mechanic who has a tow service and will pick us up. I'd be much obliged."

"Welp, I guess but make it quick. Ray'll have a fit if he finds out. He don't like nobody on his property unless he's invited 'em."

The old man looked down at his feet and rubbed a knuckle down the bridge of his nose before he pulled a cell phone out of his back pocket.

"Tell ya what, here's my cell phone. Go ahead and call, and I'll take you to your car."

"Thanks, Mr. uh ...?"

"Just call me Trini, short for Trinidad. I'm Ray's daddy. Ray owns this ranch. My daddy left it to him. I used to live here with Ray but I live in Santa Fe now. I come out to the ranch every day except weekends, unless Ray's out of town. I supervise the hands and look after things. What'd you say your names are?"

"I'm Dan Wickam and this here is my bride to be, Diane." Dan took the phone from the old guy. He nudged Trini with his elbow and said in a conspiratorial tone, "She's quite a prize, don't ya think? Especially for an old geezer like me." He smiled and raised an eyebrow while the old man looked me up and down. Dan dialed a number and waited a moment before talking.

"Hey, Sis. We've hit a little snag. ... No, we're fine, just broke the timing belt on the car. It's deader'n a dad burn doorknob. ... Yep, just outside a Santa Fe. ... Not too far. Would you call your mechanic with the tow truck and have him come get us? ... We walked up to this ranch house to use a phone. Ole gent, Trini, loaned us his cell phone. ... No, no, don't bother. It's so dad burn perdy up here that we'll just walk back to the car and enjoy the fresh air while we wait for the tow truck. See ya soon. ... Love you too."

He ended the call and handed it back to Trini and thanked him.

"No problem. Hop in the truck and I'll take you to your car."

"That's okay. I know you must have a lot to do. I worked as a ranch hand in my college days. Keeps ya busy. And besides, we have a bit of a wait for the tow truck. Like I told Sis, it'll be nicer to take a stroll to the car instead of just getting dropped off by you and standing around waiting."

"Ma'am, that okay with you?"

"Oh, yes, Mr. Trini." I gave him a demure smile. "Thank you for the offer, but I enjoy a morning walk. Thank you so much for your help. You have a beautiful day."

"Yes, ma'am. You too, both of you. And, mister, since you're a mechanic as you say, you should have known better than to take a trip and not service that car first."

"Yes, sir, you're right. I did get it serviced, and I knew it was almost time to change that timing belt, but I thought I had a few more months. So sorry to have bothered you. We'll just mosey on down the road yonder and enjoy the morning. You have a good day, sir, and thanks again."

We both started back down the drive at a leisurely pace holding hands. The tainted steaks still stuffed in Dan's jacket pocket. When we were out of ear shot I asked, "Who'd you call?"

"Jewel, of course. She's on her way to pick us up. She won't be long."

We made it to the highway and turned left toward Albuquerque.

While we walked, I started laughing. "Funny how you automatically fell into that good ole boy Texas drawl."

Dan looked over at me and grinned. "I am a good ole Texas boy."

We walked about a mile down the highway when Jewel pulled over and picked us up. On the way back to the house, we filled her in on what happened.

"So, we may not be able to get in and search for evidence." I turned to Jewel. "How'd it go for you?"

"I followed him to his office. What if we got access to the office after hours?"

"Government offices? That's pretty risky. Let's knock it around with the rest of the gang when we get back to the house." Dan sighed and laid his head back on the headrest.

"Norela and I can get in. Just sayin'."

"I don't like the risk. Let's see if there's another way to handle this."

We rode in silence the rest of the way to the house, each of us trying to come up with a viable plan.

Morgan, Norela, and John were already at the house, and once we arrived, we found a place to sit on the carpeted floor in the living room and discussed what had transpired.

Morgan advised that his team was able to observe Nylla's house and it doesn't appear to be a challenge to get in and search the place. After they staked out Agent Palmer's place, they went to Detective Marshall's house, and Norela and Morgan went in and bugged it.

"Hopefully we'll get something on recording that could be used to wrap things up," Norela said.

**********

Other than someone confronting Cortez face to face, we couldn't come up with a safe way to ascertain if Cortez was dirty.

John volunteered to try and catch him in a public setting, such as lunch, and 'chat him up', but that wouldn't be much help. Any information he got would be trivial. Cortez would not divulge important information to a stranger over a happenstance meeting.

"Hey Jeff, ahh ... Mariah, what about that scopolamine you used on Dempsey?" Morgan asked me.

"Jim supplied that. It was legally obtained through the FBI and I don't have access to it on my own."

"We could break into his house while he's asleep," Norela suggested. "I could get you in there."

"Not with those dogs. Plus ... it seems Cortez is a pretty light sleeper. If we did get in, we would have to beat the information out of him, or torture him, and I'm not willing to cross that line." I shook my head.

We decided to call it an early day, get some rest, and check out Palmer's place in the morning after she went to work.

Jewel invited us all to her favorite cantina for 'the best darned chili rellenos in the state'. Dan thought it would be too risky for Morgan and me, but Jewel assured him it was a small, out-of-the-way cantina. John assured Richard and Dan it would be okay, and we piled into the cars. I rode with Jewel, and Norela rode with Richard. Dan, John, and Morgan followed in a third car.

We pulled up in front of an ancient stucco building with a sign above the door that read, **"CROSSROADS CANTINA."** Inside, it was cool with subdued light. Across the wall to our left was a beautiful wooden bar with beer caps covering the entire top. The beer caps were covered with a clear resin so you could make out each individual cap, and yet the bar top had a smooth glossy finish. Along the bottom of the bar was a long brass rail for patron's feet and a row of round stools sat in front. Scattered around the room were small square tables with plastic, flower-print tablecloths.

"Hi, Dixie," Jewel said to the bartender when we walked in. "I've brought a group of friends in for your famous chili rellenos and some beer."

"Jewel, so glad to see you, Hon. Any friends of yours are welcome here. How many are we seating?"

"Seven altogether. Mind if we pull a couple tables together?"

"Why do you even ask, Jewel? You know you can. Do they want to look at menus, or does everyone want chili rellenos?"

"Maybe they'll want; oh ... here are the rest of them. Bring us menus, and we'll all order at the same time."

Jewel introduced us by first names only (she gave false names for me and Morgan).

Dixie hustled around to the side of the bar and grabbed a stack of menus while we pulled two tables together in the back of the room. We perused the menus, and Dixie laid out silverware and napkins. She brought salsa and tortilla chips and delivered a glass of water for each of us at which time we were ready to order. Everyone ordered the chile rellenos plate and Coronas on Jewel's recommendation. When the beers were brought to the table by a server, each bottle had a lime slice sticking out of the neck.

We stayed away from discussing anything about the case and kept the conversation light and friendly. The food was excellent. The proprietor, Dixie Cross, pulled up a chair and joined us on Jewel's invitation.

Dixie, a friendly and vivacious woman, was about five-seven with shoulder-length auburn hair and a heavy fringe of bangs. She was slender considering the amount of beer she consumed while visiting with us. She inherited the cantina from her father, who inherited it from his father, and on down the line to 1865. She advised us it burned back in 1947, they rebuilt it, and in 1969 it caught fire again. When they repaired the damage, they installed smoke detectors and a sprinkler system in case it caught fire again.

Dixie was married, now widowed, and had two boys—both college graduates employed with good jobs. She got to see them about twice a year. She was hoping she could leave the cantina to one of them one day, but so far, neither of them showed an interest in running it.

We were about ready to pay up and leave, when a group of men in suits and ties came in and sat at a table next to the front windows. Dan and Richard were facing the door, and the two of them glanced at each other before Dan leaned over the table and whispered to me and Morgan not to turn around. Jewel, sitting at the end of the table nearest me, asked what was up.

Richard nodded his head toward the group and whispered, "Cortez."

Jewel leaned over to Dixie and asked her in a whisper if Morgan and I could leave through the kitchen. She told Dixie there was a situation and it wouldn't be good if the group who just came in noticed us.

Dixie nodded and stood. "Before y'all go, you've got to come back to the kitchen and see the new equipment I installed. It's beautiful. Remember, Jewel, I told you about it when they were getting ready to install it?"

"Oh, yes. We would love to see it."

The uncles stood and came around the table to block me and Morgan from view of Cortez's group. Jewell and Norela fell in beside them to add an additional screen while Dixie led us. We made it to the kitchen without consequence.

Jewel handed Dixie a wad of cash and told me and Morgan they would meet us around the corner in the cars.

Everyone admired the equipment and with the exception of me, Morgan, and Dixie went back out to the bar area and exited the building.

Dixie hugged me and then Morgan. "Now, don't you two get caught until you get this mess cleared up. I want you to come back and visit me again, *Dr. Jeffries* and *Detective Sellers*."

"You knew who we were?" I asked.

"Of course I did. It takes more than cheap disguises to fool me. I'm sure glad that group of FBI agents didn't see you. They come in here pretty regular, especially Cortez. He's a pretty good friend."

"Hey," Morgan asked, "do you talk very much to him?"

"Oh, sure. He's a great patron, a really nice guy. Why, what do you need?"

Morgan glanced at me and then said, "We think he's dirty and part of our problem. We learned he recently had several large deposits made into his bank account. That was just before Mariah was kidnapped."

"Oh." Dixie led us to the back door and out onto the back step. "I can explain that. His older brother died and left everything to him. He told me all about it. His brother will really be missed, too. Boy, could he drink.

"Anyway, the first deposit was Junior's disposable cash value—all of those Cortez's have been really well off for generations. Ray's brother went by Junior because he didn't like the name Trinidad, and he didn't want to be called Trini like his dad. The second deposit was the profit from the sale of the small ranch his brother bought when he was eighteen."

"What do you mean by small?"

"Lets see. He told me it was two-hundred and fifty acres."

"That small, huh?!"

"Wow," I added.

"Yeah. The third deposit was for the sale of Junior's business, a real estate Agency. He had several agents working for him, and Ray sold the business to the senior agent, Gus Lyons. He's a regular here, too—very reliable and hard working."

"Thanks. That's a lot of information we didn't have. It helps a lot." I could feel my smile spreading.

"Happy to help. I'll tell you something else he told me. He doesn't believe you two are guilty. He's doing his own behind-the-scenes investigation to find out who in the FBI is dirty. He's really mad about this, and he and Hector, an agent up in Idaho who worked under Jim are good friends, so he's serious about it."

"Thank you, Dixie. That's good information, and we appreciate you sharing it with us. Please don't tell him we were here, just to be on the safe side, okay?" Morgan took her hand and squeezed it.

"Sure, no problem. Now git ... and come back when this mess is cleared up."

We each hugged Dixie goodbye one last time and walked through the alley to the street where Jewel was waiting for us.

"What took so long? Richard and Dan just went back in to check on things." Jewel was dialing her cell phone.

"Richard, I've got them. They're okay. ... I don't know, but we'll find out. Meet you guys at the house."

Once we were at the house, Morgan and I filled the group in on what Dixie disclosed to us.

"Sure glad to hear he's not on the take or involved in this mess," Dan said. "That information will help Richard track down the money to make sure it's all legit. She said he's doing his own investigation?"

"Yep, that's what she told us." Morgan nodded.

"Hopefully he'll get information for us that will help. Now all we have to worry about is Nylla Palmer and Newton Marshall."

"Speaking of Marshall," Richard said as he sat in front of his equipment with headphones on, "We've had activity at his place. It's a phone call. Take a listen." He pulled the headphones off and flipped a switch.

A voice came through the speaker. "Look, Gordon, I'm doing everything I can to find them."

"Yep, that's Marshall," Morgan said.

"You better find them. We took care of Jim, and we can sure take care of you, too."

"That's Gordon Morris!" Dan exclaimed.

"You're the head of the New Mexico division of the FBI. Why haven't your guys found them?" Marshall yelled.

"Newton, my man," Morris said, laughing. "DON'T QUESTION ME OR MY TEAM," he yelled. "I'll make sure they do their part. Now you do yours. You assured me you would find them."

"Yes sir," Marshall said with controlled rage. "No problem, SIR!" And then we heard the phone click.

"Well," said Dan. "We now know who to go after."

"Yeah, so what do we do with that information?" I asked.

"I have an idea," said Jewel. "You can make a copy of the recording, can't you, Richard?"

"Of course I can."

"Why don't you make a copy and give it to me. I'll take it to Dixie and ask her to give it to Cortez. When she gives it to him, she can say that some dude dropped it off and asked her to deliver it to him. You know, something like, 'he said you would find this interesting.'"

"Yeah," Richard said. "We can put it in a sealed envelope so Dixie doesn't know what it is. Would she do that?"

"Well, she's on our side. She recognized Mariah and Morgan and didn't say anything until we asked for help. She told us about Cortez and said he's doing his own investigation. He can present the evidence as having gotten it from an anonymous source. I bet he'll have this cleared up in record time."

"Yeah, right." Dan shook his head. "You must not be familiar with government bureaucracy, but I think it's still our best option. I can also send a copy to my FBI contact. Maybe he can do something to expedite it or at least make sure something is done with it … in case Cortez doesn't or if the corruption goes even higher. Time to clean house, I suppose."

"Do you doubt Cortez would act on the recording, Dan?" asked Norela.

"At this point, we don't really know who's on our side. Experience has taught me not to trust anyone until you have proof, not just in their words but in their actions as well."

"I'll wait and see if we get any other information before I make the recording. Maybe we'll get more to hang them with," Richard said.

**********

Early the next morning, Jewel, Norela, Dan, and Richard went to Nylla Palmer's place to search it for evidence. When they got back to the house, Jewel advised they didn't find anything.

"No, but we bugged the place like we did Marshall's." Dan grinned and raised and lowered his eyebrows. "Maybe that will give us something. We also went back to Marshall's place and removed those bugs to cover our tracks. I think we got all we need from him for the time being. At least it's enough to get him on criminal charges. Let's wait to see what Nylla's place garners us before we deliver the package to Dixie."

"Norela and I are going back to our office and take care of some work that pays the bills." Jewel came over and hugged me. "I'll come back this evening to visit and see if you need anything."

"Thanks, Jewel."

Jewel hugged me again. "See ya later sweetheart. How 'bout I bring some pizzas for dinner?"

Everyone in their own words said yes and nodded saying pizza would be good.

"See ya later then." John shoved some cash in her hand as she left.

"Good-bye you two." Dan lifted his hand in good-bye to Jewel and Norela. "See ya tonight."

We had a quiet and uneventful afternoon. Jerry stopped by at four thirty to check on our needs and to visit. Jewel showed up at six with three large pizzas as Jerry was preparing to leave. I invited him to stay and eat. It was a relaxed evening and everyone seemed to be in a playful mood, telling jokes and ribbing one another.

Jerry hugged me and kissed me on the cheek before leaving at eight. Jewel followed on his heels.

The next day, Sunday, we worked on the case of Mr. and Mrs. Andersen, from whose house the phone was stolen. We still needed to figure out what Marshall had been doing with the Andersens—at least which one of them he was coercing.

When Richard came downstairs, dressed in work clothes and a ball cap, I asked him what he was up to. He handed me a handyman business card with a fake name, and one of the burner phone numbers on it.

"I made up the cards this morning. I'm going to approach them with the pretense of seeing if they need any work done around the place. I doubt I'll get very far, but it's a shot."

"Do you want one of us to go with you to help scope the place out?" I handed the card back to him.

"I called Norela, she's going to meet me at the market on 108th Street and we'll approach the house together. I'll be back in a few hours and fill y'all in."

At that, he walked out the door.

The rest of us had a relaxing afternoon. We exercised in the backyard and kicked back— read, talked, napped, meditated, and ate. Jerry came by to see how things were going and if we needed anything, which we didn't, so he hung out for a while. He and I sat in the backyard on the grass underneath the big Japanese red maple and talked about miscellanea.

"Whatever happened to us? When did we become just friends instead of a couple?"

"Jerry, we agreed a long time ago it wasn't working out … for either of us. I wasn't ready for a relationship, and you said I wasn't what you were looking for in a partner … in a wife. Why do you ask anyway? I thought we were happy as friends. We're good friends, right? I consider you one of my most trusted friends."

"I love you, Mariah," he blurted out. "I guess I didn't realize it then, but I sensed that you weren't ready and I was, so instead of getting in any deeper I backed off. I've never stopped loving you. If anything, my love for you has grown over the years. Why do you think I've done so much to help you?"

"I thought you were helping because you loved me as a friend and that's what friends do for each other. I would do it for you."

"Can we try again? It's been a while. Maybe you're ready now?"

"Oh, Jerry!" I shook my head. "I do love you, but I'm not *in* love with you. I'm not ready to move on." I shrugged. "I'm not."

A dark look of rage crossed Jerry's countenance so briefly I wasn't sure I saw it. Then he looked sad. "Okay, I understand. I'll leave now."

"Jerry, I'm sorry."

"It's okay. I'm not going to turn you guys in or anything, and I'll be back tomorrow to see if y'all need anything." He stood and left.

I felt terrible. I had no idea he was harboring feelings like that toward me, but I couldn't lie to him. I sat there in the grass alone, a tear sliding down my cheek while I contemplated the loss of a very dear friend. Things have certainly changed between us forever. Uncle John came out and sat behind me. After a few minutes of silence, he asked me what was wrong, so I told him what happened.

Uncle John looked off at a sparrow sitting on the fence. "Was he terribly upset?"

"Yes, he looked heartbroken. He's been such a good friend over the years, and I had no idea he was carrying that torch. We never got that serious."

"Was he angry enough to turn on you ... turn us in?"

"No. He's not a violent person. I doubt I will hear from him again after this. And that's probably best. He will need to put some distance between us in order to get over me and move on but it makes me sad."

We talked for a while before going back into the house. I started up the stairs when Richard and Norela came in the front door. I turned back to greet them.

"What did you find out?"

---

They headed into the living room and I followed sitting on the floor in my usual place.

Uncle Richard went to his computer and started typing.

"Well? What's up?" asked Dan.

"Just a minute," Richard responded.

"The Andersens were out of town and the gardener was there," Norela started to explain. "Richard gave the gardener a hard-luck story about us being homeless and looking for work. Teddy Iverson, the gardener, said his hands didn't show up and asked if we could help him for the afternoon."

"Yeah, and when I asked to use the bathroom, he let me into the garage, where there is a little half bath with a toilet and sink. I tried and wasn't able to access the interior from there, but I was able to get a pretty good lay of the house from working in the flower beds all around outside.

"I also found out the Andersens are going to be out of town the rest of the week, so we may be able to get inside the house and do a thorough search. I'm trying to confirm they are out of town and ... THERE! I've got it. They're on a cruise, and look—pictures on their facebook account with them posing at the pool on deck."

"Wow, you'd think people would learn not to put so much personal information on a public forum." Dan whistled looking over Richard's shoulder. "They've told the world the dates they'll be gone, where they've gone … everything except their social security and bank account numbers. It's crazy."

"It's great! At least we know they're out of town," Norela said. "Maybe they feel their security system is impenetrable, but I can get through anything. Who do we need to go with us Richard? I can get us past the security system, but we want to be in and out fast, so if three or four of us go in and split up we might have better luck finding something quick."

"Probably a good idea." Richard turned off his computer and turned around to face the room. "I don't think Mariah or Morgan should go. They're too recognizable. How about you, me, Dan, and Jewel?"

"That makes sense to me." Dan nodded.

"I'll call Jewel right now." Norela pulled out her burner phone as there was a knock on the front door.

Morgan and I stepped around the corner into the kitchen while John answered the door. It was Jewel.

"Hey, what's up, everyone? I stopped by Mamacitas and picked up dinner for everyone—tacos and guacamole salad. Who's hungry?" She rushed past everyone to put her bags down on the kitchen cabinet. "Hurry up. I'm starved."

We followed her into the kitchen and started dishing up our own servings.

"Jewel, how do you feel about a little breaking and entering tonight?" Richard whispered in her ear seductively as he filled his plate with the beans and rice that came with the tacos.

With her mouth full of chip and guacamole, Jewel nodded. She swallowed and winked at Richard. "Sure darling. Who's the target and what are we looking for?"

Everyone moseyed back into the living room where we sat and ate while Richard and Norela filled Jewel in on the day's activities.

"Just the four of us are going? What about you, John?"

"I'll stay here with Morgan and Mariah. Someone needs to be available to bail you guys out of jail if need be."

"Oh, thanks for the vote of confidence!" Jewel threw a chip at him.

We sat and talked until ten at which time Jewel, Norela, Dan, and Richard left.

I said goodnight to everyone and went up to my room, climbed into my sleeping bag, and tried to go to sleep. This had been the worst month of my life, and now to top it off, I was losing one of my best friends—Jerry.

It was around two in the morning when Jewel shook me awake.

"Hey, how'd it go?" I rubbed my eyes trying to wake up.

"Good. We're all gathering downstairs to go over it, but I wanted to talk to you alone first. I'm worried about you; you seemed pretty down."

I told her about my afternoon with Jerry. It felt good to talk to her about how I was feeling. She never liked Jerry, and she said she was glad I told him there was no future for a romantic relationship, but she was sorry I felt the loss of a trusted friend.

We hugged and went downstairs to join the others and discuss what they found at the Andersen's house.

"At first we weren't finding anything that could be of help or give us any insight into what Marshall was up to with the Andersens. We found a collection of porn movies in the master closet, many of them made at home with the Andersens and other couples. Apparently they're in a swingers group," Dan told us.

"I don't think that's enough for the blackmail that we heard on the phone," Richard added.

"I found cocaine in the master bathroom," Norela said. "They probably use it during their sex-capades. There was a cookie jar full of pot in the kitchen, so we thought he was threatening them with drug charges."

"We searched the home office and found some large deposits in their bank statement, but they can be explained by sales of his paintings or commissions on her real estate deals," Jewel said. "We found receipts that explained all of the sizable deposits."

"We couldn't find anything that would explain the blackmail or what Marshall wanted from them until we started to leave," Richard added.

"On the way out of the home office, I tripped on the edge of the Oriental rug and fell into the wall next to the desk. My left hand slid along the wall trying to catch myself, and hit a hidden switch. A panel in the wall slid back, and you'll never guess what we found in that little concealed room." Dan's eyes gleamed with excitement.

"We found plates for counterfeiting U.S. currency in twenty-, fifty-, and one-hundred dollar denominations. That has to be what Marshall wanted from this joker. These plates looked like rough drafts, so Marshall already has the good ones, I'm sure."

Morgan let out a soft whistle. "Wow. I wasn't expecting that. Are there any reports of funny money floating around?"

"I haven't heard of any, but Richard is going to see what he can find out." Dan grinned. "We've got them now."

"I'm sending the prints we took in the secret room to Dan's contact in Boston as well his FBI buddy," Richard said.

**********

The next morning I was the first one to rise and went downstairs to make a pot of coffee. The smell of coffee must have woken the others because it wasn't long before everyone had a cup. I brewed another pot.

Richard took his mug and went to his campstool in front of his computers. Very shortly after he sat down, he hollered for all of us to come and listen.

"We've had activity at Nylla's ... a phone call. Listen to this."

"Hi, Nylla. Where's Cortez? He thought he was onto something and now he seems to be off the grid. What's going on?"

"I haven't been able to get hold of Cortez either. I know he's working on the case, too. We're doing our best to get something to clear Jim and the rest of them like you are Hector."

"We're running out of time. Whoever is behind this farce is pushing for a quick trial and taking Jim out of protected custody. He'll be thrown in with the general population, and you know what that means!"

"I know. If we get anything, I'll call you right away. Maybe Cortez is onto a lead and will have something soon. He'll get in touch with me as soon as he can."

"I hope he wasn't found out trying to investigate this, or he might have run into foul play. When you talked to Jim, did he give you *anything* that could help?"

"No, he didn't. Of course, he didn't know I was working to get him released, either. He thinks I was following up on the abduction of Mariah Jeffries."

"He's getting pretty discouraged. They let me see him every day, but I know we're observed and listened to, so I keep it to mundane topics."

"Yeah, that's why I couldn't tell him why I was asking the questions I asked. I think he got suspicious of me."

"He hasn't said anything to me about who he thinks is involved." Hector paused for a moment. "Well, don't worry about that. Hopefully we'll have something soon and know the truth. Talk to you later."

"Hey, Hector?"

"Yeah?"

"You were in the thick of that kidnapping case of Mariah along with Jim. I can't help but wonder why you and the rest of the agents involved haven't been arrested."

"I know. I figured they were going to file charges against the rest of us when I heard they filed against Jim and Riley. I went to my new supervisor and he told me new evidence came to light that proved the four of them—Jim, Riley, Morgan, and Jeffries—were involved in criminal activities. That's all he would divulge.

"I asked him what kind of evidence, and he said he wasn't privy to it. I don't think he knows. He's blindly doing what he's told like so many others. There's someone higher up orchestrating this, and I want to know who it is."

"Yeah, me too. I hope we get it figured out soon ... before it's too late. I'll call you as soon as I hear from Cortez."

"Okay, bye."

Everyone in the room was stunned into silence. Richard spoke first. "This is a good thing. There are a lot of people working on this, *AND* we have the evidence of who is on the take. We need to get that recording on Marshall to Cortez, and he'll channel it to the proper authorities to get this wrapped up. I suggest we put a note on the evidence telling him to listen to the recording so he doesn't inadvertently give it to Gordon Morris. I also suggest we note that this is much higher than the state branch. Someone higher than Morris has enough juice to bring false charges against Jim, Riley, and the two of you."

"Oh, Cortez will listen to the tapes first; I can guarantee that, but a note with it to explain who is talking in case he doesn't recognize the voices would be a good idea." Dan paused and tapped his fingers on the table. "What about also tipping him off on the counterfeiting plates at the Andersen's house? Since it's all going to him anonymously, why not?"

"I'll get to work on the note for the first recording and to tell him about the counterfeiting information," John said.

"Good," Richard said. "I think the counterfeiting information should definitely be included. Let's get those bugs out of Nylla's place ... soon."

John and I drafted the note to go with the recording that Richard made of the conversation between Marshall and Morris. We added the information about the counterfeiting plates found at the Andersen's house.

Morgan called Norela, and she said she and Jewel would be right over.

When they showed up, we filled them in on Nylla's conversation with Hector.

"Wow, that's great!" Jewel beamed at me from across the room.

"Yes, it is," Morgan said. "That's why we asked you guys to come over. We have to get into Nylla's place and remove all the bugs and we want to do that before we get the information to Cortez. Norela, are you game to help me?"

"Sure I am. Do you want to go now?"

"Now is as good a time as any. Jewel, have you been able to find out anything about my family? Where they are and if they're still okay?"

"Not yet. Norela has been working on it. I think they're okay. The people behind this conspiracy are probably holding them thinking it will give you incentive to turn yourself in—but they can't find you to relay that information. Once Cortez gets the information we have to the proper authorities, your family will be released."

"I hope you're right. Norela, let me know when you find out anything at all about them, please—good or bad."

"You know I will, Morgan. Let's go get those pesky little bugs so we can try to get this mess wrapped up."

Morgan turned and walked out of the house with Norela and Dan.

"He hasn't talked to his family or heard anything about them since we left the safe house. I think he's feeling guilty for leaving them—as though his decision to leave and investigate on his own has caused his family harm." I took a sip of my coffee. "I've tried to reassure him. If we hadn't left, we would both be in jail along with Jim ... or worse."

Richard, who had been typing away on his computer, printed off the note, folded it, and slipped it into a manila envelope with the recording. He sealed the envelope and stripped off the pair of latex gloves he donned to handle the "evidence" and threw them in the trash.

"As soon as they get back with the bugs, you can take this to Dixie for us, Jewel—like we discussed. Ask her to give it to Cortez but not to tell him where she got it. Tell her it's hot and needs to get to him ASAP."

Jewel picked the envelope up from the table.

"I will and she will. I trust Dixie with my life, and I know she'll help us any way she can.

She knows you guys are being railroaded. As soon as Norela and the guys get back, I'll head over there. I'll give you guys a call or come back by after it's dropped off."

An hour later, Norela returned alone.

"Hi, Norela." John said. "Where's Morgan and Dan?"

"Dan and Morgan dropped me off—here are the bugs—they went to pick up lunch for everyone." She handed the bugs to Richard and said she had something important to do and would be back later. Jewel left with the package, right behind Norela.

Forty-five minutes later, Dan and Morgan showed up with three big bags of fast food burgers and fries and old fashioned milkshakes.

Norela walked in the front door as we were finishing our meal.

"Grab some food and come sit down. There's plenty left, but you'll need to put it in the microwave." Morgan wadded up his hamburger wrapper.

"What did you find out about my family?"

"I do have some information for you, Morgan—all good—and also some news on

Riley, not so good."

"Tell us about my family first, please."

"Everyone is fine. They are still at the safe house, and I was able to catch Molly alone in the backyard. I called her name real soft when I saw her alone, and she came to the fence. I stayed ducked down in case someone was watching her from inside. She said they are being treated as well as before you left, Morgan. She has been worried about you, and I was able to reassure her that you are alright and working on getting this case resolved. I also told her not to let on that she has heard from anyone, not even to tell your children, and she agreed.

"Mariah, your cute little dog is fine, too. She was running around the backyard, chasing the birds."

"Thank you, Norela," Morgan said.

"Yeah, thanks. I'm glad to hear Paisley is doing well, too. I sure miss her." I couldn't help smiling just thinking about her chasing birds. "Tell us what you found out about Riley."

"I found out Riley is wanted as a conspirator in the bogus charges that you are under. It is reported that he has been seen around Rexburg, Idaho Falls, Boise, and even

Denver, Colorado. They have put out an all-points bulletin for him and believe he is headed here to New Mexico, but nobody can confirm that."

"From the Nylla/Hector tape, we already knew they had charges on him," Dan said.

"Riley will not be seen or found until he's good and ready," Morgan added.

"I know. That's the talk I'm hearing. They are saying he's like a ghost, and a deadly one at that. One guy I talked to, retired FBI, said Riley is some kind of ninja expert at self-defense. He assesses risks with an uncanny skill and knows how to take out a known enemy silently and skillfully. He can handle any kind of weapon as though it is an extension of his own hands and mind.

"Some people are getting uncomfortable knowing he's out there, maybe planning on exacting revenge for any wrongs done to him, his friends, and his family.

"But there's also the scuttlebutt that he's not all that bad—it's hype. There are reports that he and his wife were killed in an auto accident in Germany. I'm not sure that it's true, but I did find record of them flying to Germany after you came home from Idaho, Mariah. I can't get a fix on where the information on their deaths is coming from. I personally hope he's still alive and that I get an opportunity to meet the man."

"If he's still alive, you'll probably get your chance, Norela. Just keep in mind that he's married and extremely devoted to his wife." I pointed to my left ring finger to stress my statement.

"Oh, I know that. I just want to meet the guy. He's like a legend."

"What about his wife, Jeri? Any other word on her besides her death?" Morgan asked.

"No. None. I'm guessing Riley has her safely tucked away somewhere until this mess is cleaned up unless, of course, the scuttlebutt is true and they're both dead."

"They're not." John stated as a mater of fact.

"I don't think so either, John. That's not to say they're not looking for her also. They figure if they can find and take her, then Riley will give himself up."

"Then they don't know squat about Riley. He won't give himself up, but people will die if they mess with his wife. You can count on that," Morgan said. "And, they'll never see it coming until it's too late."

We finished eating and Norela left to take care of some of their own business.

**\*\*\*\*\*\*\*\*\*\***

$J$ewel came back with Norela around six that evening.

"When I walked into the Crossroads Cantina, I saw Cortez sitting at a table with Nylla Palmer and another woman, so I walked up to the bar and ordered a shredded beef burrito to go. While Dixie was taking my order, I whispered that I needed to talk to her alone, not with Cortez or his friends there. She nodded and went to the kitchen to make my order. I sat at the bar with a cold beer and tried but couldn't hear Cortez's conversation. Dixie came out with my food and told me with a wink to come back soon.

"I went out to my jeep and pulled into the parking lot a block down the street where I could watch the front of the cantina. They were in there a good hour and a half. Once I saw them come out and go to their separate cars and leave, I went back in.

"Dixie told me that Cortez introduced her to Nylla Palmer, the tall, butch-looking woman, and Joy Love, the shorter, black-haired woman. She only got pieces of the conversation at their table, but she was able to deduce that Nylla and Joy are FBI agents. I recognized Nylla, but I hadn't seen Joy before."

"Yes, Joy was part of the detail protecting us at the safe house here. I would guess she's still part of the detail protecting Morgan's family."

"Right, that's another piece of the conversation that Dixie picked up on. They were talking about the family's safety and Joy's boss was getting ready to move them. Joy was concerned as to what *that* was going to entail."

"Oh GOD!" Morgan dropped his head into the palm of his hands. He stood as though to bolt from the room.

John stepped up behind Morgan and placed his hand on Morgan's shoulder. "It's okay, Morgan. They're going to be fine. I know it. Jewel, did you drop off the evidence with Dixie?"

"Yes, and Dixie called Cortez while I was standing there. She told him she found something he might want to come back for—that it looked important. He apparently asked her what it was, and she told him it was some mail or something with his name on it.

"When she hung up she told me he was on his way back, so I stepped into the kitchen with Dixie's consent to listen in. There wasn't anyone else in the place when he arrived.

"She handed the package to him and asked if he left it there.  He told her no, he never saw it before.  He frowned and looked the package over front and back.

"He asked her where she found it, and she led him to the far end of the bar—back in the corner.  She asked if he was sure he didn't recognize it.

"'Nope,' he said, 'but it is obvious it's meant for me.  You have no idea what this might be about?'

"She told him no, of course not—called him Hon.  'But it is curious, now, isn't it?'  That's what she said, all innocent like.  I kept my hand over my mouth so I wouldn't laugh.  It was a great performance.

"'Yes it is, Dixie.'  He kissed her on the cheek and told her thanks and to watch out.

"She gushed over that.  'Oh, thank you, sweetie.  You take care, too.'  Jewel clasped her hands together under her chin, turned her face up and batted her eyes with her lips puckered.

We laughed.

"He told her to call if she found any more packages for him, or if anything odd or worse happens around her place.

"She took him by the arm and guided him to the door, and he walked out.

"After a few minutes, Dixie came into the kitchen. She wanted to wait to make sure he didn't come back to ask more questions.

"I thought she was going to tell him someone dropped it off. I asked why she didn't.

"She said she was going to, but figured he would want to know who it was, and so forth and so on. She figured this story would be the safest.

"I thought it was a smart move and told her so. She has my number so I told her to call if she heard anything from Cortez. She said she would.

"She told me to go out the back door, around the block, and up the other side to my car. 'I know Cortez, and he is probably watching to see if anyone comes out of the place,' she told me.

"Then I left and came over here." Jewel took in a deep breath and sat down.

"We've done everything we can and got the information into the hands of someone we are pretty sure will do the right thing with it. Thank you, Jewel." John gave her one of his charming smiles.

Richard leaned forward in his chair. "I also sent a copy of the recording and counterfeiting information to your FBI contact, Dan, in case Cortez drops the ball or puts it into the wrong hands."

"That's great." Dan turns to speak to Morgan, but he's gone. "Where'd Morgan go?"

"Oh no!" I ran to the front door and pulled it open. We heard a car fire up and peel out.

"He's gone to get his family. They'll kill him!" I cried.

"Mariah, you stay here. Come on, John. You and Richard come with me." Dan grabbed his gun. "Let's go be his back up. He's going to need it."

John followed Dan to the front door with Richard following.

"I'm coming too. Come on Norela, we can help."

Norela glanced between Jewel and me, unsure she wanted to leave me alone.

"Come on, then. Take your car and follow us." Richard waved his arm in a 'come on' motion as he stepped out the door behind John.

"I know the way. I'll come in from the south; you go in from the north. Maybe we can intercept Morgan and come up with a reasonable plan before he gets there." Norela followed Jewel out the door.

We could hear Uncle John's response from the walkway. "That's a good idea."

Before closing the door behind her, Norela told me she was sorry. "Don't worry, we'll be back soon."

I was a nervous wreck waiting to hear something. Left alone with my own thoughts and worries, my mind raced. I went to the kitchen to get something to eat. My stomach was queasy with concern, and I bolted for the bathroom, bile rising in my throat.

I fell to the floor and sobbed. I was so tired of this—my life in danger, my family's and friends' lives in danger, and our futures on the brink of destruction—and I missed Paisley.

I was worried about her. She was just a little dog—probably a nuisance to the people holding Morgan's family. Only Molly, Mia, and Max were there to keep Paisley safe—keep their captors from killing her or throwing her out to get run over. Morgan's family—they're like my own—may not be able to stop them from hurting Paisley.

I was okay when the others were around; we lifted each other up and supported each other. We were always collaborating to figure out a solution, and that helped to relieve the stress. At this particular moment, it felt hopeless.

I reasoned myself out of my bout of self-pity and fear. I went downstairs to wait. One of my biggest stress relievers is to cook, but I didn't know when they would be back or how many would be returning.

As I reached the foot of the stairs, the front door opened and Uncle John came in. He walked over to me and took me in his arms.

"I'm sorry, honey. For a moment, we didn't think about what you were going through. With Jewel and Norela helping, I told Dan to let me out a mile down the road and I walked back to be with you. Everything is going to be fine, I can feel it."

I sighed and squeezed him tight.

"Plus," he continued, "Dan told me while we were in the car that he was turning to tell Morgan about a dream he had."

"Another one?" My question was muffled in the enclosure of his arms.

"Yes. Morgan's family were back in their home with him at the dining room table, laughing. You know how Dan's dreams are so often prophetic."

I nodded as the tears fell from my eyes onto John's shoulder. Then I pushed myself away, wiped my eyes, and smiled at him.

"I'm really glad you came back. I was going crazy with worry."

"I know. Let's play a game of cards while we wait."

I grabbed the deck of cards, and we decided to play something light and childish. We started a game of *Go Fish* and laughed at each other.

Darkness came and still no word from anyone. John kept telling me everything would be alright, but I was becoming more concerned with each passing hour. It was after midnight when Richard and Dan came in the front door.

I met them in the front hall. "Where's Morgan? Where's Norela, and Jewel?"

Richard took me by the shoulders and stared into my eyes. "Morgan and Jewel were captured. He was ushering his family out the back gate, and when we started into the alley to help them, two goons came out of the darkness and grabbed Morgan. They told the family they would kill him if they didn't all go back into the house."

I groaned and crumbled to my knees. Uncle Richard reached down and lifted me. He guided me to a chair and made me sit.

"We waited around to see if we could get a take on the situation, and twenty minutes after taking Morgan, they escorted him out the front door and into a black SUV with dark windows. Jewel followed them in Norela's car.

I wiped my eyes and nodded.

Richard stepped back and Dan came to me. He gripped my shoulder. "We were going to try to get the family back out, but it was too heavily guarded."

Norela came in the front door carrying Paisley. I rushed to her almost knocking over Uncle Dan in my rush. I took Paisley into my arms and started hugging her and talking to her. I tried examining her little wiggling form. "Oh, poor little girl, you're so skinny. Have they been treating you right? Were they feeding you?"

I glanced up to the others in the room. "I don't think they've been feeding her. I need to go get some food. She's starving."

Paisley squirmed around in my arms, kissing my face and arms and hands and sniffing me all over.

"Oh, thank you, Norela. How did you get her?"

"When Morgan was ushering his family out of the gate, Paisley came out too, but when the goons jumped out of the bushes, she took off down the alley in my direction. I was hiding beside a dumpster, and when she ran by me, I reached out and snagged her. She yelped and tried to get away, but I held fast, and she settled down. I figured she was your dog."

"She is. Thank you. I've been so worried about her."

"I'm glad I was able to get her for you."

"Me too. You just made my day." Still holding Paisley, I turned to Richard and Dan.

"Did you find where they took Morgan?"

Paisley rested her head on my shoulder, one front paw around the right side of my neck, the other around the left side in a hug. She sighed, content to be with me.

"Yes," Dan said. "They took him to some abandoned offices outside of Old Town. He was bound and I assume gagged with a hood over his head. There were goons posted at all exits to the building, and we couldn't get any closer."

"Jewel tried to take out two guards at the door in the alley, and they took her too." Richard shook his head. "We decided to come back here and come up with a new plan."

"Give me the keys to your car," John said holding his hand out.

"Why? Where are you going?" Dan asked.

"You just never mind about that. Give me the keys and the address where they have Morgan and Jewel."

"No, not until you—"

"Dan!" John used that voice he has that makes the hair at the back of your neck stand up.

"Give! Me! The keys! I'm going to take care of this. You two stay here with Mariah. Norela, I would like you to come with me."

"John, you can't take them alone. I'm telling you," Dan said in a pleading tone.

"I'm as good as you are, Uncle John. Let me go with you," I said.

"No, Mariah. Norela and I will handle this. And Dan, don't worry about it. I know what I'm doing."

"Let him go." Richard rested his hand on Dan's shoulder. "He knows what he's doing, and Mariah needs us here."

"Then you stay here. I'm going with John."

"Nope, not happening Dan. If I have to choke you out until you're unconscious, you're staying here." John gave his 'don't mess with me' glare, took Norela's hand and walked to the door.

"I don't want Mariah left alone again. If something happens to me, she needs both of you. We'll be back."

"Be careful, Uncle John," I called after him.

He looked back at me as he opened the door, and grinned. "Everything is going to be fine my sweet niece. Trust me."

"I do. See you soon."

I stood staring at the door after he pulled it closed behind Norela and then looked at Richard and Dan.

"He knows what he's doing, Uncle Dan. I don't know why, but he needs you and Uncle Richard to stay out of it for right now. It's going to be okay. Don't ask me how. I just know it."

"You're right. I know better, but my adrenaline was pumping, and I didn't want him to go off and get taken as well. I wasn't thinking about who I was talking to."

Richard put his arm around my shoulders, guided me into the living room, and sat me down in the camp chair. Paisley squirmed out of my arms and started investigating the place.

I jumped up. "I've got to get some water down for Paisley. We don't have any food for her, and she looks like she's hungry."

"I'll go out and get some, but I have to eat first. I'm starving." Dan started for the kitchen.

"Me, too," Richard added cheerfully in an attempt to lighten the mood in the room. "Let's have some sandwiches and chips. Do we have enough for grilled cheese?"

"I think so." I went to the kitchen with Paisley following close on my heels.

As I started getting the stuff for the sandwiches together, Richard pulled out chips, and Dan started a pot of coffee.

"Good idea on the coffee. I don't think any of us want to sleep until we hear from someone." Richard's voice was rough and raspy from exhaustion.

We worked at putting together a midnight meal and took our paper plates of food to the living room. Dan told me to take the camp chair, but I shook my head and sat cross-legged on the floor, Paisley at my side. Richard took the camp stool in front of his makeshift desk with all the computer equipment, and Dan took the camp chair when I refused it.

The situation was heavy on all our minds. It was like the elephant in the room none of us wanted to talk about so dinner was quiet. I gathered the paper plates when we finished, gave Paisley any scraps that were left, and cleaned up the kitchen.

Richard came into the kitchen carrying my coffee cup and his, and asked if I wanted a refill. I did. After filling both cups, we went back to the living room and started a game of blackjack, while Dan went to the store for supplies.

"Don't you dare go looking for John or Morgan and Jewel," I admonished him as he was walking out the door.

"No worries, darlin'. I'll be right back."

Dan was back within the hour loaded with groceries: ice for the chest, cheese, eggs, milk, oatmeal, cold cereal, chips, cookies, ground beef and chili mix, beer (now I knew he was really stressed because he seldom drinks), and food for Paisley.

"Why'd you get so much food? It looks like you're stocking up for a siege."

"I bought enough for Morgan's family. We'll need it when John gets back with them."

"Oh, good thinking."

I helped him unpack and put everything away. I put some food down for Paisley, who sniffed it, took a drink of water, and sat down in front of me. She stared up at me as if to say, "isn't it bedtime?"

I reached down and picked her up, nuzzled her and whispered, "Come on little girl. I'll fix you a bed next to me in the living room."

It was a very long night filled with anxiety. We settled into a game of spades while Paisley slept beside me, and we waited.

At five, I threw the cards down. "I can't play anymore. I can't concentrate so I'm going up to my room to lie down. Hopefully I can get a little sleep."

"That's a good idea." Dan stood. "I'm ready to lie down, too."

"Sweet dreams you two. I'm going to camp out down here. If anyone comes in, they'll wake me if I'm asleep and I'll get you both."

I nodded and moved toward the stairs watching Paisley. Her head popped up and she spied me as I took another step.

"Come on, Paisley. Let's go to bed." The fourteen pound bundle of white fur jumped up and followed me up the stairs. I knelt down on my sleeping bag and patted it for her to join me before lying down. Paisley snuggled up against me and I closed my eyes. I didn't expect to fall asleep but with the comfort of Paisley's presence, I thankfully slipped into blessed, dreamless slumber.

I woke to the sun shining into the window and as soon as I moved to check the time on my watch, Paisley jumped up and ran to the door where she waited for me. It was five after seven and my thoughts went to Morgan and the rest of those I cared about who were in a dangerous situation.

Paisley followed me into the bathroom and waited while I freshened up for the day, and then she raced down the stairs and to the back door to go out.

Jerry put up a brand new fence around the backyard before we moved in. It was a six foot tall, pine board fence—sturdy with no gaps between the boards or at ground level. This was in preparation of selling the property. Because of the fence, I wasn't worried about leaving Paisley in the yard alone.

Richard and Dan were already up and talking quietly in the living room. I poured myself a cup of fresh hot coffee and grabbed a donut that Dan bought the night before. I stepped into the living room.

"Still nothing, I suppose?"

"No. We were discussing taking a trip to see if we could learn anything new. I don't think

I can sit around here much longer." Dan grimaced and shook his head.

"Hmm." I took a sip of my coffee. "I know what you mean. I'm about half crazy ... never was all that patient to begin with. What do you think, Uncle Richard?"

"I think we ought to give it until noon. If we haven't heard anything by then, the three of us should go together and stay together. Paisley should stay here. She would be safer, and you'd be less distracted."

"Good. I'm going upstairs to clean up. Will you keep an eye on Paisley? She's in the backyard."

"Sure will." Richard rose. "I'm going out back to run through some exercises. You want to join me, Dan?"

"Sure."

"Oh, that sounds great. I'll join you too, and then I'll get cleaned up. I don't know why I didn't think of this. It will help work out my muscles from the stress."

At eleven fifty, we were getting ready to head out when John walked through the front door all smiles, his left arm slung over Jewel's shoulder. Behind him were Norela and Max, and following were Morgan—one arm across

Mia's shoulders, the other around Molly's waist. None of them looked any the worse for wear. I gave silent thanks.

We crowded around hugging each other, talking and laughing when, to Richard's, Dan's, and my surprise, in walked Cortez, Joy, and Nylla.

"Well ... I can see we have a lot to talk about." Dan grinned.

"We sure do," Morgan said with a huge smile and a wink at me.

"Come on in and find a place to sit down everyone." I stood at the front door with Paisley in my arms as everyone moved into the living room. "Does anyone want something to drink? Dan went out last night and loaded us up on groceries. If you're hungry I can whip something up."

"Yes, but let's wait. I can't wait for you to hear what's been going on and what your Uncle John did." Cortez clapped Uncle John on the shoulder.

We crowded into the living room and sat wherever we could find a place. I sat on the floor where I sat the night before, expecting Paisley to climb into her makeshift bed beside me. Instead, happy to see the rest of the family, she went to each of them, tail wagging a hundred miles an hour, sniffing them and kissing their hands before finally settling down beside me.

**********

"**I** can't wait to hear what you did, John," Dan said.

"I knew this situation had gotten too big for our little group to handle, and we all knew Cortez, Joy, and Nylla were on our side. I took Norela and went to Cortez. I explained the whole thing to him and asked for his help." John glanced over at Cortez.

"That's right. The recording and information you guys got to me was invaluable. I got it to the people who could end this farce of an administration in the FBI. We were getting ready to take down Newton Marshall, Gordon Morris, and the Andersens this morning not to mention the rest of the dirty FBI and police.

"When John showed up at my door and filled me in on everything, I called my boss with the DEA. He helped us put together a detail from the correct agencies to go in, rescue the family, Morgan, and Jewel, and take down the whole kit and caboodle."

"Norela and I were allowed to attend the raid on the place where they were holding Morgan and Jewel, but we had to stay back and not get involved. The main thing is we were there when Morgan and Jewel came out." John grinned.

"Everyone looks to be okay, at least. I was really worried that Morgan was taking another beating like the last time he was held captive. And Jewel, I couldn't imagine what you might have been going through." I shook my head.

"They weren't going to beat us up. They were going to start cutting off body parts until we gave you up," Morgan said.

"I figured I was done for once they grabbed me. All I could think about was my family and making sure they would be safe, so I told them I would cooperate as long as they didn't hurt any of them.

"Molly and the kids were frantic when they got us back into the house. I tried to reassure them everything would be fine.

"They had me tied up, but they allowed me to talk to Molly and the kids, and for them to hug me under watchful eyes. After the little reunion, they gagged me and put a hood over my head. They took me out the front door and I could hear the kids sobbing as the door closed behind me. That just about killed me, but they assured me none of them would be hurt if I went without a fight.

"Once in the vehicle, they took me to an abandoned office building. They sat me in a chair in what turned out to be an office without windows and only one door, situated in the middle of a second floor office space. Once they had me seated, they unbound my wrists and tied each forearm to the arm of the chair and tied my legs to the front legs of the chair before taking off the hood and removing the gag.

"As they finished tying me up there was a commotion in the outer lobby. After a few moments, two more goons brought Jewel into the room, kicking and screaming." Morgan grunted a laugh. "It took some effort before they got her into a chair and bound to it in the same manner I was." He shook his head with a wry smile. He cut his eyes over to Jewel. "She's a fighter!

"Other than that, they were very civilized in their treatment of us, but they were adamant that I give you up. They said they would not accept the information from Jewel and that it had to come from me."

"They could have mutilated me. I was not going to give you up Mariah," Jewel interjected.

"They informed us they were not going to rough us up, and if we cooperated with them, they would make our deaths quick, but if we didn't, they were going to remove one body part at a time until I broke.

"They laid out their plan of torture succinctly. First they were going to start with me, one finger joint at a time. When they snipped off what remained of one finger, they would move on to the next. If I hadn't complied by the time they finished all my fingers, they were going to make me watch them do the same thing to Jewel."

At the telling of this story, Molly, Max, and Mia sat sobbing. Morgan reached his right arm over Molly's shoulders and rested his hand on Max's shoulder. With his left arm, he drew Mia close to him. Molly leaned into Morgan and held Max's hand in hers.

"They had my left little finger in the snipper at the end joint when Joy came in with guns blazing. She took out the goon who was about to do me damage—none too soon either. They had Jewel at gun-point to force her to watch the mutilation, and Nylla took that guy out. I've got to say, I'm sure glad I didn't lose any appendages, but there was no way on earth I was going to tell them where to find you Mariah. I knew that talking wouldn't save me or my family."

"Oh my God, Morgan. Sounds like the cavalry got there just in the nick of time." I dropped my face into the palms of my hands and sobbed.

"While that team was taking down the abandoned office building, I was with the team that was taking the house where they were holding the family," Cortez said.

"We hadn't been threatened or abused in any way, but I don't know how long that would have lasted." Molly glanced at me as I wiped my eyes.

"They kept up the pretense that we were in an FBI safe house and they were looking for you and Morgan for your own safety. Once you two left the house, the radios and televisions were removed from the house. We were told the case was dragging on longer than they planned and the cost was getting too high.

"I became suspicious even though I didn't let on to anyone, not even the kids. Now we know they didn't want us to see or hear any news. They knew if I heard about you two being wanted for crimes in Idaho, I would know they were not the good guys." Molly's voice was choked. She smiled up at Morgan with unshed tears sparkling in her eyes.

"This was all about the phone and the counterfeiting." Cortez smiled at me. "They didn't want to take a chance that you checked the messages on the phone and figured out the scheme, so they were going to kill you, then Morgan because he was helping you, then Jewel because she got involved, etc."

"Now what?" Dan asked.

"We go home," Morgan said and turned to me. "You can stay with us until you figure out what you're going to do about your home, Mariah, but for all intents and purposes, it's over."

Tears in my eyes made me see prisms around everyone in the room, and I got choked up. "I'm so glad," I managed to squeeze out. "You mean there won't be any charges against us for bugging Nylla's and Marshall's homes, or escaping protective custody, or the stuff in Idaho?"

"No!" Joy glanced at Cortez. "No one but those of us in this room knows where that tape recording and the information on the Andersen's came from, and Nylla isn't going to press charges. She's as thankful as I am for the help you gave us. As far as Idaho, we know those were trumped-up charges, and since you weren't really in protective custody but were instead being held hostage, you didn't escape protective custody. Besides, leaving protective custody isn't a crime unless you are under arrest at the time."

"Has Jim been released yet?" Morgan looked at Nylla with hope.

"Yes, he was released about an hour ago, and said to thank all of you for your help in getting him out. He's in debriefing now with the head of the western division."

"Any word on Riley?" It worried me that he hadn't been heard from.

Joy shook her head. "No. He seems to have vanished off the face of the earth. Jeri, too. We're afraid The Mongoose organization got to him and killed him and his wife. We may never find them."

"Oh no. I hope not." I was getting a headache from the emotional rollercoaster.

Uncle John put his arm around me. "I'm very saddened to hear that. I hope you're wrong about their status."

Everyone was quiet for a moment. Richard broke the silence. "So, we can pack up and leave today? ... Right now?"

"Yep!" Cortez nodded. "We'll even help you pack and load up if you like."

"No, that won't be necessary," Richard replied.

**********

After the agents left, Morgan and I gathered up our things and were saying goodbye to my uncles when Jerry arrived to check on us.

"It's over? Wow, that's great. I'm so relieved, Mariah. You can finally relax and get back to your life."

"Yes, I'm relieved too, but I have a lot of decisions to make now. I have to find a place to live, sort out all the insurance stuff, figure out what to do about my destroyed home, and on top of all that, make a decision about my career path."

"What?" Uncle Dan turned from helping Uncle Richard pack his computer equipment and stared at me.

"You have a career, dear," Uncle John said.

"But, Mariah ..." Morgan started.

"I know. I have my own thriving practice, but I don't know if I really want to go back to that. I was getting bored, and all of this brought back my love of the chase. The adrenaline rush is addictive, and I'm not sure I don't want to get back into law enforcement and working investigations."

"Give it some time, honey." Richard patted me on the shoulder. "At least six months. Get back into your practice and see if this craving is just part of the adrenaline rush. You can always decide to close your practice and go back into law enforcement later."

"I don't know what I'll do, but I think Uncle Richard is right. I need to give it some time. I have a lot to take care of in the meantime."

"Don't forget that I have rental property and would be happy to rent you a place, Mariah. I was going to sell this place, but if you want to rent it, we can work something out. In fact, I have a cute little house that will be available in two weeks. It's smaller than your house, but it's newly remodeled and has a big fenced backyard for Paisley. I think you would like it better than this place." Jerry raised his eyebrows in my direction.

"That sounds great, Jerry. Thanks. I would love to see it ... maybe tomorrow afternoon?"

"Sure. How about I pick you up at your office around twelve thirty? We could have lunch and then go check it out?"

"Perfect. I'll see you tomorrow afternoon, then."

"Jerry, we uh, really appreciate your help during this umm ... situation, and the use of your property." Uncle Dan scratched the stubble on his cheek. "Do you mind if my brothers and I stay here for a day or two longer? We want to make sure Mariah gets settled before we head home."

"Of course you can. I want to clean it up and put it on the market soon, but a few more days won't interfere with that."

"Good. Thank you. If anything comes up and we need to stay longer, we'll get a hotel room. It's just easier not to have to move everything for one or two days."

"No problem. I'll check back here in a couple of days then."

"Thank you."

We said our good-byes, hugging or shaking hands before I left with Morgan and the family, Paisley in my arms.

\*\*\*\*\*\*\*\*\*\*

# VII

It took six weeks before I had my life back on an even keel. The first thing I did was take a two-week hiatus to Texas with my uncles and to see my mom. While I was away, the insurance company settled my claims on the house and the car. When I got back from Texas, I reopened my practice and went back to work. I was still thinking of getting out of the forensic psychology field and doing something different.

Jewel offered me a partnership in her and Norela's practice, but my desire to leave Albuquerque and start over some place new was growing stronger by the day. I wasn't sure where I wanted to go, but I wanted to go somewhere I'd never been before—someplace beautiful, and a place where, to the best of my knowledge, The Mongoose's organization had not infiltrated. I wasn't sure exactly where that might be, but I was pretty certain I was going to leave New Mexico and leave the practice of forensic psychology.

The sweep this time was complete. Wade and LaRue Andersen were indicted on a number of charges, including conspiracy to commit counterfeiting, as was Newton Marshall. Marshall had evidence on Wade that he had been painting nudes of under-age girls, and Marshall had been holding that over Wade's head to get him to make the counterfeit plates.

Calvin Josephson was found to be innocent of any wrongdoing. He was duped by Mary and Romeo De Angelo and his marriage to Mary was a farce. The preacher Mary hired to perform their wedding was an actor; therefore, Josephson's marriage to Mary wasn't legal. The poor man was devastated at the news. So was his bank account by Mary and Romeo.

Romeo and Mary De Angelo were picked up on a yacht in the Pacific headed to Peru.

Tabatha, A.K.A. Little Darling, was placed in a foster home with Child Psychologists who can try to rehabilitate her. I had little hope for that child who showed no remorse for her behavior and exhibited signs of a true sociopath.

Judge Harvey was located in an abandoned warehouse—unharmed but very upset—once Craig Hites was arrested and started talking. The courthouse employees, who were involved in the false charges against Morgan and me, were arrested.

It seemed to be finally over, except for all the trials. Hopefully most of those arrested would plead guilty and save the government and the rest of us the cost and frustration of a jury trial. Time will tell.

Since almost all of my things had been destroyed in the explosion, the 1020-square-foot, two-bedroom, two-bath home Jerry had for rent was perfect for Paisley and me. We moved into it as soon as it was available. I replaced only the bare minimum that I needed to live comfortably and bought an old 2001 Toyota Corolla with 98,375 miles on it for fifteen hundred dollars. I banked the rest of my insurance money to use for my move or a new place depending on what I decided to do.

Jerry and I were back on friendly terms, and I had him over about once a week for dinner and a movie. He never approached me again about having a romantic relationship and seemed content, as was I, with the friendship we had.

One Saturday, after happily cleaning my humble little abode I was online looking for an established P.I. practice up for sale. I had a delicious brisket in the oven and fresh dinner rolls rising on the counter.

I found several practices for sale. One was in North Carolina called *Just the Facts*, and another in Pennsylvania called *P.I.'s Inc.*, but I didn't want to move east. There was one in Texas that was available, one in Baton

Rouge, Louisiana, and another in Portland, Oregon called *The Watchers: Investigation and Reporting*. I called the number to inquire about it and spoke with a Rand Larson.

"Hello, I'm calling to inquire about the P.I. practice that's for sale."

"Oh, yes. Let me get Mr. Larson for you. Just one moment please," a young woman stated before hold music started playing in my ear.

"Hello, this is Rand Larson. How may I help you?"

"Hi, Mr. Larson. My name is Mariah Jeffries and I'm looking for an established P.I. business to purchase and operate. I found your ad online. Could you tell me a little bit about your practice and what kind of cases you handle?"

"Sure. It's a small practice. I work mostly insurance fraud cases, some divorces, but I try to avoid those—they can get messy sometimes. Occasionally I'll pick up a criminal investigation from a defendant, but it's usually small-time stuff. Portland is a nice little city. It has its problems like any place, but it's not riddled with high crime. It's a diverse city with lots going on culturally. Have you ever been here?"

"No, but I've heard it's beautiful."

"It is. There's enough business and money here to make a living and even get ahead a little bit."

"May I ask why you're selling the practice?"

"I've been doing this for the last thirty years. My wife and I are ready to retire and do some travelling while we're young enough and healthy enough to enjoy it. Have you ever had a P.I. job before?"

"No, but I'm an ex-cop and currently have my own forensic psychology practice. Due to a series of events, I'm ready for a change of scenery and a change in career. This seems like the next logical step to me.

"The name of your company is *The Watchers*—plural. Do you have a partner or partners?"

"No," he said with a little chuckle. "I had aspirations that my son would join me when he got out of college, but it didn't work out that way. I never saw the need to change the name since it was established by then."

"Oh, I see. That must have been a big disappointment for you. What field did he go into?"

His voice became subdued. "I lost my son his junior year of college in a terrible automobile accident."

"I'm very sorry for your loss. I didn't mean to pry."

"Would you like to come out and see the city and the business ... and talk about it in more detail?"

"Yes! I would very much like to come to Portland and check it out. When would be a good time for you?"

"Anytime is good for me. Just let me know when to expect you, and I'll clear my calendar."

"One more question, please."

"Sure."

"If I bought your business, would you be around long enough to teach me the ropes and help me get my feet under me?"

"We could negotiate that."

"Great. Thank you, Mr. Larson. I'll be in touch."

I googled Portland, Oregon, and got a little information about the city and its demographics. Seemed like a nice enough place. The crime rate is no better or worse than most large cities.

Jerry arrived for dinner at six that evening. I had prepared, for our dining delight, the best brisket in Albuquerque (if I must say so myself), a beautiful spinach and strawberry salad, baked beans, and homemade dinner rolls, along with my favorite Pinot Noir. I told Jerry about the business in Portland, Oregon.

"What? You're leaving?"

"Yes." I gave him a little pout. "I need to move on. I'm not happy here anymore. I'm constantly looking over my shoulder, and I'm really burned out as a forensic psychologist. I feel the need to relocate to someplace new and start all over with a new career."

Jerry's face turned red with rage. He stood in a rush knocking his chair over and banged his fist on the table making the wine glasses jump. He started shouting at me.

"NO! I won't let you leave. I won't let you get away with it anymore."

"Calm down, Jerry." I rose from my chair and walked around the table to stand before him. I didn't understand his reaction. I frowned.

"You won't let me get away with *what* anymore?"

"You'll see. I'll show you." He slammed his fist into my face. I didn't feel the pain at first because of the shock, but it didn't take long for my broken nose to scream at me.

Blood gushed and ran down my face. I shoved Jerry against the wall and he fell. I ran to the bathroom. Jerry regained his balance and followed close behind me. I slammed the door and locked it. He rattled the doorknob, banged on the door, and called to me, asking me to open up. He apologized through the door saying he wouldn't hurt me again.

I grabbed a clean hand towel, wet it, and held it to my nose, my head back, and yelled for him to leave before I called the police.

"I'm sorry, Mariah. I'm so sorry. I just lost my head. I was shocked. I don't want you to leave. Please forgive me and let's talk."

"No. Ged oudda here. Ged oud, Jawy."

"I'm sorry. I'll leave for now, but we need to talk about this. I'll leave and we can talk later, okay?"

"Yeah sure."

I heard him move from the bathroom door, his keys rattle, and the front door open.

He called out, "Bye, Mariah. I'm really sorry." I heard the front door close.

I waited in the bathroom for a while, trying to get the bleeding to stop and listening for him to come back in. I needed to get my phone from the kitchen and call Morgan.

I was rattled. I couldn't think clearly. How did this happen?

I couldn't breathe through my nose and my eyes were starting to swell. I eased the bathroom door open and peaked around the facing. All was quiet except Paisley who was howling and barking at the back door. She wanted in and I wanted her with me.

I moved through the living room toward the kitchen. Just as I entered the doorway to the dining room, I caught a glimpse of Jerry out of the corner of my eye. He was prepared, I wasn't. He struck me in my right thigh with an old bat I kept in the corner of the living room.

At impact, I heard the femur snap and I could feel the bone shift, one end of the break sliding up along-side the other end. The pain was excruciating—not like anything I had ever experienced before—and I fell to the floor screaming and writhing in pain.

As I fell, I saw Paisley in a frenzy snarling and barking. She was jumping at the door trying to get to me.

Jerry grabbed my right arm and jerked me up, sitting me down hard in one of the chairs at the table.

"Shut your trap," he yelled putting his hand over my mouth. My nose was already closed off. He was smothering me.

I shook my head, trying to get a breath of air, but I couldn't. I lost consciousness.

**********

When I came to, I was in the trunk of a car moving over what felt and sounded like a dirt or gravel road. It was a rough ride, and I was still in excruciating pain. My hands were tied behind my back. I guessed my ankles were tied together too, but I couldn't tell from the pain in my leg. Every time I tried to move my feet, I thought I would pass out. Every movement of the car sent waves of pain and nausea through me.

I tried to concentrate on trying to pick up sounds outside the car, or the number of turns and the direction, but my head was pounding, my face hurt, and my leg was screaming pain so loud I couldn't think.

The last thing I remembered before waking up in the cabin was the car skidding and then hitting a deep rut or something in the road. I bounced off the floor of the trunk and landed back down hard on my broken leg and hit my head. I lost consciousness again.

I must have been unconscious for quite a while. Jerry slapping my face brought me around. I found myself tied up to an old wooden office chair in Jerry's rustic hunting shack up in the hills above Albuquerque. My left leg was tied to the leg of the chair and my forearms were tied to the arms, much as I imagined Morgan had been tied up when they were going to cut his fingers off. I started whimpering in pain again, and when I looked up Jerry's face came into focus. He was bent over at the waist staring at me.

"Oh, look who's decided to wake up." His voice was different—snide ... cold and unfeeling. I could tell all reason had left him. He was in a rage like I've never seen before.

He slapped me hard across the face.

"Jawy," I sobbed. "You broke my yeg. I need to go to the hothpital. Pleathe, help mbe."

"I'll help you, you selfish, arrogant whore. I'll help you die."

"Why? Whad I ever do to you?"

"You don't even have a clue, do you? You have no idea what you've done to me and how you've ruined my life."

He started to cry and sat down in the chair in front of me, his hands over his face. When he dropped his hands and raised his eyes to mine, his face was twisted and distorted with sheer hate. I could see murder in his eyes and for the first time in my life I was truly terrified.

"You've spent your whole adult life looking for and wondering who set the fire that killed your father." He was calm now—it was a cold, dispassionate calm. "Do you really want to know who it was, Mariah? Do you really want to know the truth?"

*Oh, my God. Please tell me he hasn't known all this time.*"

"Pleathe Jawy ... taw mbe you han't known ah dis time." I couldn't say more. I couldn't pronounce my words right. He was looking at me like I was a science experiment.

He smiled. It was a smile of cold pity, his eyes devoid of life.

"Your father, the renowned Officer Jeffries— the esteemed firefighter who couldn't help but investigate every fire he ever worked and find the cause or the arsonist. He was warned off a warehouse fire in the shipping district of Dallas by his chief. Do you want to know why, my dear?"

Jerry glared at me with his now cold, lifeless eyes.

I nodded and choked back a sob.

"Because the fire was set by Compton. An employee at the warehouse snitched to the cops about some smuggling. The fire was payback. Because of that snitch several of Compton's transport drivers were arrested. The chief wasn't in on the arson, but he knew not to mess with Compton. He knew Officer Jeffries was getting in over his head and tried to warn him off. *We* knew Officer Jeffries wouldn't listen."

I sniffled. "Doe you're teying mbe Conton set da fire?"

"Yes, in a manner of speaking. Compton was informed that your father would be on duty that night. Your father was a big thorn in Franklin's side. There was a woman who was making trouble for Franklin too. Franklin wanted her shut up, so Compton tied her up and torched the place.

"She wasn't gagged and your father heard her screaming for help. Being the big hero he was, he couldn't resist another headline. Franklin and Compton knew he wouldn't resist running to the rescue and it was fixed so when he did, he would never return."

"Tank you for teying mbe. I'm gyad I had a part in putting Conton behind bars..." I groaned.

Jerry jumped up, and waving his arms, he screamed, "HE WAS MY FATHER!" He swung with his right fist in a wide arc connecting to the left side of my head knocking me and the chair over on our side.

My head banged against the wooden plank floor, my little finger was crushed by the arm of the chair, and my broken leg screamed with added pain. My mind was racing as I tried unsuccessfully not to cry out.

"Who was your fadder, Jawy? What did I haff to do wiff him?" I tried to control my sobs.

"Compton! Jerry Compton was my father. You and Morgan sent him to prison where he was executed. He was my *father*, my best friend, and a good man. He was framed. You and Morgan created a bunch of false evidence and sent him to that prison where he was fried. I've wanted to pay you back for years, but I fell in love with you."

He combed his fingers through his hair and looked away from me. He sat back down in the chair across from me and started weeping.

"Your fadder? Your nange's not Conton. What do you mbean, he wath your fadder? Your nange is Fowyer."

"That's right, Mariah." He wiped his eyes.

"I had to change my name when my dad was convicted and sent to prison. I took my mother's maiden name and changed schools. I lost my scholarship, moved away from home to Albuquerque and enrolled in a management degree program. I would have been a great lawyer, but you ruined that for me. I would never have been able to get into a law school after you ruined my life. NEVER!!!"

He kicked me hard in the gut before he righted the chair with me in it. I was gasping to get a breath but passed out.

I was brought back to consciousness with a bucket of cold water in my face and a hard slap that wrenched my neck.

"Oh, Mariah, don't you dare try to sleep through the best part of this. I'm going to give you what you gave my father. I want you to know the real truth first, and then I'm going to watch your face as you die."

He went to the corner of the little cabin and pulled out a small galvanized tub. He untied my left leg and raised it, dropping my foot in the tub. He then raised my right foot, the pain racing through me from the broken femur. I wanted to scream from the pain, but I couldn't get enough breath and whimpered instead. He dropped my right foot into the tub, and again the pain was searing and jolting.

"My life was ruined when you stole my father away from me. We were more than father and son—we were best friends. We did everything together. He taught me how to be a real man, and he supported me in everything I chose to pursue.

"Because of you he was sent to the pen, and because of you he fried. Now I'm going to fry you.

"Too bad you didn't return my love, Mariah. You could have avoided all this, but *NOOOO!* You think you're too *good* for me."

He methodically poured water into the tub, one gallon jug at a time, until my feet were covered up to my ankles.

"I said 'In a manner of speaking' when you asked if Jerry Compton set the fire that killed your dad. It's true; it was Jerry Compton, but not my father. You see, dear Mariah. It was me. I'm the arson you have been looking for all your adult life. I've been right here, under your *sniveling* nose." He kicked the chair in front of me out of the way.

"Franklin paid my college tuition in payment for my work. Now I get to finish the job and end the great Jeffries lineage. I'm going to put you to rest too.

"Don't go anywhere, Mariah. The fun is just about to start." He stepped behind me and it sounded like he opened the cabin door. I heard a generator start up, and the end of a long extension cord came flying in, bounced off the rim of the tub, and hit the floor.

He walked in without closing the door and stepped in front of me.

I was crying from the pain, and I tried to plead with him. I hated that I was begging for my life but I didn't want to die.

With a perverse calm, he bent toward me, his face close to mine.

"My father was beaten repeatedly by the guards before they executed him. Now it's your turn."

He started wailing on my face, my head, and my upper body—left punch, right punch, left punch. The chair was rocking and he had to grab it several times to keep it from tipping over. My eyes were swollen closed and my jaw was broken—or at least it felt like it. I bit my tongue and blood was gushing again—running across my chin and down the back of my throat choking me. The last blow tipped the chair back and it fell.

I hit the back of my head on the floor. Jerry kicked me in the side before righting me and the chair. He put my feet back in the vat of water.

I could barely see him through the slits of my eyes. He bent over and plugged something into the extension cord. I couldn't tell what it was.

He stood up straight before me.

"Time to say goodbye, Mariah."

I was gasping for breath and choking on my own blood. I was resigned to the fact that I was going to die in that filthy cabin, beaten and electrocuted. I closed my eyes and waited for the pain to finally end. Nothing happened. Through the loud buzzing in my ears, I heard a thud and tried to force my eyes open.

Through slits in my swollen face, I saw Jerry laying in front of me, slumped against the wall, a single, bloody, round hole in his forehead between his eyes. Brain matter and pieces of skull were splattered against the wall in front of me. I passed out.

**********

Four days later I woke up in a hospital room. Morgan was asleep in the chair next to my bed. I guess the pain brought me out of my drug-induced sleep, because it was pretty bad and I started moaning. Morgan jumped up from his chair and came to the bed. He grabbed the call button and started pushing for a nurse.

"How ya doing?" he asked me with genuine concern on his face.

I shook my head and moaned again.

"Try not to talk. Your jaw's been cracked and the doctors want you to keep still while it heals."

The nurse came in with a hypodermic and shot some wonderful drug into the IV tubing. Within a few minutes I was feeling sweet relief and floating on a cloud.

When I woke again, Molly was in Morgan's chair watching me.

"How you doing, sweetie? We've all been worried sick about you."

I nodded and tried to smile. "The drugs have been good," I croaked out.

"You'll be getting more." She called for the nurse. I was soon relieved of my pain again.

The next time I woke, Molly was walking into the room.

"How long have I been in here?"

"This is day ten."

"I thought I was a goner."

"Just be quiet and we'll talk when you can say more. Try to rest and I'll let the nurse know you're awake again." She pushed the magic button and I was soon gone.

Eventually I woke and no one was keeping vigil over me. It hurt to move so I stared up at the ceiling and waited.

Jeri walked in and rushed to my bedside. "You're awake. I'm so relieved. We've all been terribly worried." She took my hand and smiled down at me.

I started crying. "Jeri. You're alive." I groaned from the pain of trying to speak.

"Yes. Of course I'm alive. Riley wouldn't let anything happen to me."

"I'm glad. I was worried about you. How's Riley? We thought y'all were dead."

"Shush! He's fine, honey. You're going to be fine, too. Riley and Morgan will be here a little later to fill you in on what you missed."

Jeri pushed the call button for a nurse. "Do you need anything? Water? Anything?"

I smiled and quipped, "A cheeseburger and sweet potato fries with a large IV infusion of coffee, please." I tried to laugh before my dry throat stuck together and I started coughing, which caused my rib cage to hurt.

"Water would be great instead," I finally croaked.

After a couple sips, I laid my head back down and closed my eyes. The small exchange with Jeri had taken everything out of me. I was suddenly exhausted and couldn't keep my eyes open.

It wasn't until the next morning I awoke to find Riley standing beside my bed. "Wake up, slacker." He grinned.

Peeking my still-swollen eyes open I asked, "Who's the slacker, buster? You're the one who disappeared."

"I'm the one who saved you in that cabin."

---

"Really? How did you find me?" I winced but didn't wait for a reply. "Tell me what happened. I was ready to welcome death because of the pain." I started coughing and Riley gave me a couple sips of water.

"Thanks." I laid my head back and groaned. "Auuugh. I hurt all over." I was exhausted again and closed my eyes for a moment.

"I'll let you rest," Riley said. I groaned and told him to stay.

"How bad is the break in my leg, and what are my other injuries? Am I going to have any permanent damage from the beating?"

"Whoa, girl. I can only answer one question at a time." He raised his hands in a defensive motion trying to ward off the questions.

Morgan came into the room and stepped up to the foot of my bed with a vase of beautiful mixed flowers, tied with a big, yellow ribbon.

"Who'd you steal those from?" I quipped.

"Ha ha." He smiled. "I'm glad to see you awake. Your allotment of scaring the bejesus out of me has hit its maximum limit. You're not allowed to do that anymore."

I smiled back the best I could. "I hope to never frighten you with my safety again."

Jeri and Molly walked in and came up next to my bed across from Riley. Molly took the flowers from Morgan and set them on the counter.

"Thanks for the flowers, everyone. They're beautiful." I looked at Riley. "What happened? How did you find me?"

"Are you up to it right now?"

"Oh yes, please fill me in, and I'll try my best to stay awake."

"Okay, I'll fascinate you with my story." Riley grinned. It was wide and beautiful.

"Story away. I can't wait to hear it."

**********

"When your place was bombed and Jim tried to reach me, he left me a cryptic voice message stating the madness wasn't over and to watch my back. I tucked Jeri away in a peaceful little hamlet in the south of France and came back under an alias I bought in Paris. I followed Jim's arrest and yours and Morgan's false charges. I kept an eye on Morgan's family and was prepared to slaughter the whole house of thugs if one member of that family was harmed. I tried to keep up with as much of it as I could, but I didn't have the resources, and I didn't want to trust anyone with the knowledge I was in the country.

"When you and your *'gang'* managed to get everything wrapped up, I decided to stay incognito for a while. I spent the last few weeks keeping an eye on things and making sure it was really over. I didn't know who to trust anymore and wanted to keep all of you safe.

"I saw you spending a lot of time with that creep, and I had a gut feeling he was up to something, but nothing happened. I was just about to give it up and bring Jeri home, when I decided to break into his house and do a thorough search first."

"Why was everyone except me able to see him for what he really was ... a twisted and hate filled monster?" I turned my gaze on each person in the room.

"You were too close to him, Mariah. And he genuinely cared about you. That's what you saw." Morgan rubbed the top of my foot and gave it a gentle squeeze.

"Have you ever been to his house?" Riley asked.

"Yes, of course. It's usually kind of messy but not dirty and a nice enough place in general."

"Were you ever allowed in the back bedroom?"

"Uh, no. I never had a reason to go in there. Besides, he kept it locked. I asked about it one time, and he told me he had a lot of old family heirlooms—mostly old furniture and bric-a-brac stuff that he hated but couldn't part with for sentimental reasons. Why?"

"It was ugly, girl. He'd been stalking you for years ... since your cop days. There were all kinds of pictures of you plastered all over the walls, some of them mutilated. There were reams of paper with notes about your activities, habits, friends, and there were diaries full of fantasies about you—all kinds of fantasies, including ways he wanted to kill you. It sent chills up and down my spine, and I knew beyond a shadow of a doubt you were in eminent danger.

Everything from the cabin started rushing back at me. I began to cry ... loud wracking sobs and hiccups.

Jeri patted my left knee. "I'm sorry, honey, but you need to know this."

I could only nod and try to get my tears under control.

"Then I came across another diary. This one was about his father. He blamed you for his father's death."

I couldn't stop sobbing but I heard what Riley was saying and nodded. I knew what he was going to tell me, but I couldn't get the words out that I already knew.

"Riley, stop. You're upsetting her." Morgan put his hand on Riley's shoulder.

"Na ... na ... nooo," I sobbed. "Pa ... lee ... ease go ... oh ... oooon."

Riley nodded. "I headed straight to your place, Mariah, but I didn't get there in time. I'm sorry I didn't get there sooner. I'm so sorry." He was shaking his head, his eyes filling with tears.

He took a deep breath and wiped his eyes. "As I rounded the corner at the end of your block, I saw him open his trunk with you slung over his shoulder like a sack of potatoes. He tossed your body in and slammed the trunk closed.

"I was so stunned I sat there in my truck in the middle of the street with the engine idling. I think he snapped. He wasn't afraid of someone seeing him.

"I watched him get in behind the wheel and drive off. He didn't even look around to see if anyone was watching. He was demented, Mariah." Riley shook his head and sighed. "Anyway, I would have called for back-up, but I didn't have a phone or radio, and I wasn't about to let him get away with you, so I followed.

"I lost him on the dirt road up to the cabin. I hung back a ways so he wouldn't know he was being followed, and I lost him, so I got out of my truck and started listening.

"I heard the engine of his car and followed that sound and his tire tracks on foot before I lost the sound of his engine again. I didn't know if he turned it off or if the sound was out of range. His tire tracks were distinctive enough I could follow them, so I did."

I got my crying under control, but I couldn't speak. I kept nodding that I understood.

"When I found the trail where his tire tracks turned off the rutted dirt road I'd been on, I followed. After about eighty yards I could see the cabin through the trees.

"Good thing I grabbed my sniper rifle when I left my truck. I sighted in and saw him pounding on you. When he stopped and stood up straight, I had a clean sight on him and put a single round right between his eyes dropping him once and for all."

I was sobbing again and blubbered my thanks.

"Thank you so much. I was certain my life was over and I didn't want to die. Thank you, Riley." I looked around the room through the tears in my eyes at those I loved and who loved me.

"Thank you, all of you. I love you so much." I settled my gaze on Morgan.

"How's Paisley? Did he hurt her?"

"No." Morgan shook his head and gave me a gentle smile. "He left her in the backyard. She had water and the shelter of the covered patio. We've got her at the house now.

"Your uncles came back when I called and told them of your attack. They're here ... in town but left to get something to eat a few minutes ago. They'll be back and happy to see you awake."

"Compton was his father." It was a matter-of-fact statement and the only thing I could think to say.

"I know. It was in the diary." Riley grimaced and shook his head. "He blamed you for everything. He was crazy, Mariah. Even though he recounted some of his father's crimes in the diaries, he believed his father was innocent."

I tried to stifle a yawn, and Molly began to shoo everyone out so I could rest.

"Please don't go. I don't want to be alone." I pleaded for them to stay as they started toward the door.

"It's okay, Mariah." Morgan moved up to my side and smiled down on me. He patted me on the arm. "I'm staying with you until your uncles get back. One of them will stay with you through the night."

I smiled and nodded. "Thank you."

When I awoke in the dark room later that night, I panicked and started thrashing around until I heard my Uncle John's voice telling me I was safe. He switched on the light, and I saw his face looking down on me with concern.

"How ya doing, kiddo?"

"I didn't know where I was for a moment. When I woke up and it was so dark, I thought I was dead. It scared me."

"You're safe now. You have a long road of recovery ahead of you, but you will recover. You'll bounce back. You *will* have to be diligent about your rehab, and I'll be staying on to help you with that."

"He set the fire that killed Dad." It was a simple, quiet statement. "It was a trap to kill him."

"What? Who set the fire?"

"Jerry. He was Compton's son, and Franklin hired him to get rid of dad and a woman who was making trouble for Franklin. They paid his college tuition for doing the job."

Uncle John was quiet for a long time.

"Uncle John?"

"I'm here, honey. I'm glad we finally have answers. It doesn't change the fact that your father was a hero, and we already knew he was murdered. I'm glad we know who the murderer was, and that the killer is dead now, too. I'm real glad of that."

"Me too."

Uncle John patted my shoulder. "Now get some rest. You start physical therapy in the morning. I'm sticking around until you're on your feet, and I'll help with your martial arts training to get you back in shape. I'm not leaving until I know you're strong enough to take care of yourself."

"I'm glad you're here," I said. "It's been a terrible year, and I don't know how I'm going to recover from the trauma of it."

Uncle John rested his hand over mine.

"You will, Mariah. You'll get through this and find your happy place again. We'll be here for you to help you all we can. Now get some rest. I'll be here the whole night so you don't have to worry. Nothing is going to happen to you under my watch."

"Thank you." I smiled and closed my eyes.

**********

My recovery was too slow for my liking and very painful. I had the compound fracture of my femur, an orbital fracture of my left eye, a flattened nose, two crushed fingers—all of which required surgery to repair—two broken ribs, a cracked jaw, and a fracture in my skull. I was astonished I didn't have any missing teeth, although several were loose. My face was one big, puffy, purple bruise when I finally got to look at a mirror.

Uncle Richard and Uncle Dan returned to Texas after I was released from the hospital.

I had to put aside any plans to close my practice and move until I was healed, and I decided to wait until then to make any plans for my future. After my bone fractures healed and physical therapy strengthened my leg, Uncle John started me back on my Tai Chi exercises.

I was on my own—Uncle John, having declared me fit, went home—and back to work. There was a big shoot-out with a group of drug runners in which a couple officers were injured and another one was killed. Anytime there's an officer involved shooting, it is standard procedure to evaluate and treat them for PTSD (Post Traumatic Stress Disorder) and make sure they're ready to return to work. I was busy.

I walked into my office and put my purse (with my Five-seveN snuggled in the holster compartment) on the new credenza behind my spanking-new desk, both of which my uncles purchased for me. My grandfather's Colt Python was recovered from Gordon Morris when they arrested him and searched his home. It's still in evidence, but I will eventually get it back, unlike my baby Glock that was taken from me when I was abducted. That has never been recovered, but Riley and Jeri bought me a new one for my birthday. I shuffled through the mail Norah left for me and dropped everything when I came to the card from Jeri and Riley.

***Dear Mariah,***

***We're so glad to hear that your cast is finally off and you are recovering nicely. We hope life has returned to normal for you as it has for us. Riley is retiring next month and I am throwing him a retirement party. Morgan and Molly have graciously agreed to come and we hope you will too. There's plenty of room at the house and we are asking you and the Morgan family to stay with us while you're here.***

*Actually, JEFFRIES, I'm not asking, I'm pleading. I have a proposition for you and Morgan that I would like to present to the two of you in person. Please say yes. —Riley*

**We love and miss you, Mariah. Hope you can make it.**

**Jeri and** *Riley*

*Hmmm, I wonder what he's up to,* I thought as I dropped the card on my desk and picked up the phone to call Morgan's cell phone.

"You got the card finally, didn't you?"

*No 'Hello, how ya doing Jeffries?' He's been waiting for me to call him, the dog!*

"If you already knew about this, why didn't you call and give me a heads up?"

"Come on, Jeffries. You've had a lot on your plate, and I didn't want you worrying about what Riley might be up to any sooner than necessary. I told him to hold off inviting you until you had your cast off and you were getting around better. How ya doing, by-the-way?"

"Good. My leg is getting stronger, and I'm running again with my physical therapist's approval—mostly on the treadmill at the clinic right now, but I'm ready to start jogging again. I'm getting fat and have to put the kibosh on that nonsense." I laughed.

"So what is Riley up to? Do you know?"

"Nope! He refuses to say anything to me about it until he sees us in person. Can you get away?"

"Oh, I'll make it happen. I owe them so much, and I have really grown to care about both of them. You know Morgan, I've always loved you, Molly, and the kids like family, and now I feel like Jeri and Riley are family, too. I can't wait to see them again and see Riley into retirement in style."

"We all love you, too. So we'll fly up together? Molly's excited and is planning a shopping excursion this weekend to find the perfect retirement gifts. You should go with us if you're free."

"I'd like that. I have some heavy evaluations starting today, and I'll have to make sure I can get through them before Saturday. I'll call you Friday afternoon and give you a progress update."

"Sounds great. Talk to you then." In typical Morgan style, he hung up without saying goodbye.

**********

# VIII

Riley and Jeri were both at the airport to meet us when we arrived. Hugs were shared all around. We stopped at a great little Italian restaurant for dinner before going to their house. After we got settled into the guest rooms, everyone met in the living room—Morgan, Riley, and Jeri with their beers, Molly with her iced tea, and me with my rum and Coke. Max and Mia were in the back yard with Paisley.

"I'm so glad you guys were able to come this weekend." Riley raised his beer in cheers. "My last day was Tuesday, and I've spent the rest of this week helping Jeri get ready for the big party tomorrow. But I'm hoping we'll have something else to celebrate tomorrow, too.

"I'm going to open a private investigation agency, and I want you two to be my partners. We work well together.

"Morgan, between your time served in the marines and your time at the PD, you have more than your twenty years needed to retire. Would you be interested in retiring if you could go into business with me, equal partners?"

"Don't tell Molly, but the only reason I haven't retired is because I know she would work me to death with all the honey do's."

Everyone laughed, and Molly punched him in the shoulder.

"Oh, be quiet!"

"Honestly, I've been thinking about retirement, and I'm intrigued about being a P.I. but I don't want to make a hasty decision about it. Besides, it will have to be Molly's decision, too. I'm assuming you'll want to work out of Idaho. What town?"

"Actually, Jeri wants to be closer to her sister, especially after everything that happened. We found a well-established practice for sale in Portland, Oregon. It's beautiful there.

"I know you said you're ready to start fresh someplace new, Mariah. Would you be interested in being a full partner?"

"Is it called *The Watchers: Investigation and Reporting*?"

Riley's face opened up in surprise. "Yes, it is. How did you know?"

"Because I called Mr. Larson about it the afternoon Jerry went killer on me. I was going to schedule a flight to go see the city and talk to Mr. Larson about the business, but I never got the chance before I was ... almost killed."

"So you're the one. He told me some woman called inquiring about it, but he never heard from her again and he couldn't find the note with her contact information.

"I'm sorry, Mariah. If I'd known you wanted it, I would have backed off, but the up side is we can go in as partners together. What I would like to do is draw up a contract and have you both invest equally in it with me ... if you want to."

"Hmmm. I can't think of anything I would like better." I couldn't wipe the grin off my face.

"So you're in?"

"Well ... yeah! I'll have to wrap up some current cases, and I have a few regular clients I'll have to find a new doc for, but that shouldn't be a problem. My house is gone, and I just closed the sale of the land yesterday. So yeah, if you can give me, say..." I shrugged. "...six months to make sure I get everything wrapped up, then I'm in."

"I can wait, but we'll need you to go ahead and sign on the dotted line with me and get some earnest money to Mr. Larson since this will be an equal partnership. I don't want Rand to lose his patience and sell out from under us; he needs some cash up front. I'll split the earnest money with you if Morgan isn't ready to commit. Will you have any problems in that area?"

"No. I have a small inheritance that I get income from every month, I just sold my property, I'm debt free, my car, such as it is, is paid for, and I have the money from the insurance settlements. Hopefully I'll be able to sell my office building and the psychology practice with it. I may have to close it up and refer my existing patients to a new doctor, but the building shouldn't be a problem to sell. Even without that, I'm solvent and a good credit risk."

"Great! So Morgan, how much time do you and Molly need to decide if you're in?"

Morgan glanced at Molly, who was already looking at him. "A week, babe?" he asked her.

"I think a week should be enough time, certainly no more than two," she responded, looking at Riley. "Will that be okay?"

"Yep. Once you make a decision, I'll contact the bank. They can handle the paperwork via fax so you won't have to come back here. And I'll call Mr. Larson and let him know. Mariah and I will go ahead and put up the earnest money and we'll settle up once you join us."

"You're confident!" Morgan laughed.

Riley shrugged with a wide grin. "Hopeful!"

We sat around, and Riley filled us in on all the research he'd done for the P.I. business. I was so excited about the new venture I could hardly sleep that night, tossing and turning until two in the morning.

The next morning was hectic. After cooking breakfast, eating, and cleaning up, we started cooking and setting up for the party. The party was going to start at six o'clock. We all stayed busy. The weather report promised clear skies and mild temperatures for the event. Morgan, Max, and Riley were busy setting up tables and chairs in the backyard. The covered patio was hosed down by Mia after locking Paisley in a room (I did not want to bath her again before the party), and Jeri, Molly, and I set up a couple of tables on the patio—one for drinks and one for food.

I was excited at the prospect of seeing Jim, Hector, and the crew from the local FBI office.

Kenny Rhode of the NSA promised to come and meet us all. Jewel, Norela, and Dixie were also invited to come and celebrate along with Cortez, Nylla, Slim, and Joy from Albuquerque. It was going to be a great reunion. Even though Riley didn't know all of them, he wanted to meet them and thank them for their help in the case.

At three, we took a break in the dining room and shared delivered Chinese food and cold long-neck beers. Max and Mia were jumpy. They acted like they were waiting for the winner of the lottery to be announced.

After we finished eating, Morgan wiped his mouth with his napkin, wadded it up and threw it on his plate. He leaned back in his chair, and clasped his hands behind his head.

"I'm in," he announced.

"What? You're joining the partnership?" Riley's eyes were bright with excitement.

"Yep. Molly and I talked about it until the wee hours of the morning, and we both want to do this. We talked to the kids this morning and they're excited about the move. We'll start packing and prepare our home to be put up for sale when we get back.

I turned to Max and Mia. "You two don't mind leaving your school ... your friends?"

Mia shook her head. "It's not the same since everything that happened ... you know, being held captive. A lot of the kids look at me funny and some I caught talking about me when they didn't think I was around. Max has experienced the same thing."

"Yeah. We want dad off the force." Max took his eyes off his dad and turned his gaze on me. "We're ready to start over someplace new where no one knows what we've been through."

I nodded. "It sounds to me like you've both given this some serious thought. I'm glad."

Morgan gave his children a glowing smile. "I'll have to retire and get that taken care of, but we can be ready in six months, too. The timing will be perfect for getting the kids enrolled in their new schools."

Morgan reached over and laid a hand on Molly's shoulder. She turned a sunny smile on him.

"Molly is going to start researching the schools when we get home so we'll know what neighborhood we want to live in. Once that is done, it will be house-hunting time. Six months will fly by, I'm sure."

Riley jumped up and came around the table to clap Morgan on the shoulder. Morgan jumped to his feet before Riley reached him, and they bear hugged.

Jeri picked up her beer and yelled, "Cheers! To a new adventure!" We all picked up our beer bottles and clinked necks together. The kids joined in with their soda cans. Everyone was laughing and talking all at once, on our feet and hugging each other in celebration.

**********

## Her Husband's Wife
## CHAPTER 1

He stood, concealed in the bushes as the nondescript, white pick-up truck—slightly lifted with steps on either side at the doors—turned down the narrow, dirt drive leading to the old abandoned house. The truck came to a stop beside his own faded-red Chevy pick-up. Dust from the truck's passage drifted south over the field in front of the house. The driver's door opened and a slender, shapely ankle above a three inch, high-healed, black pump appeared beneath the door and landed on the side step. The foot turned as the second foot, toe pointed to the ground, touched down on the dirt drive—the first foot following a half minute behind. The woman took a step back and slammed the door closed, adjusted her purse over her right shoulder, and turned. The well proportioned woman, with short blond hair swept from the sides of her face, a feathering of bangs across her forehead—turned and looked around. In the perfect oval of fine porcelain skin, her beautiful blue eyes peered out from heavily lined lids and long, thick, dark lashes. Her mouth, the perfect bow, and painted bright red, accentuated the flawlessness of her skin. She wore a black, long-sleeved sweater adorned by a three strand necklace of pearls, the longest tier brushing the swell of her breasts.  Below the sweater, a matching pencil skirt stopped just above her knees.

"Quit acting like a fucking peeping tom and get out here," she yelled, belying her beauty with the coarseness of her vocabulary.

He was angry with himself for being so easily deceived by her beauty.  He imagined there was virtue where none existed simply because she looked like an angel.  He didn't know what happened in her past that broke her beyond repair, but he learned too late how heartless she had become since their childhood friendship.

*Just plain mean and hateful!*  He thought.

Her goal in life seemed only to destroy everything good in the world.  He wished he'd realized the depth of deception in her before he got involved—regretting, as he stepped from behind the bush and pretending to zip his pants, that he ever knew her.

"Sorry.  I had to take a whiz.  Are you ready for them?"

She turned at the sound of his voice and glared.

"Noooo." she said slow and precise, her voice rising at the end of the word as though correcting an errant child.  "When I'm ready for them I will tell you.  I told you that before."

"You never told me the job would take this long.  My wife's really sick and I need the money now or they won't start the treatment."

"Yes dear," she sneered.  "That's one

reason I called you. Here's half the money."

She reached into her purse—he flinched, expecting her to pull a gun and shoot him. She pulled out a wad of cash instead.

"This should be enough to get the treatment started."

She sauntered toward him, arm outstretched and waving the greenbacks.

"I have another job for you too. That means even more money for you." Her grin was forced and to him looked sinister.

His stomach churned.

*This is bad, I know it is,* he told himself.

"Now what?"

The whine irritated her. She despised this man who showed no backbone. She was thankful he was weak and pliable—easy for her to use, but she hated being in his presence.

He took the money and stuffed the cash in his back pocket. She reached up and he flinched again. She gently brushed the hair from his forehead and caressed the side of his wrinkled face.

"Why do you fear me? I told you I would pay for your help, didn't I? I'm only trying to help you take care of your sick wife. I *never* said I would hurt you."

She smacked her palm hard against the side of his face and pinched his cheek between the heel of her palm and all four fingers.

"And yet you fear me," she sneered.

She released his face with a push,

throwing her hand into the air. She turned and walking toward her truck. He reached up and rubbed his throbbing cheek knowing it would be bruised the following day.

"I'm hurt," she yelled turning back to face him. "Be here tomorrow with your van at four P.M. I'm bringing another one. You'll need to prepare tonight to have the place ready."

"What?" He swallowed hard. "The deal was only for one, and there's two already. I agreed to only one."

"I'm paying you extra. You'll need the money for your wife's treatment, after all."

She paused and glared at him. "Or you can quit. Keep what I've paid you for your troubles."

He watched her as he thought about the offer. She would kill him before she would let him walk away. She told him that before, when she took the second girl.

"How long is this going to continue?"

She advanced on him until she was a hands width away. "Until I'm done," she snarled, her upper lip curling like a rabid fox.

He backed up a step and whined, "But we need to wrap this up before we're caught."

"Yes. We. That is the operative word—*WE!* If I go down, you do too and where will your wife be then? Huh? Just shut up and do what I tell you. Everything will work out fine."

His heart pounding in his chest, he looked at the ground in front of his feet and nodded his head.

"Okay. I'll be here." There was no animation in his voice. He had no choice. If he refused, she would kill him on the spot.

**********

# THANK YOU

Thank you for choosing Deadly Intent, and giving me the opportunity to entertain you.

If you enjoyed this book, please tell your friends, and take a few minutes to leave a written review on Amazon.com.

Authors depend on reviews and word of mouth recommendations to increase our readership. Your written reviews reach out and influence other readers—helping them decide to give our books a try. They are important. *Your* tribute is important, and I would appreciate your help.

Thank you in advance for your help in increasing my readership and fan base.

Made in the USA
Lexington, KY
15 November 2019